Don't You Want Me?

Ian Borrett

ISBN-13: 9798356814099
ISBN-10: 1477123456

Cover design by: Art Painter
Library of Congress Control Number: 2018675309
Printed in the United States of America

For my Dad, who enjoyed writing and
would have been proud I got this far.

CONTENTS

CHAPTER 1 – NAPLES: 7 JULY

It was a typically warm Neapolitan summer evening but, since it was Naples, most of the sounds were man-made, with car horns constantly blasting, as if they were pre-recorded in a studio and blaring out from speakers throughout the city. Lots of animated talk and debate drifted out from the bars and restaurants that huddled together in this crowded city – the largest city in the south of Italy, and generally looked down on by the rest of the country as being dangerous and dirty.

The smell of fresh coffee hung heavy in the air. Jake was excited, but his nerves were a little frayed, his fingers trembling as he took a deep breath and walked boldly up the steps between a traditional trattoria on his left and a tour company on his right, which had bright blue and white banners promoting tours to Pompeii, Capri and up Mount Vesuvius. His Italian wasn't the best, but '*bella*' he recognised. Jake loved travel and was happy being in Italy, but this was work and he didn't expect to have much time for sightseeing. He looked around as he reached the top step. Vespas were weaving around the streets, young and old Italians alike impressing each other with their skills, often missing walkers by a hair's breadth.

Not for the first time, Jake wondered why he was here. He'd walked from his hotel across the Piazza Dante to get here, sensing he was about to start an unpredictable, but potentially exciting, journey that could – finally – give him purpose. This year had been good to him. The previous year had been traumatic, his life turned upside down.

Jake had arrived in Naples two days ago to settle in and ensure his cover story was sound. He was on a mission. He was desperate to make a good impression on the person who had contacted him; he was totally on his own in Naples.

He cleared his throat. By the door, an elaborate plaque displayed the name 'Villa All'Alba' which, he found out later, meant 'sunrise' in English. He pushed open the door. As he entered the hallway, he saw a mix of old and contemporary furnishings which seemed to his untrained eye to work well together. It was quite different to his own living space. There were a couple of paintings and plants, but Jake, who wasn't well up on horticulture, didn't know what they were. The hall opened into a small living room which had a retro 70s feel to it. A hum of conversation came from a room to his left, where other guests were gathered. Then a beautiful Italian woman emerged, slightly older than himself, her shoulder-length chestnut hair flowing behind her as she raced towards him.

Isabella Bellini was genuinely pleased to see him.

'*Ciao*, Signor Taylor, I'm so glad you're here. This is my home – it's small but homely, and the food and drink are good.' She smiled, then her face became serious. She whispered, 'You'll find what you want is already here.'

Isabella had phoned him three weeks ago. Her call had captured his imagination. They'd met for lunch at the Ivy in Winchester, and she had asked him to investigate Dave Constantinou. She hadn't given him much background info, and Jake was pretty sure she was concealing her real motivation for wanting to engage him. Why pick a rookie investigator like him? But this could be a big deal – the sort of investigation he'd been hoping for and something he could really get his teeth into.

They'd agreed that Jake would have a pseudonym for this evening. He would be known as Harry Taylor. This added to the intrigue and made him feel as if he was undercover, which in many ways he was.

'Grazie, Signora Bellini.' Jake smiled. He downloaded an app a couple of weeks ago to learn the basics of Italian but hadn't spent too much time listening to it. He ran his hands through his wavy dark brown hair. He had a small scar on his forehead from falling off his bike at the age of seven: this always stood out more when he was tired or stressed, and his friends always gently mocked him for it. In his last career, he had been known as Harry Potter.

This evening Jake was neat, tidy and well-groomed. He was modest, but even he thought he'd scrubbed up well when he looked in the hotel mirror. He summoned up the confidence to stride into the dining room to meet the others. His gaze was immediately drawn to the slightly overweight figure who he knew as Dave Constantinou, but he was careful not to spend more time observing him than the other guests, for fear of drawing his attention.

Isabella introduced her other guests. There were six people altogether, including Jake and Isabella: John Warr, a Maltese property developer; Lucy Cornish, an American socialite; the rather squat-faced Claudette, who appeared to be with Dave; and the man himself. Isabella introduced him and Jake immediately felt a twang of inferiority, which he knew he would have to conquer.

Isabella sat Jake next to her. Dave glanced at them both. He picked up the decanter and poured Jake a glass of Chianti without asking him if that was what he wanted. However, in true British style, Jake had drunk half his glass before Dave had placed the decanter back on the table. More Dutch courage, topping up the glass he'd had before leaving his hotel room. Jake looked at the people around him, trying to suss them out. It was early days, but they were an interesting bunch. It almost felt like being on a film set, something from an Agatha Christie movie. They weren't people he would normally associate with. He remembered the affirmations his therapist had taught him. He'd struggled for most of his life with the feeling he was not quite as important as other people. He'd never resolved why this was, but he was getting better.

Dave Constantinou was the reason he was here. Jake noticed he had a long scar on his left cheek and was immediately curious. How had he got it? He already imagined some kind of mafia disagreement.

'How do you know Isabella?' Dave said, cutting into Jake's thoughts. There was a certain tone to the question, slightly condescending.

'We met through mutual friends in London,' Jake replied. 'I had planned to visit this area of Italy. I've a keen interest in geography and the natural beauty of this area. Isabella very kindly invited me over for a meal while I was here.'

Dave frowned. Jake wasn't sure that he had sounded convincing; he had detected a slight nervousness in his own voice.

'Ah, London – not one of my favourite places, although I haven't been there for years.' Curiously, Dave appeared a little sad.

'That's a shame,' Jake replied. 'Any reason?'

'Circumstances have meant I haven't needed to.'

Jake raised his eyebrows; sensing Dave was

holding back. 'I'm fond of London. I wouldn't want to live there anymore, but it has a lot to offer.'

Dave frowned. 'London was cruel to me once. Many years ago.'

Jake nodded. 'A bad experience can cloud your judgement of a place.' He really wanted to ask what the 'cruelty' had been, but it was a bit early for that. He hoped somebody else might ask Dave, as they appeared to be listening to their conversation, but there was silence.

Lucy suddenly laughed. 'Remember Amsterdam, Isabella? I have no desire to go there again.'

Isabella put her head in her hands and smiled.

Dave turned his attention to Claudette and topped her glass up with Chianti. Her eyes bulged and she shook her head from side to side. It was hard to work out if she wanted more wine or didn't like to say no.

Jake sensed a melancholy air about Dave. He wondered what danger he would pose. Maybe at this stage it was best he didn't know; he wasn't always the best at keeping a poker face.

Jake loved food, and only regular running and walking kept his waistline from expanding. He was looking forward to the food this evening: he loved Italian food. He tried to stop dipping into the antipasti, which included bread, prosciutto, olives, nuts, and cheeses, but his will was weak.

There was a great deal of talk by the guests, although Dave and Claudette were quiet. Isabella cleared the antipasti away and came back with a risotto, then a seafood platter with squid, clams, and mussels.

Jake couldn't help glancing in Dave's direction. It wasn't pleasant to watch him eating. He frequently talked with his mouth full, his sparse dark hair was already damp with sweat, his full round face was red. But there was something fascinating about him.

The conversation was mostly superficial. Lucy seemed to want to hold court, dropping in names of people she knew and had met, clearly wanting to impress the other guests. Jake didn't detect a great friendship between her and Isabella, as they both subtly tried to put each other down. He wondered why Isabella had invited her.

Typically, strong coffee was served at the end of the meal. Jake felt full and a little drunk, but not satisfied that he'd gained as much information about Dave as he had hoped. It was time to tread carefully but find out a little more about the man. He thought he would remain subtle, so he started with Lucy.

'So, Lucy, where do you live? Are you here in Naples?'

'No – this cesspit? I'm just here visiting Isabella; we've known each other for years. We used to knock around together in New York when she was there. Currently I'm living on a very expensive yacht in Nice, owned by my current love, Charles Lang. I expect you've heard of him?' She'd mentioned Charles several times already this evening.

Jake shook his head, feigning ignorance. He was relaxing, getting into his stride, and starting to enjoy himself. He had to hold himself back at times; he was in danger of sounding like a detective, so was conscious to remain interested, but not too inquisitive.

'You obviously don't read about celebrity culture, Mr Taylor. It sometimes feels like all social media and the paparazzi are living with us, commenting on everything we do.'

Jake bit his lip and thought carefully about his reply. He wasn't here to make a friend of Lucy, but he also didn't know when he might need her help. It was always important to bear in mind.

'That must be tough at times, but I suppose that's the attention you attract moving in those circles... What does Charles do?'

'Shipping, darling,' she said, nodding to him to refill her glass. Jake obliged, but he resented being asked. Lucy had a sense of self-importance about her.

'I think he owns half the coast of Spain – he's involved in lots of new developments that are going up, although that's not something we tend to chat about over our langoustines and Dom

Pérignon of an evening.'

Jake bit his lip. He had noticed she'd had a certain amount of work done on her face: her forehead didn't crease, lips that were boosted by collagen, and cheeks that didn't move when she smiled. She was wearing a gold and rust-coloured dress, probably made in Milan by an expensive designer he'd never heard of.

He waited to see if she would ask him something back and was not surprised when instead she turned her attention to John, amusingly he seemed to ignore her and started speaking to Dave. Jake decided to listen to the other conversations going on around the table and sat back, glancing from one person to the other. Isabella was talking to Claudette about France, Dave was talking to John about a hotel venture, and Lucy was quiet, checking her phone.

Dave mentioned that he lived mainly in Menorca, so Jake stepped into the conversation. 'Whereabouts? My family has a holiday home on the east coast.'

Dave frowned at Jake, then softened his reaction. 'In the middle, away from the tourists. Near a place called Alaior.'

Jake nodded and raised his eyebrows. 'I know it. Do you mind me asking exactly what you do Dave?'

'Tourism,' Dave replied. 'I own a couple of hotels here in Naples and we're thinking about building another in Malta, which is how I know John here. We're working on a leisure development for the island.' He paused to dab sweat from his forehead. 'I don't think I asked you what you do?'

Finally, someone had asked Jake. It had only taken two hours. He and Isabella had talked about this and decided to choose a profession that wouldn't raise Dave's curiosity or be of any interest to him; the objective of the evening was that Jake should be thought charming but rather dull.

'I work for the local council,' Jake replied. 'It's not very interesting, but it pays the bills and is worthy work.'

Silence descended. Jake suddenly felt anxious, he sensed that Dave was a bit anxious all evening, abrupt with Claudette.

'So, what's your game?' Dave looked directly at Jake.

The question rocked Jake. 'I'm not sure I know what you mean. I'm not into games. That's for other people.'

'Bullshit.' Dave was smiling at Jake, a slightly menacing smile that said, 'I've got your number'. Jake needed to think quickly, and he could sense Isabella's tension.

'OK,' Jake said, running one hand through his hair. 'You got me.'

Isabella stiffened, but he daren't glance her way.

'I'm also a writer. I met Isabella in London and we chatted about my work. We thought Naples would be a good setting for a scene in my current book, so she invited me to dinner.'

Isabella relaxed. Jake tensed.

'So, is Harry Taylor your real name?' Dave narrowed his eyes as he asked.

Jake calmly replied that it was, and that this was his first book. Dave looked unconvinced. Jake steeled himself for more questions, hoping he had plausible answers.

CHAPTER 2 – WINCHESTER: 16 JUNE, THREE WEEKS EARLIER

Jake's train pulled into Winchester at 10.45 a.m. – perfect timing for a short walk down the hill to the Ivy on the high street. It was another warm day. Tourists milled around, taking photos, studying maps, and drinking coffee. The sun was high in the sky, the shadows sharp on the flagstones, which were dotted with dried lumps of chewing gum. Looking up, Jake could see that many of the old buildings had been through an early summer clean. Down the road there was a banner across the street promoting 'Winchester Hat Fair, 4–8 July'.

When he reached the restaurant, the outside tables were full of Prosecco-drinking forty-somethings wearing designer sunglasses and expressing opinions of their friends' house renovations. There was clearly money in this city.

A smartly dressed young woman in a crisp white apron greeted him at the reception desk and showed him to the table. She poured him water and he ordered a flat white. He was starving but wasn't sure whether Isabella was intending to eat. He had his eye on eggs Benedict, which he spied being delivered to a middle-aged woman with several bangles jangling up and down her wrist.

He was studying the vast range of whiskies behind the bar when Isabella arrived at the table. He stood up and, before he could do anything, she grabbed him and kissed him on the right cheek. He expected the same on the left cheek, but she immediately sat down. She studied him for a few seconds across the table as if she was mesmerised, which Jake found a little unsettling.

Isabella had called him out of the blue, asking him to meet her here as she had an important job for him. His investigation business was in its infancy, and this sounded like an intriguing prospect.

'Mr Stone, thank you so much for meeting me.' She sounded much warmer than she had during their phone conversation two days earlier.

'It's a pleasure,' Jake replied. Isabella looked younger than she sounded. She was undeniably attractive and very smart in a grey tailored jacket and matching skirt. She had an Italian air about her, but with hazel eyes and light brunette hair, which he decided was natural. Her eyes matched his own. She had a friendly-looking face, but he noticed that she continued to scrutinise him. She seemed cool – in all the ways that meant these days.

She ordered a double espresso and asked Jake if he wanted to eat. They settled on eggs Benedict.

'I'm sure you're wondering why you're here, Mr Stone,' Isabella said.

'Jake's fine.'

'Thank you. Please, call me Isabella.' She reached for her water, took a sip and met his eyes. 'I need to know about a man I met recently.'

'Go on.'

Isabella put her water down carefully. 'The man I want you to investigate goes by the name Dave Constantinou, but that's not his real name. And he claims to be a Greek Cypriot, but I don't believe that either.'

'That doesn't explain why you picked me.'

'He lives in Menorca. I understand you have a house there?'

Jake raised an eyebrow. She'd researched him. He was intrigued. 'One I inherited from my parents, yes. And your involvement with this Constantinou is … what? A romantic one?'

'Goodness, no.' She reached for her water glass again with an unsteady hand. 'Let's just say he came into my life recently. And I need to know for sure that he's not the sort of person I suspect he might be.'

'I see. And what sort of person would that be?'

Looking uncomfortable, Isabella met his eyes. 'A dangerous one, Jake. A very dangerous one.'

'You need to give me more. Why don't you just walk away from him?'

'Can I ask you to just trust me?'

'That's a big ask. I'm new to this game, and I didn't anticipate a case like this so early on.'

'I'm a good judge of character. You've got the balls for this.'

Jake half smiled and knew he wouldn't let this opportunity pass by.

The eggs Benedict arrived, perfectly cooked. Conversation turned away from the business at hand and they talked casually about the state of British politics and Jake's recent lifestyle change. She seemed fascinated by what he had to say, and he found himself opening up to her. This took the conversation onto a friendlier level, and Jake found himself warming to her, although she wasn't giving much away about her life. When their plates had been cleared away, Isabella had further instructions for him.

'I'm having a dinner party on the 7th of July at my home in Naples. Dave will be there, and I'd like you to attend as my guest. If you can arrange a flight, I will reimburse you; I will cover all your expenses if you work for me. I'll email you later with suggestions where to stay and my address. Is that OK?' Her formality had returned. 'Now I need to go. I'll pay the bill on my way out. I have a solicitor's appointment, but it's been nice meeting you. I'll be in touch later.'

Jake was pleased that she'd picked him, and he wondered idly why she was seeing a solicitor in England. Maybe she has more connections here in the UK, which he found curious. He decided to park that thought for now.

Jake stood up, and Isabella kissed him on both cheeks this time. 'One thing. This Dave appears to make you nervous.' This wasn't a question. Isabella smiled unconvincingly and said, 'Ciao for now.' She shimmied between the tables to the front desk, phone in hand.

He sat back down for a couple of minutes, checking his messages and taking a last swig of water. It was just after midday. Office workers on their lunch breaks were mingling with the tourists and pensioners in the warm sun outside. Jake could feel a headache coming on, so he popped a couple of paracetamols in his mouth which he found in his back pocket and stepped out of the restaurant onto the high street. His next train wasn't for another forty-five minutes, so he decided to wander round to the cathedral grounds, where he could sit and think about the meeting and the potential new case.

The grass was brown through lack of rain, and there was little space available in the shade. He grabbed another coffee from the caravan by the side of the cathedral and debated whether to add a raspberry flapjack. His willpower was surprisingly strong, and he resisted. As he looked for a spot to sit down, he noticed the number of young couples on the benches – probably from the local college. He found a space under the shade of an oak tree and sat, admiring the west entrance to the cathedral, which was framed by the cloudless blue sky.

He sipped his coffee and promptly scorched his tongue. 'Fuck,' he muttered at the cup. He looked at the cathedral again, reflecting on the last two years and how his life had changed.

Jake had been in Lymford since January – a new year and a new start. Previously he had lived a miserable life in London, working as a civil servant in Whitehall, a career he'd fallen into at the age of nineteen – partly thanks to his father, who had lots of connections. He didn't have the will or inclination to dutifully network with people to improve his prospects, and a previous boss had told him that 'his sarcasm was holding him back' and that perhaps 'he was a bit too popular with his colleagues to gain loftier promotions'. At the start of his career, Jake had dreamed of knuckling down and seeing if he could get into MI5 or MI6, but numerous people had told him that it wasn't as glamorous as it seems. You could spend days on mind-numbing tasks, alone in a room, not speaking to anyone. Jake had probably been too easily put off.

Eighteen months ago, tragedy had struck. One snowy evening his parents had been driving home and they had hit a stationary car on the M3. His parents' car had flipped several times. His father died instantly, and his mother survived for three days before succumbing to head injuries. Jake had no siblings, and his parents' deaths left him with an inheritance of £1.5 million and, at thirty-three, a burning desire to leave London and the civil service behind him. The shock made him re-evaluate his life and career, as money was no longer a priority. It gave him the freedom to hand in his notice and seek out new ventures. He loved the calmness of being by the sea and knew he wanted to live on the coast. After spending some time visiting several south coastal towns, he plumped for Lymford. It was an attractive town in a beautiful area – not too big, not too small, but with good connections. It also had some great pubs and restaurants. It was a big move for him, and something of a risk. He knew no one there. He no longer had any family in London, and he was leaving behind all his friends. He wasn't naturally gregarious, but he pushed himself to be; he came across as a sociable person, although people didn't realise that it wasn't always easy for him.

His thoughts went back to Isabella. For some reason, he felt a little nervous. He sensed danger, as he felt there was a lot she hadn't told him. Was he a lamb to the slaughter? Someone to be used and chewed up, if necessary? Is that why she had come to England for an investigator rather than using someone in Italy? She lived in Naples, a place renowned for its mafia connections. He thought about *The Godfather*, especially the horse's head; he wouldn't fancy finding that on his houseboat. His mind was running away with itself. Although he was excited and intrigued by the prospect of this case, he also felt a little unsure. Some people had said it was a pure flight of fancy that he became a PI, but he was lucky that he could indulge in it and not worry about income. Isabella must have worked hard to find him.

His shirt sticking to his back, Jake got up and made his way back to the station. He decided to start his research on Dave Constantinou as soon as he got home, but he had a stop to make on the high street first.

CHAPTER 3 – MILLY: 16 JUNE

The train whirred as it pulled out of the station, gathering momentum. Jake checked the carriage and was pleased to see he was the only passenger – the benefit of taking a lunchtime midweek trip on a slow train. There was a bald chap with a SWR – the railway company – badge on his lapel further down the carriage, but he was glued to his phone.

Although Jake was in the quiet carriage, he picked up his mobile, hoping the employee wasn't a jobsworth and would ask him to stop. Milly was a local radio presenter who presented the afternoon show across the south coast. She wasn't on air today so he speed-dialled her number, eager to speak to her.

'Yes?' she answered, rather formally.

'Hi, it's me.'

'I know – your name comes up on my phone.'

'Phones are so clever, aren't they?'

'Oh, Jake. What am I going to do with you?'

'You know I'm an idiot, but did you like the flowers?'

'They're lovely,' she said, her tone softening.

'I've got some chocolates here as well.'

'Look, Jake, I'm trying to be a bit cold and offhand, but you're not making it easy for me.'

They'd had a stupid disagreement over

where to go for a weekend break; he wanted quiet sightseeing, she wanted adventure. Because they couldn't agree, he had gone home. This had been two days ago. Jake knew he'd been in the wrong and wasn't the best at handling these situations. Today he was on a charm offensive.

'I know. I'm an idiot at times, but you've been great for me, and I really do care for you.'

'You are an idiot at times. Look, I've got to go. We'll speak later.'

The phone went dead, leaving Jake unsure whether he was forgiven.

Out of the window a plane was taking off from the local airport, flying alongside the train before gathering speed and height. He wondered if he could fly to Naples from here.

*

Milly sat back in her office chair in the broadcasting studio she had set up at home. She mostly travelled to the studios of Coast FM, which were about fifteen miles away, but the station had installed her home studio when Britain went into its first COVID-19 lockdown so she could work from there. Jake called it the 'Starship Enterprise'.

She'd been pondering their relationship all morning. She knew she was a very confident character, strong in her views and a woman of her time. She'd married Ben when she was twenty and they divorced six years later; they had been too young, and their marriage made

21

her realise that she wanted more from life than just being a wife and mother. They had remained friends, and he even came to her thirtieth birthday party.

With her shoulder-length dark hair, slim figure, and soft, symmetrical features, she had no trouble attracting male attention. She pondered what Jake had just said and it brought her a warm glow. Jake was a little complex, he was an enigma, simultaneously laid-back and on edge, which made him unpredictable. He seemed confident but also quite self-deprecating. He had an inquisitive mind, which suited his new business, but he lacked self-esteem and could be quite humble. He wasn't good at small talk, but when he had something specific to say, he was fine. At the end of the day she knew that was part of the attraction she found in him.

Many of her friends had told her they would happily get to know him better if she ever dumped him. He would consider this ludicrous. She thought there was more to his background to uncover – that it had shaped him. She found that interesting.

She recalled their first proper chat, in the pub three months before their first date. She knew he wanted to ask her out, but she had to engineer it.

She took a sip from her mug and considered life without him. He was kind, funny, interesting, and good-looking. They had common interests: they loved travel, food, drink, running and Chelsea Football Club. He had just bought them both a season ticket, which was his birthday present to her. She loved it, although her friends had laughed, considering a necklace or nice earrings more appropriate.

Her relationship with Jake felt very natural: they both enjoyed sport and it provided a connection between them. Her next task was to get him to support Hampshire Cricket Club rather than the county of his birth, Middlesex.

She remembered the first time they slept together. His houseboat was not the easiest place to have wild, passionate sex; they had smashed two lightbulbs along the windows by the bed.

No, she decided. She was fond of Jake, and she shouldn't have dismissed him without saying more. She checked her watch and realised she'd better get on. She had a meeting soon.

*

Jake's train rattled over the bridge then gently pulled into Lymford station, where a group of college students were waiting to catch the train on its way back up the line. The students tried to crowd on the train before Jake got off. He muttered, 'Excuse me', but they ignored him. Jake hopped off, then made his way through the ticket hall, to be met with a cool, refreshing sea breeze. Beads of sweat trickled from his hair down his neck, while others rested on his forehead, waiting to gather force to run into his eyebrows. It was an unusually warm summer, and the aircon on the train had been less than adequate. He debated whether to head straight over to Milly's but decided to go home and collect his thoughts first.

When he got home, Jake checked his email. There was already one from Isabella sitting in his Inbox. His thoughts about Milly evaporated for now as he opened it, eager to see what she had to say. She gave him her address in Naples, the time and date of the dinner party, and a link to a hotel she recommended, which was close to her home. A pang of excitement danced around in his stomach, as well as a slight feeling of panic. But this was what he had signed up for when he decided to be a private investigator. Wasn't it?

Jake suddenly had the idea of surprising Milly and booking a ticket to Italy for her as well – maybe they could have a romantic break at the same time, drive along the Amalfi Coast spending afternoons drinking Barolo and gorging on pasta in the cafés that line the bay. He'd never been there before but he had researched it in the past. He had nearly got there three years ago when he had been living with Karen, but he'd been a poor civil servant then and they had settled on a weekend in Jersey. Karen had dumped him for a bohemian artist in Hoxton the week after.

On second thoughts, maybe it would be a bad idea to mix business and pleasure on his first major case. He booked a flight on Alitalia's website with an open-ended return, including four nights at the Relais Della Porta Hotel, an attractive hotel near the Piazza Dante, one Isabella had recommended.

With that, Jake closed his iPad cover. It gave the familiar ping as it switched off. He looked around the houseboat, wondering what to do now. He checked his watch. It was 4 p.m. He remembered that his mum used to say it was that in-between time if you're not working: too early for dinner, too early for a beer, but too late to get into anything too involved.

In times of stress Jake would always go for a 'thought walk'. It was his own form of meditation, giving him time to think and piece things together in his mind. These walks worked well for him and often ended with an idea or solution to whatever issue he was dealing with. He recognised this as a positive trait for an aspiring investigator.

But today he was restless. He decided that a walk wouldn't cut the mustard. Instead, he changed into a T-shirt and shorts and decided to go for a run. He put his wireless pods in his ears and selected a playlist on Spotify. He had a lot to think about.

He kicked himself for being a bit of a prat and was now worried that Milly had second thoughts about him. It had only been three months since they met but he already felt a deep attraction to her. She had a certain amount of confidence that he didn't always have, everybody seemed to love her, and she was able to talk to anyone with ease. She was a popular radio presenter.

As he ran, KLF pounding through his head, he looked up and saw Milly coming the other way. He didn't recognise the slightly built man she was with. His first thought was that he was someone to do with the station – maybe someone she was interviewing, or a producer. He was quite impressed by the people she met through her job, although she always seemed genuinely unfazed by them. She glanced up at Jake and gave him a wave. Hopefully that meant he'd been forgiven, he nodded at them as he ran past, although he was desperate to know who she was with. Jake guessed he was about twenty-five, blond, fresh-faced, and sporting a golden tan. He had a Scandinavian appearance about him. Jake carried on running, now accompanied by Prodigy telling him he was a twisted fire-starter. He certainly felt a bit mixed-up, but also excited.

CHAPTER 4 – NAPLES: THREE WEEKS LATER

The other guests then asked him questions about his book: what was it about? What was its inspiration? How long had he been working on it? Jake thought fast. Although he could feel sweat around his collar, he thought he had blagged it pretty well.

Dave got up and excused himself to go to the toilet. Claudette looked up at him, asking that he not take too long. She was a very inconsequential woman, and clearly in Dave's shadow. Jake had asked her a couple of questions, but she seemed quite reserved and had only known Dave for a few days, so she probably wouldn't be able to enlighten him on anything about him. While Dave was away, Jake took the opportunity to switch the conversation and ask John how the Maltese development was going.

'Slowly,' he replied, in a manner that suggested exasperation. 'Let's just say, me and Dave have different ideas.'

Somebody who called themselves a property developer was often a conman in Jake's book, but John came across as quite genuine. He was witty and didn't seem to take himself too seriously. His dark Mediterranean features were clearly attracting the attention of the ladies. Jake wondered if he was on intimate terms with Isabella.

Claudette looked at him, twitched her nose, but said nothing.

John carried on. 'He wants a very contemporary appearance to the hotel, but it's not in keeping with the area and the other developments we've planned around it.' He glanced at Jake as if to say, 'there's a lot more I could tell you'. Jake made a mental note of this.

'I'm sure we'll get there, but he'll need to be a bit more sensitive to the local population rather than breezing in like some Greek wide-boy, thinking he can bulldoze his way in.' John's English was impeccable, but he had a slight accent, typical among people from Malta.

Jake was interested. 'Does everyone speak English in Malta?'

'More or less. Everyone speaks Maltese, most people speak English, and because we get Italian TV programmes, Italian is spoken more now as well. Maltese and English are officially taught in schools, so children grow up speaking both.'

More conversation followed, including a heated debate about the European Union. Jake decided to stay out of this one now that the UK was no longer a member. He had been strongly anti-Brexit at the time of the vote, but now he wasn't so sure. There seemed to be quite a bit of tension between the nations left in, and Dave started to criticise the Italians, which Isabella tactfully ignored.

The evening was drawing to a close, but Jake wasn't satisfied that he knew enough about Dave, so he decided to be more direct. 'I can't quite make out your accent, Dave. Is it Greek Cypriot?'

'I didn't know you were an expert.'

Jake was feeling mischievous and wanted to shake Dave up a little. 'I had a girlfriend when I was younger. She was from Athens and would often tell me about the differences between the Greek and Cypriot-Greek language.'

Isabella smiled. Jake wasn't very clear about the differences between the dialects, but he felt this would provoke Dave so he could get an idea of his character.

'Where do you come from?'

Dave shifted in his seat, looking uncomfortable. 'Nicosia,' he replied curtly. 'Cypriot-Greek, south of the Green Line. Why do you ask?' This came out a little aggressively.

'Just interested. I thought your accent was more Greek mainland, but I'm rusty. Do you go there much now?' Jake asked.

'No, I haven't for some time.' Dave clearly didn't want to go into detail, but Jake pressed on.

'Any reason why?

'I'm a soul of the Mediterranean,' Dave declared flamboyantly, his eyes going around the other guests as if expecting approval.

'But is Menorca your base? Is that where you run the business from?' Jake already knew it was.

'I do, Mr Taylor. I'd call it home.' This sounded a little sarcastic.

'Harry, please.'

'You ask a lot of questions … Harry.' Dave was frowning, and his mouth was turned up on one side.

Jake raised his eyebrows and gave an unconvincing apology. His next question was going to be why Dave was so defensive, but he realised that that would appear a little too aggressive and counterproductive, although his guise as a writer seemed a good reason to ask probing questions.

Everyone went quiet. Shortly Dave stood up and thanked Isabella for a lovely evening. He took Claudette by the elbow, and they left.

Lucy had been quiet for the past hour. Now she smiled at Isabella as she wobbled across the room, thanking her effusively for the evening. She kissed her on both cheeks, and they arranged to meet again when Isabella was next in Nice.

That left the three of them. Isabella, now relaxed, toed off her shoes and picked up a bottle of Asbach brandy. She gestured for them to go through to the sitting room, while she collected three clean glasses.

'Right, let's talk.'

CHAPTER 5 – DAVE: 7 JULY

Dave jogged down the steps of the Villa All'Alba, pulling Claudette behind him. He'd had a very unsatisfactory evening. Claudette hadn't been sparkling company and he felt lumbered with her, he knew it was a mistake to bring her along. He should have ignored her when they met in a café in Sorrento instead of buying her a coffee. He'd had a good afternoon of sex from it but should have stopped at inviting her to Naples as well. She'd told him how she was travelling Europe on her own in search of adventure. Dave felt tense.

It was gone midnight, she had no transport, and her other bag was in the small apartment he owned nearby – one of several scattered across southern Europe, dutifully she followed him through the back streets and down to the apartment complex close to the shore.

Once inside, Dave grabbed a bottle of Glenmorangie and took a swig straight from it.

'What is it, Dave? What's wrong?' Claudette asked tentatively.

He looked at her with contempt and took another swig, looking at her as he did so.

He eventually replied. 'There's something about that English kid I didn't like. Why was he there tonight? It was like he was trying to get at me. He was charming to everyone else.' He took another swig, not looking at Claudette. His voice rose. 'There's something odd about him.'

'I should ignore it. I think he was just interested in you.'

'Bullshit! Him and that bitch Bellini are up to something. I saw them glancing at each other.' Dave grabbed a crystal glass and poured whisky into it without offering any to Claudette. Dave saw Claudette get up to gather her belongings, her bag was in the bedroom. He felt red mist descending and it took all his reserves not to fall in the old trap of acting irrationally.

'Where the fuck do you think you're going?' he shouted, grabbing her arm, and spinning her around.

'You're scaring me.'

'Good.'

'Can't we just talk about it? Isabella seemed nice and Jake was quite nice.'

Dave glared at her. 'I think we've done all our talking.'

'What does that mean?'

'I want you to go.' There were a few seconds of silence between them.

She then hesitantly said, 'can you just tell me how to get to the train station?'

'I could.' Dave glared at her.

Quietly, Claudette edged over to her bag and checked what was in it. The only thing missing was her purse, which was in the kitchen.

Dave refilled his glass; he'd drunk a lot this

evening and as Claudette started to get upset, he couldn't stand to have her in the apartment a second longer. He grabbed her bag and threw it at her.

'Find the station yourself.'

Claudette muttered, 'please just give me some directions.'

'Use your phone. Or are you too stupid to follow a map!'

Claudette stumbled to the front door, grabbing her purse from the kitchen. Dave shouted, 'you wanted some adventure.' He threw his glass in her general direction which smashed on the floor behind her. He watched her fumble with the door handle and with what sounded like a yelp she opened the door. Dave just stood watching her and then shouted.

'Go on, fuck off out of here. I can't bear to look at your ugly face anymore,'

He listened to her sobbing down the corridor and out of the building. He then felt a pang of guilt.

CHAPTER 6 – NAPLES: 7 JULY

'Well, he's an interesting character, wouldn't you agree, Jake?' Isabella said as she handed him a brandy in an expensive crystal glass.

'Um, I think that's what I would say,' Jake said diplomatically. 'But I'm not sure about dangerous. I quite liked him, in a funny sort of way, although I can see there's a lot to unravel there.'

Isabella looked concerned. 'So, it's probably time to give you a bit more background.' She sipped her brandy. She appeared more relaxed, as if something she'd been dreading was now over, although she still looked nervous. John was running his finger round the rim of his glass, then unbuttoned his shirt further hoping that the night air would cool him down somewhat.

'So, the big question is...' Jake frowned at them. 'What's the problem here, and why is Dave so important?'

Isabella pursed her lips, looked up at the ceiling and considered her reply carefully. John focussed his eyes at her, his head slightly bowed.

'Straight-to-the-point answer. We think he might be a murderer – or, at least, linked to the disappearance of at least two people.' She looked across at John, who nodded.

'And your evidence is?'

'Before I answer that, I need to confess

something. You're not the first investigator I've hired.' She paused and took a larger sip of brandy. 'Dave, who we know is not called Dave, has little connection to Cyprus. His father was stationed there with the British Army, where he met and married Dave's mother, who was from Paphos. When his tour of duty was over the family moved to London when Dave was eighteen months old. His father came out of the army and set up a video rental store in Chingford.'

Jake nodded. 'So, his accent is fake? What's his real name?'

'Daniel Welby,' John replied, looking at Isabella. 'It seems that at the age of twenty-four he severed all connections with his parents, changed his name, went to live in France, and then started to build up a timeshare business in Spain. This was a good move at the time. Now, at fifty-six, he's wealthy, with several properties across Europe.'

'And your private investigator, or should I say previous investigator, found all this out?'

'Paulo's his name. Yes, he did. But now he's disappeared.'

Jake pondered what Isabella was saying. Was she implying that Dave had murdered him? If so, what the hell would he be getting into?

'So, this Paulo uncovered this and now you think something has happened to him, and that Dave is responsible?'

Isabella put her empty glass down on the

table next to her. 'I don't know, but that's not all of it. John has heard other stories about Dave's business associates disappearing. They may be legitimate, but each time a disappearance seems to have been preceded by them disagreeing over something, then suddenly they're gone. He's not a pleasant character, and I've heard other stories, about women he's mentally and physically abused.'

Jake gave a sharp intake of breath, 'So, may I ask what *your* relationship is?'

Isabelle hesitated, 'you mean me and John?'

'Yes.'

She smiled. 'It's not what you probably think it is. We met at a fundraising event and somehow got talking about Dave and found we had a mutual distrust of him. That's when we decided to hire an investigator.'

Jake narrowed his eyes. 'You know, I'm not buying this. I asked you this in England three weeks ago and I'm asking again: why do you want to get involved with this Dave bloke?' Jake downed his drink and frowned at her.

'He's my father,' Isabella replied.

CHAPTER 7 – NAPLES: 8 JULY

It was 3 a.m. before Jake returned to his hotel, thoughts swirling around his head. He and Isabella had agreed to meet up tomorrow; John needed to get back to Malta, but they had agreed to keep in touch. Jake had to decide whether to take this case. It could be big, and it could be dangerous, but wasn't that what he wanted?

Naples was quiet: it was a short interlude between the night-time revellers making their way home and the newspaper kiosks, cafés and fishermen starting theirs. There was a peaceful still in the air, which was humid but had the fresh smell of a new day about to arrive. Mount Vesuvius loomed over the city, dominating the landscape. Although it was dark, Jake thought he could see a hint of red light from where the crater would be. Vesuvius was an iconic sight which you couldn't help admiring. When Jake used to draw volcanoes as a kid, they looked exactly like Vesuvius.

The fresh air had made Jake feel even more drunk. He knew he'd have a terrible hangover in the morning. He was never good at mixing his drinks. Isabella had been a terrific host, but he couldn't help feeling like a fish out of water. This was where his apparent confidence on the outside conflicted with his inner reserve.

He let himself in through the front door

of the hotel. The door banged behind him just a little too loudly. His room was on the first floor, so he walked quietly up the carpeted stairs and managed to put his key in the slot at the third attempt. He decided that he had finished thinking for the day. He stripped off his clothes and threw them onto a chair, went to the bathroom without putting the light on, then collapsed into bed.

It was noon before Jake woke. For a minute he didn't have a clue where he was. A big wide bed and a room that you could comfortably walk around; this certainly wasn't his houseboat. His head was thumping, and his stomach was flipping and gurgling. He sat up, rubbed his eyes, and instinctively ran his hand through his hair. It was a habit of his which Milly teased him about, he always this did first thing in the morning, as well as when he was tense. Seeing himself in the mirror opposite the bed, he said aloud, 'You look like shit.'

He went to the toilet but found the act of standing to pee too much; he was swaying and his insides seemed to be moving up his body. He sat down and stayed there for a while, going back over the night before. He shouldn't have drunk so much on potentially his first big investigation, but he found himself going with the flow.

He was having to piece the events of the evening back together slowly. Before he'd left the villa, he'd found out a little more about why

Isabella had chosen him, although he wasn't convinced. John had come across Jake's website and Facebook account. It seemed a bit odd; his website was basic, and he wasn't a frequent user of Facebook. This was still work in progress and unlikely to attract clients outside of the immediate Lymford area, let alone Italy.

He also discovered that Isabella had been adopted. Although Dave/Daniel was her biological father, she had been brought up since the age of five by an Italian family living in Rome, which she said had been idyllic. She remembered nothing of him or her real mother and what would have been her early life in north London. There was more to learn there, she had been reticent when he had pressed her on this.

Jake turned on the shower and walked back into the bedroom to look for his paracetamol, eventually finding them in the pocket of his jeans. He opened the bottle of water on the side and swallowed the tablets, followed by the water. His phone pinged. Picking it up, he noticed he had three messages from Milly. He made a mental note to reply properly as soon as he got out of the shower but sent a smiling emoji and a text saying *Give me ten minutes*.

He discovered that the man on the towpath with Milly was called Elias, he was from Malmö, and he'd just joined their news team from a station in Sweden. This was a big move for him, so Milly had been showing him around. He liked

Lymford and had decided to rent a flat in the town. Milly assured Jake he would like Elias.

He was due to meet Isabella at one o'clock. The Etto Restaurant was just off the Piazza Dante, so he had a quick shower then threw on his jeans and a light blue polo shirt. The paracetamol was starting to kick in when he headed out of the hotel. Jake had a bit of an obsession with knowing exactly where he was. Everywhere he went he would buy a map, checking where he was going and studying how far away particular landmarks were. He read in advance about the places he was visiting, and Naples was no exception. Consequently, he knew exactly where he was going and had no need to check the app on his phone.

Isabella hadn't yet arrived. He chose a table on the street and ordered water and a cappuccino. Surprisingly, he was tempted by a beer, but sensibly chose to leave that for now. The smells coming out of the restaurant were enticing. He could see plates of fish and vegetables lined up inside. It appeared unpretentious but, according to TripAdvisor, the buffet-style food was good. Jake had also read that you paid for the weight of food you ate, which was an interesting concept, although he was more dehydrated than hungry and quickly downed the glass of water. He was wondering why he'd worn jeans again when his app told him it was thirty degrees and he had two pairs of shorts in his bag.

His cappuccino arrived just as Isabella did. She reminded him of Sophia Loren, in large sunglasses and a stylish light-brown two-piece suit. Her skin was more tanned than when he had seen her in England, and she had a chic Italian air about her.

'Good afternoon, Jake. How are you feeling today?'

'A little jaded, but I'm recovering.' He smiled.

Isabella ordered sparkling water and confirmed that they would be eating as well. She seemed to know the waitress, as they started to have a chat. Jake couldn't understand a word but was fascinated by their animated interaction.

'I come here regularly for lunch,' she told Jake as she turned back to him.

He felt nervous for some reason. 'I do love Italy,' he said. 'It's the way you're all so emotional and dramatic – you can see why it's the home of opera. And I love the food.'

Isabella smiled. 'This is Naples; I can't argue with that. I hope you've had one of our pizzas?'

'Oh yes. It was the first food I ate when I arrived, in a tiny back-street restaurant. It was out of this world.'

'Now,' said Isabella, 'I need to know if you're going to take on this case. It may take time and it may put you in some tricky spots.'

'You mean, my life could be in danger?' Jake

interrupted.

Isabella hesitated. 'Possibly, but I doubt it.'

'Thanks for your honesty. So why didn't you go to the police with your suspicions?' Jake was starting to feel a little pressured.

'Several reasons. This is Italy, and the police can be bought. Dave has the money. Since I first met Dave I've heard quite a few rumours about him, people have disappeared, John has the contacts and he's been told he's shady and can be ruthless if anyone stands in his way, but there's no real evidence so the Italian police just wouldn't be interested.'

'How do you know this?'

'I don't want to sound pompous but the wealthier communities across this continent can seem like a small world. Stories circulate and both John and I have heard them.'

'But he's your real father?' Jake questioned. He sat back in his chair, stirring the froth in his cappuccino with his finger.

'I don't feel any emotion towards him.'

'That's cold.'

'Maybe.'

'So, why consider having anything to do with him?' Jake was frowning. 'I think you need to explain yourself a bit more.'

Isabella took off her sunglasses and, with a heavy sigh, stared into the distance over Jake's head. Then she lowered her gaze and looked directly at him.

'I think he also killed my real mother.' She paused.

Jake raised his eyebrows. He hadn't imagined that was coming.

She continued. 'Paulo, the investigator I mentioned before, found that my biological mother went missing at the same time Daniel changed his name to Dave. Her name was Amara. And that was when I was taken into care. I was five. I will send you the details that Paulo discovered, but my mother was last seen driving away from their house thirty-two years ago. Paulo hit a brick wall, but I think his lack of knowledge of England and police procedure was a problem. He was more interested in the more recent disappearances, but he wasn't getting far with those either.'

'Amara – is that Greek?'

'Yes, her parents were from Cyprus as well.'

'So, this is what you want me to focus on? Presumably you're not trying to establish a long-lost relationship, but you want revenge for what he might have done. I'm not sure I understand it. You've a nice life, you don't remember him and, as you say, you've no proof, so why spend a lot of money putting yourself through it?'

Isabella put her hand up, indicating to Jake to shut up. This annoyed him.

'Whoa, slow down,' she said. 'He's dangerous, and if he did kill my real mother then I want justice. I don't think that's too much to ask.'

There was a pause. Jake shifted in his chair, then reached out and poured himself another glass of water without offering to top up Isabella's. He could feel her gaze fixed on him as if she was trying to delve into his soul.

'I apologise,' he said. Head bowed. 'I'm still a bit hungover, and I'm new to this game. I suppose murder was not the type of case I thought I'd be taking on when I came to live in Lymford.' He continued. 'I don't think we clarified this last night, so how and when did you first come across Dave – or should I call him Daniel?'

She replied. 'Pure coincidence. I was at a dinner in Menorca about twelve months ago, he was there, and quite good company, so we kept in touch as I was interested in his business and even considered investing in it. We met a couple of times after that, which is when I saw through him a bit more and the rumours came to my notice. If I was going to invest, I needed to know more about him, so I hired Paulo, thinking it would be a straightforward investigation. He managed to find out about his change of name, which led him to the mystery of what happened to Amara.' She paused. 'Then he found out that a child had been adopted and taken to Italy.' Another pause. 'Who became known as Isabella Bellini.'

'Wow, revelation number two – they say

fact is stranger than fiction. That's an incredible coincidence. What a shock,' he eventually replied.

Isabella nodded. 'I didn't confront Dave, but then Paulo went missing. That's when I contacted you.' Jake noticed a slight sense of hesitancy with this response.

'So how did Paulo find out about Dave's change of name?'

'Not sure, he hasn't really explained that, but Daniel's life does appear to end when Dave's started.' Isabella was now looking across the piazza and seemed to be avoiding Jake's gaze.

He was pensive, taking it all in. 'I'll be honest. I didn't find Dave a particularly offensive bloke last night. A bit preposterous, but he didn't strike me as evil.'

'If it's too much of a challenge for you, then that's fine.' The frown on Isabella's face made it clear it would not really be fine.

Jake felt his hackles rise again, although he knew she was deliberately baiting him. She really wants me to do this, he thought. 'And your history? I need to know more,' he asked, changing to a more casual tone.

'When I was eighteen I found out that I was adopted. I didn't do anything about it. My parents in Rome wouldn't talk about it anymore, so to respect them I've never taken it further. The Anglo-Cypriot connection was a surprise, as I'd assumed I'd been born in Italy.'

'But your English is very good.'

'I was always encouraged to learn it and found it quite easy. That now makes some sense, because I had a grounding in it when I was very young. My parents have always been great travellers, so it was good for them to have English as a second language. It's funny, I always felt a pull towards the UK, but I never knew why. I put it down to being so very different to Italians – less emotional. I'm a bit more like that.'

They both ordered food. The day was quite cloudy and extremely humid. Thunderstorms seemed to be brewing – the first distant rumble echoed across the bay as they finished. The conversation became more personal when Jake found himself confessing his recent relationship with Milly, and Isabella talked about her now estranged husband, Luca. Jake found her extremely easy to talk to, and finally felt a bit of a connection with her. However, he still felt she was holding something back. He debated whether to say this, but decided against it for now.

Jake then remembered that he'd forgotten to reply to Milly.

CHAPTER 8 – MENORCA: 8 JULY

Dave classed Menorca as his main home: he'd bought a modest house several kilometres from the capital, Mahon, twenty-five years ago when he decided he needed a more permanent home. Thankfully this had been before the days of money-laundering checks and God knows what, so he'd been able to turn up at an estate agent, look at the house, say yes, transfer the money over, and have no further questions asked. Menorca suited him. It was not so quiet that everyone knew everyone else and would go poking into his business, but also it was not overrun with tourists, apart from two or three resorts in the middle of summer. He avoided them like the plague.

Dave flew into the island just as Isabella and Jake were finishing lunch in Naples. He had decided to leave as quickly as possible; he hadn't enjoyed his visit to Italy. Claudette had been a mistake and he didn't trust Isabella, although he was intrigued by her. John had seemed very shifty the previous evening, and Dave didn't like the fact that Isabella was friendly with him. His business in Malta wasn't going well – or at least, not going the way Dave liked. He preferred full control and to be in charge. Decisions should be his decisions, he didn't like having to compromise, and John was making him compromise. He reminded himself that he'd always been better off working on his own. He had his secrets and had always kept people at arm's length, and he didn't trust John. He didn't understand John and Isabella's relationship.

Dave drove out of the airport and headed north. The sun was hidden behind a shield of cloud, but there was a sharp dividing line with blue sky ahead. He turned right onto the main road which cut through the length of the island from Mahon to Ciutadella. Just before Alaior he turned right onto a well-maintained road that snaked through the red soil fields bounded by the stone walls that were a feature of the island. Here, the land was abundant with trees growing peaches, apricots, and oranges. A small drive took him to a small enclave of villas, which included his own. Fairly modest but still quite impressive, it was two storeys with a big semi-circular balcony on the first floor which overlooked a pool. Whitewashed with a terracotta tiled roof, the villa had a large array of aerials, including a satellite dish. Dave liked his TV. The villa was decorated minimally but in a contemporary style, with sand-coloured walls and light grey furnishings. This was Dave's private place and very few visitors crossed the threshold, apart from his housekeeper, who lived nearby and was very discreet.

He checked the fridge. She had stocked up on bread, cheese, milk, and ham, as instructed when he'd rung her from Naples earlier. He opened two cold bottles of Estrella and wandered onto the terrace, where he slumped into a chair.

The beer slipped down quickly and started to take effect. He considered a line or two of coke then thought, maybe later. Dave was unhappy. He couldn't remember when he had last been happy, and not for the first time he wondered about giving everything up and retiring quietly to a place where he could leave his current life behind him. He'd done it before, and he had secrets to conceal. He could have a clean life and perhaps finally learn to connect with people. Surely at his age he didn't need the power he had always craved, as well as the violence and loneliness that had gone with it. He'd always been careful and perhaps he'd been lucky; he'd never been inside a police station. Dave was clever. This thought brought a wry smile to his face.

It had been creeping up on him for some time: the feeling that he was done now. He wanted his life to change. He had delegated most of his business dealings, had set up companies to manage his hotels and apartments in Italy, Spain, and Corfu. Malta was a venture he now found less appealing, so maybe it was time to leave business behind him and lead a normal life on another continent. He could even find a good honest woman who he would be kind to and settle down. He thought fondly of his lost love, the one he should never have let get away.

Could he do it? He looked across at his brochures, packed neatly on top of a small table, guides on countries in South America and what you would need to do as a European if you wanted to move there. If he was to do it then Argentina had appealed to him, Patagonia, off the beaten track. Maybe that was the next big life challenge for him. He decided to think it over and tidy his affairs.

His mobile rang, startling him out of his thoughts. It was Nico, the manager of his hotel on the edge of Corfu Town. Dave debated whether to ignore the call then decided to answer, even though he'd had enough for the day.

'Nico, what's up?' Dave could speak Greek quite well but insisted on English for all his business dealings, much to Nico's annoyance.

'Dave, we've got a situation here. Demetrious is insisting he use the hotel for a conference, but we're fully booked – what do I tell him?'

Demetrious was a local gangster who was involved in several extortion rackets locking many local businesses into protection deals. A 'conference' meant a meeting of his 'soldiers', as he called them, to discuss what new screws they were going to apply to the local populace. They usually stayed at the hotel for a few days, which meant that several of the bedrooms would be needed. Demetrious was getting more involved with the Albanians, who were a ruthless and deadly group of thugs. Dave had flirted with them a few years ago then decided to back out, but this had come at a price.

'Fucking hell,' Dave said, raising his eyes to the sky. 'I don't suppose we have a choice, so you're going to have to cancel some of the other bookings.'

'Do we have to? I'm not happy about it,' Nico said tentatively, knowing it would be a waste of time.

'We've no fucking choice, Nico. You know how these things happen. Just manage it and do it – that's why I pay you so handsomely,' Dave replied with more than a trace of sarcasm.

Nico rang off with an audible tut. Dave owed Demetrious. He'd covered for him a couple of years ago, over a deal that would have seen Dave locked up until his old age, and Demetrious was always keen to remind Dave that the debt wasn't yet fully settled.

CHAPTER 9 – NAPLES/ LYMFORD: 8 JULY

Jake had another twenty-four hours in Naples. He left Isabella agreeing that he would think it over and let her know as soon as possible if he would take on the case. It was half past three, so he didn't have much time to do any sightseeing. If he'd had a full day to himself he would have taken a taxi past Vesuvius to Pompeii and onto the Amalfi coast. He kicked himself for not doing that when he had arrived in the city. There's a good chance he'd be back, he consoled himself.

On his first day in the city, before dinner, Jake had wandered around from street to street but with a keen eye on his app to know where he was. He found himself in the raw back streets where a large proportion of Neapolitans lived. He explored crumbling narrow alleyways, where exposed pipework and cables jutted out into the streets and people hung out smoking and drinking, leaning over balconies which looked as though they would collapse at any moment. Masses of aerials pointed in the same direction, as if they were paying homage to a local god. He was fascinated by real life and enjoyed this walk as much as seeing the tourist sites.

He knew that he would take on the case. Why not? The life of a private investigator is always going to have an element of risk – at least if you watch TV and films. He would be a coward not to, and his sleuthing head was already ticking over with thoughts of 'Who is this Dave Constantinou really? What about his parents? Who were they? And where is Paulo?'

On Isabella's recommendation, he decided to take the short walk to the National Archaeological Museum, which was filled with artefacts from generations of Italian life. He was particularly interested in seeing the sculptures from the Roman period.

The air was oppressive. He felt as if he was wearing a heavy coat and flapped his shirt to cool himself down. Again, he regretted wearing jeans. Hopefully the museum would be air-conditioned, he thought. The clouds were ominous above his head, and the wind was getting up. The first drops of rain fell, huge round black marks appearing on the pavement and quickly disappearing, unable to compete with the heat of the stones. The rumbles of thunder were getting louder, and the first streaks of lightning briefly brightened the sky. Jake checked his messages from Milly, which she had sent over the past four hours.

> *Hi Jakey, how is it there?*
> *Can you reply so I know you're OK?*
> *You're annoying me now, Jake.*

He hurried to the front entrance of the museum as the rain started to get heavier and sent her a reply before going inside.

Hi Mills. So sorry, I was tied up meeting with Isabella. Really need to talk to you. I'll give you a call about 6 pm your time.

He knew she would be on air now, and he really did need her opinion on this case. He decided to tell her how much he was missing her. For the past two months they'd seen each other almost every day.

He could have spent hours in the museum, fascinated by the collections, especially in the Temple of Isis room, which was a shrine discovered at Pompeii to the Egyptian goddess Isis, and included paintings, ornaments, and furnishings. When he'd finished, he ambled back to the hotel in time to ring Milly. The rain had cleared and the sky just had a few, almost stationary, jagged clouds looking down on Naples. It was cooler and less humid, but still warm.

Jake put his key card in the door, thinking about how rough he had felt when he left the room at lunchtime. The room had been made up and smelt a lot sweeter. He was feeling quite invigorated after an interesting couple of days so had a quick look at the guide for somewhere to eat this evening. He decided on a restaurant that promised a healthy Italian food experience. Jake settled himself onto the bed and pressed Milly's number on his iPhone.

She answered, then explained that she was driving home and about to grab a ready to cook lasagne from Morrisons.

'Interesting,' Jake replied, unable to prevent himself sounding sarcastic. 'You spoil yourself – I'm having a traditional hand-made Neapolitan pizza.'

'Nice one. I was actually getting a bit worried that the mafia had picked you up and you were dangling off the edge of a cliff somewhere.'

'Nothing quite as dramatic as that, but I've had an interesting twenty-four hours.' Jake gave Milly a rundown of what had happened and how the case could be pretty involved, maybe dangerous, and would probably take up a lot of his time.

'So, do you think I should take it?' he asked Milly.

'Ah, I love the fact that you're asking me, but what's your gut feeling?'

'I ... think ... so.' He drew the words out.

'Then do it, you idiot. If you want to be a PI, then this is priceless. Your hero Cormoran Strike would jump at it,' she teased. 'Oh God, Jake, it could be really exciting. Maybe I can help you?'

Jake grunted. 'OK, decision made. I'll see

you later tomorrow.' He paused, then added, 'I've missed you.'

'Bloody hell,' came the reply. 'Naples has made you soft.' She laughed.

He ended the call.

Milly smiled the remaining miles home, feeling smug but a little guilty that she hadn't said she'd missed Jake. I really should have, she thought, because I do.

CHAPTER 10 – LYMFORD: 9 JULY

It was December when Jake had decided to make Lymford his new home. Initially he had planned to rent a house, then look for something to buy, but a chance encounter with a local in a pub, The Seafarer's Rest, led him to the houseboat. It wasn't the warmest or quietest of abodes in a winter storm, but he really liked it, and on 5th January he moved in.

It was blue and yellow and called *Endeavour*. It was an old canal barge rather than a houseboat, but that's what he preferred to call it. It was originally owned by a holiday company that had used it on the Grand Union Canal. After fifteen years they wanted rid of it, so a local Lymford millionaire bought it and transported the barge to the quayside. He'd used it as a retreat to write his memoirs, but after a few years he decided to rent it out. The boat needed a bit of TLC, but it suited Jake. He agreed to rent it for six months at a very favourable rate. It was hard to keep warm and he had to get used to the wind occasionally buffeting the boat, but he made it a home and never regretted the decision. He spent the first couple of months repainting it, getting some new fittings for it, and exploring the area.

Jake landed back in England the next day, leaving Naples behind for now. Gatwick was busy, the holiday season starting to ramp up. He picked up his car, patting the grey Audi A3 on the roof as he got in. He was back in Lymford mid-afternoon, absolutely shattered. He opened his case and turned it upside down so all the clothes fell onto the floor, then threw the case down the end of the boat. He grabbed a glass of water and collapsed onto the bed. He was asleep within thirty seconds.

He woke up several hours later, feeling his shorts and pants being slid down his legs. He kept his eyes closed as his shirt was unbuttoned and gentle hands explored his chest.

'I hope that's you, Milly,' he said, keeping his eyes closed.

No answer.

He slowly opened his eyes as he felt himself rising to the occasion. Milly was already naked. He loved her breasts – not too large, not too small, and very pert. She had a great body. This was Milly dominant, and Jake was happy to be submissive. She took his hands, placing them on her breasts so he could caress them, then she moved his arms back above his head, tying his wrists together with a scarf. Jake closed his eyes again. Milly straddled him and, using her hand, helped Jake to enter her. Both groaned. After just a few minutes it was all over for now, and they lay naked on the bed, Milly's arm across Jake's chest, him gently rubbing her back. They spoke for the first time.

'So, what's next for the super-sleuth then?'

'You mean, apart from a personality change?' Jake joked.

'No need for that … much.'

He went into more detail about his meeting with Isabella, Dave, and Isabella's suspicions about him and Paulo's disappearance. Milly bit her lip.

'Argh, would you miss me if I disappeared?' Jake asked, pulling the bed sheet over her.

'Maybe for a few days, then I would move on.'

'Your life would be tormented without me around.'

'It's torment with you, love.'

Jake scoffed and kissed her on the nose. 'Ain't you the lucky one,' he said, smiling, as he rolled onto his back. 'I think I need to find out a bit more about this family he's meant to have left behind in London. Are his parents still around? Then I'll go over to Menorca and see if I can suss things out a bit more over there. What sort of life is he leading? I'll see if I can arrange a chance meeting with him, maybe try and befriend him.'

'So many questions. I hope you're being handsomely paid by this Isabella woman. Is she attractive?'

'Nothing compares to you.' Jake smiled at her.

Milly glanced across at him, a pitiful look in her eyes. Jake often laughed at his own jokes, although she was quietly comforted by the words. 'For God's sake, don't start singing it – you're no Sinéad O'Connor.'

It was getting dark, and distinctly cooler outside; the ropes were slapping against the masts, making the tinkling sound Jake had got used to. The yacht marina was right next to his boat, protected by a manmade spit of land from the open sea. Milly needed to get back as she had an early call in the morning: she had been asked to do the breakfast slot as the regular presenter was ill. She couldn't turn it down, as it was the holy grail of radio broadcasting. Jake watched her walk to her car, which was parked the other side of the towpath opposite his boat. Then he jumped into his cramped shower, but not before downing a can of Carabao to revive him. He was happy they were back on an even keel after their first tension as a couple, three weeks earlier.

At the end of the houseboat was an area that could almost be classed as a study. It had been put in when the millionaire was writing his memoirs. This also worked well for Jake so, after getting out of the shower and grabbing a beer from the fridge, he switched his iPad on and started searching for what he could find out about Daniel Welby, aka Dave Constantinou. He had an email from Isabella with an attachment, which he assumed would be the information that Paulo had put together. As useful as that would be, he liked to do his own research as well.

There wasn't much to be found on the internet. Daniel had changed his name before the internet had been a big thing. Strange to think how vital it is to our lives now, mused Jake.

He came across an article written by a journalist a few years later entitled 'The Mystery of the Welby family'. Not particularly insightful, it went into the disappearance of Amara and Daniel and how their children had been adopted. He noted there had been two – Isabella hadn't mentioned this, so he jotted it down. The author also indicated their suspicion that Daniel may have murdered Amara before disappearing, but there was no evidence and police investigations had hit a brick wall. Jake looked at the date of the article. July 1996. 'Probably a cold case now,' Jake said aloud, as if someone was listening. He often did this when alone in the houseboat.

He closed the iPad, deciding to read Isabella's email in the morning, and switched on his small TV to watch the news – one of his must-dos. He took another beer out of the fridge and sat down on the small padded bench with a large bag of crisps – his dinner for today.

The next day Jake woke at seven. He sighed, rubbed his eyes, and looked across at the remains of a late-night cheese sandwich he hadn't finished; the bag of crisps had been enough. He got up and poured water into the kettle. He thought about why he liked the houseboat so much. Maybe it reflected his personality: he didn't want to commit to a permanent home in the same way he struggled to commit to a relationship, but he wanted things to change. The last few years had been difficult, but he really liked Milly and felt she could be the one. As he poured the boiled water into a blue mug, he told himself he had been reborn in his new life, and it wasn't too late to change his ways and be more committed.

He climbed back under his duvet, put the mug of tea in a recess next to his pillow and picked up the crossword from yesterday's *Times*. This was another of his weekly must-dos, although he rarely finished it. He ran his hands through his hair when nine across was eluding him. His mind wandered to Milly again.

She and Jake had met on the towpath in March. He'd seen her several times walking a cockapoo called Henry before he decided to find a lame excuse to talk to her. It still made him cringe to think about it: he'd pretended to stumble and twist his ankle just as he was approaching her. They were already on nodding and smiling terms, so he played the brave soldier and she the concerned passer-by. It turned out the cockapoo wasn't hers; she was dog-sitting for a friend, and that day was the last time she would be walking Henry.

She confessed later that she'd also been looking for an excuse to talk to him, but his stumble had been some of the worst acting she'd ever seen. A couple of days later they were both in the pub. Jake was propping up the bar when Milly walked in with a friend. He was talking to Felicity, a bartender. Milly had felt a pang of jealousy and had asked him how his ankle was. Remarkably, it was cured, but this encounter led to dinner at a not-so-reasonably priced restaurant in the New Forest and, four months later, here they were.

Today would be his first proper day investigating Dave. He grabbed a coffee and put some bread in the toaster. He switched on the breakfast news to see that another bland politician who wasn't saying anything was being interviewed following another report being published into the recent COVID-19 pandemic. Thankfully, life had now returned to normal, but the politician was reassuring the interviewer that the government had done everything they could. Jake gave a cynical laugh; he had been working in the civil service at the time. He switched over to an episode of *Frasier*.

When his toast and coffee were ready, he opened the iPad and found Isabella's email. Reading Paulo's report, he found out that the Welby case had been unofficially closed in 1995, four years after Daniel and Amara's disappearance. It seemed that the police had not linked Daniel Welby to Dave Constantinou, this was understandable, it would have been a tricky link to make. Paulo said he was going to get in touch with the Metropolitan Police. Did he do that? Jake wondered. There was also information on Dave's parents. His father died in 2009 from cancer and his mother was in a care home suffering from dementia. Paulo had visited her, but she hadn't been much help; she just seemed puzzled when he asked her about Daniel. That probably knocks any idea of talking to his parents on the head, Jake thought. But there must be other relations. He grabbed a pen and paper to start making notes. He hadn't found any concrete information on other people disappearing linked with Dave, so that was a blank canvas. What Paulo had discovered was circumstantial. Dave met one person in Crete and three days later they were discovered floating in the Adriatic with their skull half blown away. Paulo hadn't found any reason to think Dave was responsible.

Who *is* Dave Constantinou? Jake thought, frustrated.

'What about Amara's family?' he said aloud. He was still troubled by Isabella's claim that she had only found out that Dave was her real father when Paulo had been investigating him.

He went back to Isabella's email. Right at the end it mentioned that Amara had a sister called Stelia, which indicated a Greek Cypriot background as well. Amara's maiden name was Markou.

Jake did a Google and Facebook search on Stelia Markou. There were plenty of Stella Markous but not many Stelias, so that was a break. This would be his starting point. A small fee through an information website allowed him to track down addresses and phone numbers. He started making calls and felt his investigation had started.

CHAPTER 11 – STELIA: 12 JULY

Jake's second call got him a result. Stelia Markou from south-west London was sixty years old, had never married, worked at a local supermarket, and sounded like a very sad and bitter woman. They agreed to meet in a coffee shop later in the week. He could tell that she was wary. Jake needed to turn on the charm to persuade her to share more information, and they agreed to meet three days later in Wimbledon. He was lucky, she said that she usually put the phone down on strangers.

The heat was back as Jake drove up the motorway. The air-conditioning needed a service so Jake was struggling to keep cool. He hated the M3 and always avoided the section between junctions 5 and 6, so he came off at Basingstoke, took the A30 to Hook, then re-joined the M3. His parents' accident had been between these two junctions; he still couldn't drive past the scene.

Jake parked close to the coffee shop and checked his watch. It was 10.45 a.m., and he was due to meet Stelia at 11 o' clock. He'd given her a description of what he would be wearing – beige chinos and a blue collarless shirt – so he took a seat and kept his eye on the door and pavement outside.

Ten minutes later, a small woman wearing

a flowery blue dress that looked like it had been bought back in the 1970s gently pushed the door open. She had very dark hair, quite long and tied at the back, she was pencil thin, and she appeared as though life hadn't been kind to her. Jake lifted his head and attracted her attention. Nervously she walked across, banging into a chair on her way.

'Ms Markou?' Jake said and held out his hand.

'Hello, call me Stelia.'

'And I'm Jake. It's so nice to meet you.'

She was a little wide-eyed, as if people didn't normally say that to her.

'Can I get you a drink?' Jake asked.

'A strong coffee, please,' she replied, almost gasping as she said it.

Jake went up to the counter to order. He saw some cakes on the counter and checked if Stelia wanted a piece. She didn't, but Jake asked for a slice of lemon drizzle anyway.

He settled back into his chair. 'I'm sorry if this brings back painful memories but, as I said on the phone, I'm looking into what happened to your sister Amara and her husband Daniel Welby.'

'But I don't understand why,' she said, head bowed. Instead, she fiddled with the salt cellar.

Jake wasn't sure how much to tell her. Should he mention Isabella, the lost niece? He decided that he had no choice, so he explained how Isabella had contacted him. Stelia became visibly upset at the news but said she was glad that her niece was OK and doing well.

'I've always wondered what happened to little Zoe and Christopher, but I could never get any information from the adoption agency. All they said was that both children were well cared for and happy. Christopher was only three years old, while Zoe was five.' This agreed with what Isabella had told him about herself. Jake had known that Isabella was christened Zoe, but now he had confirmed that she had a brother as well.

The coffees arrived, and Jake decided to leave the cake for now. Stelia shakily popped three spoonsful of sugar into her latte.

'What I'm trying to find out is what you know about Amara's disappearance. Do you think she's still alive?' he asked diplomatically.

Stelia stiffened and looked up at Jake, almost for the first time. 'That beast killed her.'

'Daniel, you mean?'

'He was a brute – arrogant, aggressive, he was the son of Satan.'

'What evidence have you got that he may have killed your sister?'

'I haven't. All I know is they had a blazing row, she got in her car, and he followed her. She hasn't been seen since. He went off abroad and by all accounts changed his identity. But what I do know is he very nearly strangled her to death a week before. Amara called me, saying she needed to take the children and leave, but she was scared he would track her down. In those days you didn't tell the police as they would just laugh at anything resembling domestic abuse.'

Jake felt very sorry for the woman. Her parents had died several years ago, having never got over losing Amara. At least now she has Isabella ... perhaps, Jake thought, then told himself not to get emotionally involved. He pursed his lips and stirred his coffee again. He looked up at Stelia. 'What about the police investigation when Amara disappeared?'

'Bloody useless,' Stelia said angrily, with a steely-eyed gaze. 'We were a Greek Cypriot family, so they thought we were probably mixed up in some organised crime and it was some sort of gangland killing. We're not like that – we're not Albanians or Romanians, they're the scum around here. The police spent a month appealing for witnesses and investigating what might have happened to her and where Daniel might have gone, then they seemed to give up. Typical of the Metropolitan Police,' Stelia hissed.

She continued. 'There was one policeman who kept in contact with us and was pretty sympathetic. The last time we saw him was about a year later, when he admitted that my sister had probably been killed, likely by Daniel, and she may be buried somewhere in Epping Forest, but police resources had basically wound down, although the case was not closed. I always felt he knew more than he said.'

Jake thought about Epping Forest: a huge area where many bodies were rumoured to be buried – people who had crossed the line and upset various gangs over the years. They quietly went off the radar leaving few people interested, the Met Police included.

'What made you sure that Daniel hadn't died as well?' Jake asked.

'The people he worked for would have looked after him. They helped him,' Stelia muttered, staring into her cup.

They sat there for another half an hour, Stelia giving Jake a good insight into the family and the characters of Daniel and Amara. It seemed that their children had a troubled childhood. He asked her why they were taken into care and why Stelia hadn't offered to take them in. She simply said she couldn't. He promised to let Isabella know about her and said he would leave her to see if she wanted to get in touch.

As they got up to go, Jake paused. 'One last question. Do you know the name of the policeman who kept in touch with you?'

'I'll never forget – his name was Richard, Richard Warr. I believe he was Maltese,' Stelia replied.

Jake raised his eyebrows but said nothing.

CHAPTER 12 – LYMFORD: 12 JULY

Jake promised to keep Stelia informed as she headed for the Underground to take the short trip back home to Putney. He climbed back into the A3, which was stinking hot inside, the steering wheel burning his hands. He started the ignition and switched the radio on in time for the twelve o'clock news. Another politician was being accused of falsifying information during the COVID pandemic.

Jake said to the radio, 'Let it go, we've heard enough now. Let's just put it down to history.' He made his way onto the A316, which would give him a straight run onto the M3 until he got to the New Forest. Time to think.

Richard Warr. Was Warr a common name in Malta? Was he related to John? If he was, then it couldn't be a coincidence. John knows something about this – and he hasn't told me. Jake was getting a little frustrated by this thought. Something else to ask Isabella. There was something else about Stelia that he couldn't put his finger on; she had displayed a mix of emotions, but she looked scared as well.

He checked his watch. Milly was still doing the morning show so she should be available now. He speed-dialled her number. She answered quickly, and he gave her a brief rundown of his morning. He probably shouldn't be talking to her about the details, but he needed a sounding board, and she always had an opinion.

He finally arrived back in Lymford. His car temperature displayed 33 degrees travelling through Hampshire, but fortunately there was a sea breeze on the coast, where it was a slightly cooler 28 degrees. He went straight to Milly's flat, which was in a renovated brewery just off the high street. She was on the top floor of a four-storey block with a good-sized balcony that looked across the town to the English Channel. The Isle of Wight was normally clearly visible. A haze obscured it today, but it was still a beautiful view. He thought again what a good decision it had been to move to Lymford.

Jake went onto the balcony and checked the betting app on his phone. Most days he had a flutter of some sort, on football, racing or golf. He was able to be strict with himself, sure he wasn't addicted. He never bet more than £5 a day, but his run of luck had evaporated recently. The 3.15 at Newbury was another loss – maybe it was time to give it a rest. Milly brought him a cold beer as he sat in a deckchair, so he filled her in with more detail on his meeting with Stelia.

'So, what's next?' she asked.

'Like I said before, Menorca, I think. See what I can find out about his life there, and how best to engineer a meeting.'

Milly frowned at him over the top of her sunglasses. 'You didn't expect this when you relocated for a cosy life on the coast.'

Jake huffed and gazed over the rooftops. There was silence for a couple of minutes.

'You don't have to do it, you know,' Milly said. He glanced back at her, and his frown turned into a smile.

'We both know that I'm already hooked. I was after that first meeting, but it's still a big step up.'

'I know – I'm just playing devil's advocate by saying you're able to pick and choose. Financially you don't need it. After all, it's not local, is it? You've already been to Italy and London, now Menorca.'

'Ha – you're going to miss me, admit it,' Jake exclaimed, smiling at her again. He waited for a reaction but there wasn't one. He finished his beer instead.

He looked across at Milly who was now smiling at him. Jake just raised his eyebrows.

'At least you can stay at the apartment there, check everything's OK with it. Isn't it time you went out there again?'

Jake shook his head, wincing as a stab of pain shot across his head – a sign that he was getting stressed. He knew what Milly was getting at, she'd hinted before about them having a break there, but he needed more time. Yes, it would be nice to go away properly together, but Menorca had always been his family's special place. Since his parents' accident he'd been reluctant to go there because of the happy memories he had of it. They bought it twenty-five years ago as a holiday home and as a family they would always go at least once a year. But this was a trip he needed to do on his own, so he could deal with it. Then maybe he could take Milly in the autumn, if she was still happy to put up with him by then.

Milly interrupted the silence. 'You've drifted off, Jakey boy. Another beer?'

He nodded. She got up and headed into the kitchen.

'I stink,' he said, smelling his left armpit. 'Any plans this evening?'

Milly fixed herself a gin and tonic, grabbed a beer and walked back out onto the balcony. 'I've got the new boy coming round for a chat,' she replied.

'Oh yeah, Elias, the Swedish smorgasbord. He likes a good spread, male or female!' Jake laughed at his own witticism.

'Fuck off,' Milly said quietly. 'He's just enlightened. To be honest, he makes me feel old. It must be exhausting, the way he gets about. He's spiced up the station gossip, I can tell you.'

There was a pause.

'He's tried it on with me,' she added, glancing back at him.

Jake averted his eyes. Oh, here we go, wind me up, get a reaction, he thought. He shrugged. 'I should think so – you're the best-looking presenter on radio.'

Milly smiled. 'What does that mean? You can't be seen on the radio!'

Jake just raised his eyebrows.

'Maybe tonight?' she said, suggestively stirring the ice in her glass.

'Good luck,' Jake said, shielding his eyes from the sun, which was getting lower in the sky. 'If you don't have rampant sex, what's he here for?'

'Just station stuff,' Milly replied dismissively. She was keeping an air of mystery.

Jake started to laugh. 'You know why we like each other so much, don't you?'

'We love a good wind-up?' Milly replied.

'Exactly.'

Jake checked his watch. It was half past five. 'I think I'll pop to the Seafarers for a pie and a pint then, see if Luke's around.'

Luke was his new best friend in Lymford a builder by trade. They'd bonded on a drunken night at the Forest Inn not long after Jake had arrived in town. They started chatting at the bar about new housing developments and ended the evening four hours later, arms around each other, staggering through the town telling each other how brilliant they were. Luke was gay and had once subtly hit on Jake. Jake had promised that, should he ever turn gay, Luke was welcome to try it on, but for the time being he was happy being straight. They were able to laugh it off and become good friends and drinking partners.

Luke had inherited a yacht and introduced Jake to the fun of sailing in the Solent a couple of months ago when the weather had improved.

He got up to go, feeling tired. 'I won't call too early tomorrow in case you have a late night.'

'I'm serious, Jake. Despite what I said the other day, you don't have to carry on with this case.'

'I can't give up now – I don't know what's going on. The more I think about it, the less I trust this Isabella. She's my client, but I don't think that all is as it seems.'

The next day Jake rang Isabella and asked her if she knew where Dave was. She was sure he was in Menorca, as John had been trying to get hold of him there. They had finally spoken yesterday, and Dave had told John he was going to be staying there for a while. She went on to explain that it seemed Dave might be pulling out of the Maltese development. She told Jake that John was pretty pissed off. Jake again wondered about John and Isabella's relationship.

Isabella asked if there were any developments. Jake told her about his meeting with Stelia and asked whether Isabella knew anything about her. She confirmed she didn't, Paulo just mentioned her name in his report.

'Stelia has no love for Dave,' Jake said. 'She's convinced he's guilty.'

'Interesting,' Isabella replied. 'She's my aunt … I suppose I should make contact.' She hesitated. 'But I'm not ready for that. I'm not sure I ever will be.'

'There's one other thing I don't understand.' Jake knew his tone was slightly accusing, but this was deliberate. 'You have a younger brother that you've never mentioned.'

He heard a slight but discernible intake of breath at the other end.

'He's not important now, I'm afraid.'

'What do you mean? He's dead?'

'I'm not saying that. He's just not part of the investigation.'

Jake was about to protest but decided to leave it there. He decided to come back to it later: it was very much part of the investigation, as far he was concerned. 'I need to talk to John as well,' he said.

'For what reason?' Isabella asked brusquely.

'There's something I need to clarify with him.' Jake was being deliberately vague, playing Isabella at her own game. He didn't think she would know about the Warr connection Stelia had mentioned.

They agreed to talk when Jake was in Menorca.

*

Isabella put her phone down on the table. She was troubled. When should she tell Jake some of the truth? Not yet. She suddenly felt that maybe she was doing the wrong thing. Let sleeping dogs lie, as the British would say; she wasn't used to having doubts about her actions, but she also knew that she probably wasn't of sound mind and hadn't been for a while. She looked at herself in the mirror and struggled to recognise herself. A few days ago she felt confidence with what she was doing, but now she just looked scared, and she had every reason to be.

*

Jake got back on the iPad and booked a flight to Menorca later in the week. He would go to the apartment at Es Castell, a harbour town just south of the capital Mahon, and plan his meeting with Dave. He grabbed his notepad to write down what he knew so far, and the questions he needed to try and answer. What happened to Paulo? Who was Richard Warr? What did the Met Police have on Amara's disappearance? What happened to her? And, above all, was Dave a killer?

CHAPTER 13 – MENORCA: 15 JULY

Dave was getting frustrated. Bloody John was harassing him about the Malta development, Nico kept phoning him from Corfu about Demetrious, and the local police had dropped by asking him about that fool Paulo. This all made him think again about cutting loose and disappearing – for the second time in his life. There would be a lot to clear up before he did that. Where would he go? His contacts were better now; he could get a new identity pretty easily. He could fake his own death – a clean break, and maybe an opportunity to leave this lonely life.

He hadn't thought about his first life in England for many years, but now he was reminded of what had happened then. This sudden pang of curiosity surprised him. Maybe he was just getting older, but part of him wondered what had happened to his children. He had never wanted them in the first place, not with Amara. They got in the way. He knew he'd made a mistake the day he married Amara; they were very young, and she wasn't the obedient wife he expected. She had opinions. He was also young and easily influenced by the Stefanov clan, dealers in many of the new drugs that were coming out at the time. The rave scene became hot, and the Stefanovs were getting richer, wanting Daniel to give up the car dealership where he worked and get involved full-time in the underground drugs business. The glamour and prestige of it fascinated and impressed him, and he didn't take much persuading.

Amara didn't approve. Her parents owned a restaurant in Elstree which was often visited by actors working at the nearby studios. He'd met her there. She was quite small, outwardly demure but attractive, with traditional Cypriot looks, long dark hair, olive skin and a wide smile. He had to work hard to arrange their first date, she considered him a dodgy car dealer, but he had more charm then and he was one of the best dressed around. Their first few years together were ok, this was before he got fully involved with the gangs.

The Stefanov family were Macedonian, and gradually influencing life in North London. This was causing resentment in the local English gangs, resulting in skirmishes, notably the fatal stabbing of one of the Stefanov heavies in a chip shop in Southgate. Daniel was put under increasing pressure and had to make a choice: join the Stefanovs properly and be protected or stay with the dealership and have nothing to do with the gang. The latter option left him open to reprisals and exposed the dangers of having only one foot in with the Macedonians, so he became a permanent gang member instead.

His first 'job' was to shoot – but not kill

– a member of the Butcher gang. This was to send a message following the chip shop stabbing, and his first real test. They were fierce rivals trying to take control of an area of Harrow that had long been under Macedonian control. Dave – or Daniel – had found this a remarkably easy shooting, that would leave the victim hobbling for many years. However, the head of the Butcher gang was a matriarch by the name of Brenda. She was a disciple of the Krays, so Daniel had to keep a low profile for weeks afterwards. Brenda Butcher was something of an enigma: rarely seen in public but with a fearsome reputation. Legend had it that she had left three men hanging in a warehouse in Willesden, tied up by their hands, alive, their stomachs slashed. They slowly bled to death over three days and were eventually found by kids playing hide and seek.

After a while, Daniel was a rising star in the gang and was over the stigma of not being Macedonian. Amara was horrified by his career choice and went on and on, day after day, until he could take it no more. One Saturday evening he arrived home following several visits to local clubs to ensure the drugs were being mixed with cheap alternatives to maximise profit, Amara was treating him like a leper and showing him no respect. He told her to leave and take the kids with her, but she wouldn't go. She was stubborn, so he decided to give her no choice. The kids had cried endlessly until he hit them to shut them up.

As he sat on the terrace in Menorca thirty-two years later, he recalled what had happened that night. The striking of the kids had brought out an anger in Amara he'd never seen before, she lunged at him with a knife and slashed his right cheek from ear to lip. His rage then got out of control, and he had punched her in the face; two teeth went flying across the room. She had been scared, with a look of terror in her eyes that gave him strength. He had enjoyed their fight. Despite the pain in his face, he had moved towards her with a grim smile. His immediate thought was to grab her by the neck and squeeze until her last breath was gone. The gang would protect him. But as he had pinned Amara against the kitchen wall, the bitch had stretched out her hand and grabbed a saucepan that sat on the stove. She had swung it round and hit him on the back of the head. He had staggered back, dazed and confused, lost his footing and fallen onto the kitchen table. He'd been out for the count until he heard a car door slam and Zoe screaming 'Mummy!'

He looked across the orchard to where the sun was setting. Dave was still troubled following Paulo's visit several weeks earlier. He'd thrown a spanner in the works and stirred up events and memories that Dave had thought were dead and buried.

*

On the plane to Menorca, Jake was surrounded by holidaymakers. He sat with a couple of blokes from Basildon whose families sat behind and in front of him, so there was a cacophony of Essex noise. The children were not keen to stay seated. Jake plugged in his wireless earbuds and listened to music. That soon drowned them out, and he felt himself drifting off to sleep.

He didn't wake up until the flight had touched down. The sky was a deep blue and a heat haze shimmered off the tarmac. He moved his watch on an hour, noting it was now 3.30 p.m. The Seat rental car he had ordered was waiting for him. Once out of the airport, he turned right on the main road towards Mahon. It was a short journey, and his first stop would be a supermarket to stock up. This took him longer than expected. He was starving and probably bought more than he needed, but he was determined to eat and drink well this evening. He couldn't be bothered to go out again, so he bought a fillet steak that he would cook in a Béarnaise sauce and a few vegetables, because he knew he should, and plenty of bottles of Estrella.

As the apartment had been closed for so long, he'd called Louisa, who'd looked after it for the family for twenty years. She was going to open it up, give it a good spring clean, and get rid of any out-of-date food.

As he arrived in Es Castell and turned down the road towards the apartment, Jake felt a wave of sadness. Suddenly he wished he wasn't there on his own. The last time he'd been here, he'd had a great weekend with his parents for his mum's birthday.

He pressed the button on the remote control and the garage door opened reluctantly. Clearly it needed some lubrication. There was a sloping steep kerb in front of the garage, and you had to go in at an angle to avoid scraping the bottom of the car. Jake parked, then grabbed some shopping bags and made his way to the front door. The apartment was one of six in the block, which shared a swimming pool and outdoor area. All the other occupants were Spanish but had always been welcoming to Jake's family.

Miguel from next door rushed out and hugged Jake like a long-lost brother.

'So happy to see you,' Miguel said in his heavily accented English.

'*Gracias,*' replied Jake. '*Me alegro de verte.*' His Spanish was better than his Italian.

'So sorry, Senor and Senora Stone – tragic!' Miguel continued. 'You want anything, you see us.'

'*Muchisimas gracias,*' said Jake, smiling at the elderly Spaniard. He had often popped in for a Menorcan gin with his father. 'I'll join you one evening for gin and tapas.'

'*Si, si, si,*' replied Miguel. He smiled at Jake and stepped back into his own apartment, wiping a tear from his eye.

Jake entered his apartment and put his suitcase on the floor. The main bedroom and en-suite were on the ground floor. Upstairs there were two smaller bedrooms, a living room with a galley kitchen off it, and a narrow balcony. This had always been Jake's parents' favourite spot in the evening, as it had a view down the road to the waterway that led from Mahon harbour to the Mediterranean Sea. You could see expensive yachts, ferries and fishing boats going up and down the waterway. There was a hill on the other side of the water with a large villa at the top. Jake had always wanted to go there but never quite made it. It would have a tremendous view of the capital and the coast.

He went back to get the alcohol and shut the door behind him. The beers went straight in the fridge, apart from one, and he put the rest of the food on the table. He was going to have a beer on the balcony before he did anything else and send Milly a text to confirm he'd arrived. He now wished she was here.

Text done, he leaned back in his chair, kicked off his sweaty trainers, and put his feet up on the other chair. He took a swig of beer and couldn't stop himself letting out a loud sigh as he relaxed. He was not going to think about Dave tonight; he could wait until tomorrow.

Then his phone buzzed. He had thought Milly would still be on air, so he was surprised to see her name.

Cool, everything ok?

Jake debated how to answer this. Should he tell her he wished she was there? He decided not to. He was here for a reason and didn't want to get too sentimental.

Yep, all good.

He saw the flashing three dots pop up, so waited for her reply. After two minutes nothing had come through. This always made him curious. What had she been going to say? Why had she changed her mind?

He tapped out *Good show this afternoon?* For some reason he didn't know what else to say. His mind felt exhausted.

Average.

Jake decided to leave it there but kept checking his phone to see if Milly had anything else to say. Nothing. He sighed and trudged back to the kitchen to put the food away and get another beer from the fridge.

CHAPTER 14 – DEAD ENDS: 16 JULY

The next day was cloudy but still warm. Jake decided to have a shower and take the short walk down to the harbour at Cala Fonts. Es Castell was a mix of local Menorcans going about their business, a couple of highly rated hotels, and a mix of more sophisticated Europeans with holiday homes. It was not spoiled by package holiday tourism, which was strictly controlled on the island.

Cala Fonts was an attractive harbour ringed by restaurants and bars. Jake had a favourite café there, which he hoped was still there. As he came down the slope leading onto the harbour, he was relieved to see that the café was open, and quiet at this time of day. He took a seat and ordered a cappuccino and a Spanish omelette. Slipping his sunglasses back on, he sat back with his notepad and phone, deciding what to do next.

Back in the UK, he hadn't been able to find out exactly where Dave lived, but it didn't take him long in Menorca. He could log on to a local website and was able to track him down as his company was registered in Spain. There were few Constantinou's here, so Jake was able to pinpoint him to a fairly central spot on the island. So should he drop by and say hello? he wondered. Or would that make Dave suspicious?

Jake didn't know him very well, but he guessed he would be on his guard – and it wasn't as if he'd made a good impression on Dave in Naples. It then struck him that Miguel's son was in the local police. Maybe he could see if Dave had come to their attention. Jake made a mental note to speak to Miguel today.

Now, Richard Warr – Jake needed to speak to John. He didn't have contact details for him, so would speak to Isabella. She still bugged him. What was it about her? Paulo and Christopher – what had happened to them? Why didn't Isabella want to talk about her brother? That was a secret she was going to have to reveal. It was all very strange.

His coffee arrived, and he decided to call Isabella first. He looked around and saw that the café was pretty empty. In the evening it would be a thriving bar and restaurant and every table would be occupied.

Isabella answered immediately. 'Hi, Jake. Are you in Menorca now?'

'I am, sitting in one of my favourite cafés, overlooking the harbour, watching the world go by,' he replied. 'Listen, can you give me a number for John? I want to ask him about his father.'

Isabella hesitated, but then read out his mobile number.

Jake told her about his intention to find out any local intel on Dave and asked her a bit more about Paulo. The last she'd heard; he was in London. He had been going to speak to the Metropolitan Police before going to see Dave in Menorca. Since then, his phone had been dead. He didn't have any family and it seemed that no one was worried about him. The Italian police weren't interested, partly because he was a private investigator and partly because he didn't go missing in Italy.

'I think I made a mistake with him anyway,' Isabella admitted. 'He wasn't that clever, was a bit long in the tooth, as you say in England, and he drank too much. I can't be bothered to worry about him unless his body appears, or the police knock on my door.'

Jake was slightly taken aback by this slightly aggressive tone which he hadn't heard from her before.

'Um, that's not much to go on. Did he find anything more about what happened to Christopher?'

'No,' Isabella snapped. She clearly wasn't going to elaborate on this.

Jake could feel his frustration rise again. 'Look, I know you're holding out on me, Isabella. You hired me to dig into this Dave, and that means me knowing everything you know about him. I'll find out sooner or later.'

'I understand,' Isabella replied. She ended the call, and Jake shook his head. He drank his coffee and the omelette he'd ordered arrived. He decided to eat it before calling John. His call went to voicemail, so Jake left a message saying that he needed to speak to him urgently.

Jake paid and promised he would be back that evening for mussels. He decided to go for a walk around the harbour to see if anything had changed. Comfortingly, he found that much was the same, and a favourite bar, which served the best mojito he'd ever tasted, was still open. He decided to visit it this evening too.

He took the long way back to his apartment. The sun was breaking through the clouds, and it was going to be a hot day. As he reached the end of his road, which was a dead end, he watched a cruise ship coming out of Mahon about to enter the open sea.

'Good morning, Jake.' It was Miguel, heading towards the nearby market.

'Ah, Miguel, just the person I wanted to see.' Jake replied. He asked if Miguel's son Cesar was still in the police. Miguel confirmed that he was. Based in Mahon, he was now a sergeant, hoping to become an inspector soon. Jake asked if he could meet him, but he was on holiday in Portugal at the moment, although he would be back next week. Miguel said he would let Jake know when Cesar was back and free to talk to Jake.

He returned to the apartment and decided to search the internet again for information on Dave/Daniel/Paulo/Richard Warr/Isabella/John Warr and Dave's original family. He sat on the balcony, scratching his unshaven chin, his laptop open. It hadn't been a very productive morning so far; he needed to make some progress.

*

Meanwhile, Isabella was feeling like she was about to be engulfed in a wave of panic, she was sleeping badly and had lost her appetite. It was a week since the dinner party. She felt as if she was standing on the edge of Vesuvius, looking into the fiery crater. What was she doing?

CHAPTER 15 – PAULO: 25 MAY

Paulo didn't know what to do. His brain was clouded by whisky, as it had been every day for the last three years. He was in a cheap hotel at Gatwick Airport, with a ticket to fly to Menorca. He'd just spoken to Isabella, who was pretty pissed off with him. He'd just lied to her – not for the first time – saying that he'd made great progress in finding out what had happened to Amara, and he had a contact in the police in London who was going to assist him. This was not true. He'd spoken to a detective constable in Scotland Yard, but they hadn't been interested. He suspected they could smell the whisky on his breath, but they claimed they were too busy to investigate a cold case. A lot of police time was being spent on the continuing protests over climate change that had erupted across Europe this summer.

Isabella had threatened to drop him and find a new investigator. Paulo needed the money, so he needed results.

Isabella had contacted him six months previously, saying that she was adopted and wanted to find her real parents. Not too tricky, Paulo had thought. Her parents had adopted her in London after her real parents had disappeared. They were wealthy, able to pull a few strings, and were soon back in Italy. Records showed that her birth parents were Daniel and Amara Welby, who lived in Borehamwood on the northern outskirts of London. Both had gone missing, so Isabella – who was originally called Zoe – was taken into care. The police were suspicious that Amara may have been killed. Daniel was a small-time gangster, so Paulo suspected that the police hadn't tried too hard to find him. Something wasn't right in the case being dropped so quickly, why didn't they try harder to find out what happened to Amara? The detective inspector leading the case had later been accused of corruption over another incident, maybe that was significant.

Paulo had been troubled that Isabella hadn't seemed surprised when he reported this back to her. It was almost as if she already knew. She wanted him to dig deeper and find out what had happened to Daniel: she was keen to know if he and Amara were still alive. Paulo also found that Isabella had a brother called Christopher, but she didn't ask him to check what might have happened to him.

Investigations into Amara seemed to come to a dead end, quite literally. He'd tried to contact her sister but seemed to have no luck finding the right person. One person hung up on him, but then he'd had a lucky break with Daniel. He'd spoken to a former police officer who had also worked on Daniel's disappearance. He was retired now but had advised Paulo to try and find a Dave Constantinou, who he believed was living in Spain. The former officer had been vague about how he knew this, but it was a line of enquiry that the police were no longer interested in. The former detective was not happy with this, but the orders were final.

Paulo looked in the mirror, which opposite the bed. It was battered around the edges, as if visitors had deliberately scratched it with knives. He'd been here for a week and had put the 'Do Not Disturb' sign out every morning. The room was hot, smelly, and becoming quite grubby. He hadn't shaved for a week, and it was three days since he'd showered.

In the mirror he said to himself in Italian, 'You disgust me. Pull yourself together.' He was forty-seven years old, divorced, not a spare gram of fat on him, with thick, wiry hair that was half grey/half dark. He was known as the Badger to the few acquaintances he had. His kids were in their twenties and hadn't had anything to do with him since their parents had divorced. He'd never been violent or abusive; he had just neglected them. He developed a liking for whisky, and that had become his friend. His wife had begun a new relationship; he'd barely spoken to her for four years. He managed to keep earning enough to pay his bills, but he knew he needed to break the cycle.

He was a pitiful sight, and he hated himself. He fell back on the bed and thought about getting something to eat. This was tricky. He didn't find eating in the UK a pleasant experience. He drifted to fast food restaurants or proper Italian restaurants if he could afford it. The lack of choice around his hotel meant that it was probably going to be burger and chips again. He slapped himself and decided to have a shower.

While in the shower, he decided that he would take a flight to Menorca and confront Dave at his villa. Tomorrow, he vowed, he would not drink. He would take the first steps to changing his life. The prospect scared him, but when he got back to Italy, he would attend an Alcoholics Anonymous meeting and bare his soul. He would get back on track. He'd told himself this before.

He felt slightly more in control the next day. He'd shaved and generally cleaned himself up. He didn't have a drink at Gatwick or buy any spirits in the duty-free shop, just a large bar of chocolate, which more than likely would be his lunch.

As he sat on the plane, gazing out of the window at the plane opposite, Paulo thought about Isabella. He didn't understand her motives. Why him? She seemed not to be short of money, and he came cheap. He'd traced her parents, but she was very cool about that, why not use an English investigator? It would be easier for them. His English was basic, and quite frankly he felt out of his depth. Paulo needed the money so had ignored this thought up to now, but the reality of the investigation brought it to the front of his mind. He was panicking about his lack of results. He needed to give Isabella something. And what about her brother, Christopher?

He decided to give Isabella a call. She picked up immediately.

'*Ciao*, Paulo,' Isabella said in her usual cool tone.

'*Ciao*, Isabella. I just wanted to check something with you. I'm just trying to understand what you want from me now that we know about your birth parents,' he asked.

Isabella sighed. 'I want Dave Constantinou to admit to his past, that he's my biological father and what happened to my mother. I want him to acknowledge his life before he changed his name.'

'And Christopher?' Paulo asked.

'No need to worry about him. He's dead,' Isabella replied icily.

'OK. I'll email you over the next few days.' He ended the call. He knew she was frustrated that he hadn't discovered more about Amara.

Paulo decided to go straight to Dave's villa and ask him some straight questions. Which questions? He wasn't sure, but he would tread carefully. Paulo knew where Dave lived. That wasn't hard to find out. If nothing else, he had good connections with immigration. It helped that Spain and Italy were both in the EU. He'd had it confirmed that Dave arrived from Malta two days ago on an Air Malta flight.

*

When his plane landed, Paulo picked up his hire car and drove out to Alaior. The sat-nav took him to Dave's front door. He pulled up, realising that he was a bag of nerves. His stomach was flipping but driven by a new-found determination, he pressed the bell to the right of the door. He prepared his opening speech.

CHAPTER 16 – JOHN: 16 JULY

John sat back and looked at his phone. He'd just spoken to Isabella. He was too involved in their 'business' together and she had a steely determination that was impressive. He liked that but he loathed it too; he didn't like her enough not to do something about it. He'd manipulated her for his own ends and she had been desperate enough to go along with his plan, but she was also strong-minded.

He glanced across the bay at Sliema towards Valletta, the capital of Malta. Sliema was where it all happened. John had played a major part in the town's development. At the time it had caused some unrest, as many people felt that the town development was out of control. John had successfully stubbed out any opposition. High-rise apartment blocks were starting to dominate the traditional Maltese villas and townhouses that made Sliema so attractive to tourists and the affluent locals. He wasn't too concerned.

He was enjoying a coffee in a café on the so-called Sliema Front. It was the height of summer, so tourists thronged the promenade. Most of the locals were in the shade, protecting themselves from the fierce July sun. The northern Europeans were easily identifiable, thanks to the various shades of sunburn on their skin. At this time of year John much preferred the early morning or late evening – better still was the quiet of winter.

Isabella was troubling him today; he didn't like being troubled. She'd been full of fun in Naples, but she was now back to her usual cool self. She'd just advised him that Jake wanted to speak to him and reminded him to be careful. She didn't need to do that. He was aware of the requirement for care; he'd been in this game since he was in the womb, and he had more to lose than she did. He would turn on the charm, be helpful, but also be on his guard when Jake called him. Isabella had warned that they were going to have to let him in at some point, but she was unaware of his own deceit. It just highlighted the confusion he was feeling about his own endgame. He was being drawn into an elaborate ruse, which wasn't what he needed.

John sighed. He knew that Isabella was out of her depth. He'd broken one of his own rules by getting more involved than he wanted to, and no longer felt in control. He was going to have to take back that control.

His job was straightforward, and he was ready to act when needed, but she was the coordinator, and she had to keep track of the tangled web she was trying to master. Little did she know that John was the real puppet master.

Admittedly, to begin with he had hoped for a romantic relationship with her, but that hope had been flatly trounced when he was in

Naples. She was too savvy to add in that type of complication, and he was mightily impressed by her ability to compartmentalise aspects of her life. Sex was on the table, but romance was not.

John was approaching forty, and now he had to work harder to keep his body fit and active. His waistline was expanding, but there wasn't a grey hair on his head. He kept his dark hair short and was olive-skinned with dark brown eyes and a face that many women found easy on the eye. At 5 feet 8 inches he wished he was slightly taller, but his height allowed him to blend into a crowd when he needed to.

John owned a large villa just outside Sliema. It had six bedrooms, a swimming pool and a magnificent terrace that faced west and came into its own as the sun was setting. His wife, Andrea, had designed the house a few years ago. Now that it was exactly what she wanted she needed another project, and at the moment her project was Christos, a Greek restaurant owner on Gozo. She knew John knew about her fling; John was quite laid back about it. Christos kept her entertained and off John's back. He hated Greeks. He knew this would pass and Andrea would find someone – or something – else to occupy her thoughts.

They'd never had children, and they had drifted apart in recent years. Children may have made a difference to his life choices, he didn't know, but he enjoyed the excitement that life brought him now. He knew Andrea suspected him of a darker side, she would question his sudden disappearances, but he always had a good supply of excuses. It had now got to the point where she didn't bother to ask, and he never told her. John always had twenty-three-year-old Leanne to call on when he felt like it – his romantic distraction on the island.

John was a top dog in Malta, and his business interests had been good for the Maltese economy. He'd encouraged inward investment, but whether this was always legitimate was open to question. He no longer got involved in much of the day-to-day business; he'd developed a side-line which he found much more exciting. Dave Constantinou and Isabella were part of this side line. He'd got Dave involved in his project in Valletta, not intending it to succeed. He just needed to get close to him. That was what Isabella wanted, and she thought she was in charge.

His dad always used to say, 'Keep your eye on the past to ensure the future works for you'. John knew that ghosts of the past were coming back, and it wasn't even his past. He knew it would end in at least one death.

He finished his coffee, crossed the road, and walked down the steps to the promenade. He found a bench in a quiet, shady spot and listened to Jake's voicemail, then called him back.

Jake had already added John as a contact, so

knew it was him before he answered.

'Hi John, how's Malta?'

'Hi Jake. It's very warm – even by Maltese standards.'

'I've never been, but it's certainly on my list.'

'When you do, then I will look after you,' John said reassuringly.

Jake quite liked John on a basic level, although he was highly sceptical of his honesty. He'd been careful not to say anything to Isabella about why he needed to speak to him, and he knew this had riled Isabella for some reason.

Jake carried on. 'I've come across something while delving into Amara's disappearance in England.'

John nodded and grunted.

'There was a police officer in the Metropolitan Police who kept in touch with her parents after they had ended their enquiries.'

John froze.

Jake continued, 'His name was Richard Warr. I wondered whether he was a relation of yours, by any chance? I know he was Maltese, and it may be a common surname out there.'

John's mind raced; he hadn't considered that Jake might ask him this question. Perhaps he'd underestimated Jake. What should he say? Think quickly.

'You still there, John?' Jake asked.

There was a pause. 'Sorry, Jake, I think the line dipped out. I was talking but I don't think you could hear me.' John decided now that Jake knew about Richard, he had no option but to be honest – at least, partly. 'Well, my father died a few years ago. He had bowel cancer and it was a painful death, I'm afraid. We lived in London for a few years when I was younger and I believe that he was in the Met Police for a while, so it might be him. We came back to Malta when I was fourteen and we never really talked about his job back then.'

'Is your mother still alive?' Jake asked.

'No, I'm afraid not. She died in London. That was why my dad decided to come back here,' John replied.

'I'm sorry.' Jake sounded respectful. 'Oh. I thought it was worth asking, but I'll have to let it go.'

'No problem Jake,' John said cheerily. 'Hopefully we'll catch up again soon and have a beer together.'

'Sure, that would be great. Cheers for now.' Jake ended the call.

John exhaled a long gasp of air, not sure how convincing he'd been. He scrolled to, 'Father' on his phone, and pressed call. He waited for Richard Warr to answer.

CHAPTER 17 – MILLY: 16 JULY

Jake sat back, the hint of a smile on his face. He was pretty sure that Richard Warr was John's father. It seemed too much of a coincidence that John had just happened to go into business with the son of a woman that his father had investigated thirty years ago. John had tried to brush him off, so what was the connection here? He knew that he'd just hit on something significant, but then another part of him thought maybe it wasn't a big deal. At the end of the day, he was investigating Dave, and it seemed from what Stelia told him that Richard had really been trying to help the family find out what had happened to Amara, while others had given up. Nothing sinister about that. He needed to talk to someone, bounce his ideas off them, but Isabella was not the one. His instinct was telling him something though.

Jake checked his watch. Milly would be on air, so he left her a message.

Need to talk to you, Mills. Ring me when you can?

Sitting on his balcony in Menorca, he opened the laptop again, a glass of ice-cold water in his hand, which tasted like nectar on a hot day. He'd been particularly lazy this morning. He hadn't yet showered or shaved and was still in his boxers and T-shirt. He'd planned to ring John this afternoon.

He did a search on Richard Warr. It wasn't an uncommon name. He narrowed it to 'Richard Warr Malta'. There was lots of information on someone who played football for the island, but nothing else obvious. He tried 'Richard Warr Metropolitan Police'. Still nothing to easily identify the Richard Warr he was searching for. There was a 2006 article from the *Borehamwood Times* about a Richard Warr who was now living in Malta: he had apparently been at a charity event with Hollywood stars who'd been filming at the nearby Elstree studios. It could be him, as it was the area where they used to live, but anything else that identified John's father eluded Jake. He would need to try more sophisticated means.

He sat forward and looked over the balcony with a sigh. A family was carrying a couple of kayaks down the road. Clearly excited, they were chattering away in Spanish, but not listening to each other. The mother was weighed down with most of the bags but was happily joining in with the banter.

It sure beats the civil service, Jake thought. He was warming to the investigation now. And the pay was good. He might not trust Isabella yet, but she was prompt at reimbursing his expenses.

Jake decided to go on one of his 'thought

walks'. He screwed his eyes up and assessed the sky. There were a few clouds scudding across the blue background – at least they'd provide some protection against the sun. He slapped on some factor 30, put on a baseball cap, changed his boxers for shorts, slipped on trainers and made for the door.

As he closed the door, an attractive blonde walked past and smiled at him. She was probably about thirty and was slim and stylish. He smiled back. He knew he didn't look his best, so was she really smiling at him? He decided she was, and she wasn't just being polite. Jake had often been told he was handsome, but he didn't really believe it. He had a surprising lack of confidence, which his friends always found amusing.

Jake was fascinated by maps. It had started when he was about eight. His father bought him an old atlas of the world. For years, it was his favourite book, and he spent hours poring over it and studying the countries, their capital cities and exactly where they were in the world. By the time he was sixteen he knew every capital of the world, could name any country from the outline of its border, and knew exactly where it was, and its population. It wasn't a talent that he boasted about, but it proved to be handy at pub quizzes. Although map apps on a phone had their place, they weren't the same as a proper paper map that you could open up and understand the scale. He despaired of people who blindly followed a sat-nav with no idea where they really were. Unfortunately, his houseboat didn't have room for all his maps, so he kept a selection there with the rest in storage, along with his other possessions. When he first visited Milly's apartment, he couldn't stop himself studying the map in her studio which showed the area that Coast FM covered – from Weymouth in the west to Chichester in the east, and north to cover most of Hampshire. She accused him of looking longer at the map than at her and was concerned that he was more of a geek than she'd realised.

'Wait till you see my collection of beer mats,' he'd replied. She wasn't sure if he was joking.

Needless to say, he knew where he was going to walk, although it would be new for him. He calculated it would take a couple of hours, and he would think about John on the way. Jake made his way around the outskirts of the town and into the fields, which hummed with crickets. He noticed that the clouds were gathering strength, looking darker and angrier and cutting out the remaining patches of blue. What he should have done before going out was to check the local weather forecast. He checked it now. Showers were predicted until the evening. He was out in the open, trudging alongside fields of lemon trees. He had a clear view and, in the distance, could see a shield of dark cloud touching the ground, obscuring anything behind. It was a heavy rainstorm, and it was heading straight for him. Jake groaned and looked behind him. Should he carry on and let it do its worst, or head back and see if he could outrun the rain? He rationalised that he hadn't had a shower yet; it was warm, and it might be fun. He carried on.

There was a small village ahead of him, but soon the houses had disappeared behind the gloom. He could see the rain advancing across the field so he pushed his cap more firmly onto his head, which was all he could do to protect himself. He heard the rain first – a cacophony of waving sound that quickly got louder and then engulfed him. Big drops ebbed and flowed around him. Within seconds water was running down his face, down his legs, and soaking into his trainers. He squelched on. Fortunately, he was walking on stony ground, so he wasn't stepping through mud, but this was some of the heaviest rain he'd ever seen. After ten minutes, the light became discernibly brighter, and the pounding of the rain appeared to be getting quieter. A minute later he was out the other side. The smell of fresh rain on sun-scorched ground replaced the damp mugginess of cascading water. With that the familiar sound of his phone playing 'Kinky Afro' by the Happy Mondays emanated from his trouser pocket.

Jake struggled to pull the phone out with his wet hand. It was Milly. His fingers were too wet to use his thumb to unlock the phone, so he punched in the code and put the phone to his ear.

'You picked a great moment to call.'

'Oh, hello Milly, how are you, I've missed you, have you had a nice day?' she replied sarcastically.

'Hang on a minute.' Jake replied. He took a selfie and sent the picture through to her. He continued, 'I've just come through the heaviest shower of rain there's ever been. I had no choice but to brave it out.'

'Oh, my little soldier,' Milly replied without the hint of a smile.

'Someone's not amused – what's the problem?' Jake was disappointed that she wasn't interested in his plight.

'What's your problem first?' she asked.

'It's John Warr. I'm not sure about him. You know I told you about this Richard Warr? Well, I think he's John's father, but John's being very vague. He's denying knowing about a connection with the Richard Warr who liaised with Amara's family when she disappeared. Frankly, I don't believe him, and I could do with your help.'

'What can I do?' Milly asked, not sounding very enthusiastic.

'Your new Swedish friend – did you say he spent some time investigating the Met Police while he was working for the BBC?'

'Yep, he was part of a team that was putting together an item about corrupt officers in the 90s, but the team was warned off.' Milly was gathering some interest.

'Really? So, he must have contacts who may be able to verify who this Richard Warr was – and maybe find out if there's any dirt on him?' Jake asked. There was a pause. 'Please?' he added.

'I'll ask him … while I'm still there,' Milly said.

'What does that mean?' Jake asked.

'We've just had a big meeting. Coast FM is being taken over by Anderson Media, an American conglomerate that wants to mould all their stations into clones of each other. It's the way radio has gone over the last few years. It will mean repetitions of Bruce Springsteen, Coldplay and Bon Jovi.'

Jake groaned in sympathy. They had a shared love for 90s music, particularly the club music prevalent at the beginning of that decade.

Milly continued. 'They've promised that my show will continue, but I'll have little say over the playlists. I want to play music I like, not what I'm told to by faceless management.'

'I get it,' Jake said sympathetically although he wasn't fully engaged; his thoughts were still with Richard Warr.

'I don't think I can do it. They're going to rebrand the station as the Crunch – what does that mean? The strapline will be "The Crunch – the bigger bite for your life". What the fuck?' Milly's voice was getting higher, and she was clearly unhappy. Jake decided to drop talking about his own thoughts for now.

There was a pause, and Jake tried to think of something to say. No need: Milly came back in. 'I'm going to contact Giles at Original; he's tapped me up a couple of times to join their 90s station in London. I'm too old for the youth market now, and this would suit me. I'd get the chance to mingle with the artists a bit more, which might be interesting.'

Jake sensed that Milly had finished for now, so he stepped in. 'That might work out quite well – but London?'

'I may have no choice.'

'But I've just left there,' Jake said resignedly.

'Well, I'm not asking you to come with me.'

Jake bit his lip and ran his hand through his hair – another sign that he felt stressed. Her remark had stung, and he wasn't sure what to say.

'Fair enough.' Jake decided to leave it there. 'OK, I'm sorry about your news, I really am. Why don't we talk later?' He paused. 'By the way, I miss you.' He ended the call before Milly could respond. He was a little afraid that she wouldn't say the same thing back, but pleased he'd told her. He was telling the truth and he really was missing her, but he probably wasn't showing it.

The sun was blazing again, and he was drying out quite quickly, but his squelching trainers would take more time. He knew the blonde woman he saw earlier would smile at him in amusement now. He decided to carry on his walk as planned, going through the small village he'd seen shrouded in rain earlier. It was eerily quiet, but then it was still the heat of the day. Only foreigners went out now.

He rounded a headland to be greeted by a spectacular view of the sea. He stood and took it all in. To his left was the entrance to Mahon harbour, where he could just make out the kayakers he'd seen earlier. At that moment he felt lucky. He thought again that a year ago he had been in a very dark place, but the decisions he had made to change his life had all been positive. He wasn't going to let Milly get away.

CHAPTER 18 – DAVE: 16 JULY

While Jake was getting soaked on the east coast of Menorca, Dave was sheltering from the sun on his terrace, although he saw the black clouds off to his right. Thoughts were still rampaging through his head; he was confused about what to do. He thought about Paulo again, he thought about John, but most of all he thought about Isabella.

He didn't want to believe what Paulo had told him – that's why he had been so on edge when he was in Naples, and he now felt a little guilty about how he had treated Claudette. Maybe he was mellowing. And who was the Harry bloke who had asked all the questions in Naples?

Dave looked around and felt the heavy cloak of loneliness settle around him. All this money, property and, to a certain extent, power – but for what? He'd backed his life into a corner in a self-destructive way. He knew that if the police knew about all the things he had done, he could be locked up in several countries around Europe.

Since the day Daniel became Dave, he'd expected someone to call on him and ask him about Amara, but it had never happened. The gang had done a good job there, although he was sceptical that they'd done enough to ensure that Daniel went missing in the same way

Amara had. Not forgetting his own actions to try and protect himself. As the years went by, he'd almost convinced himself that Daniel had never existed, and that Dave had been born at the age of twenty-four. He always had a back story ready, and in many ways it was like going into witness protection. Whenever anybody asked, he kept his story brief, saying that he lived in Cyprus, he left England when his parents had died, moved to France, and set up a Greek food shop in St Malo. From there he'd gone into property and done very well for himself. The gang had arranged all the paperwork for him, with a little help from the Metropolitan Police.

Although he refused to believe it at first, it was easy for him to confirm what Paulo had told him. He'd provided a lot of the evidence himself. The question was, what was he going to do? Why would he do anything? He didn't need to. However, he knew it was something he wouldn't be able to forget, and, in the end, events were being driven for him. Again, he had that feeling of being out of control.

One thing Dave had decided was to pull out of the Maltese deal, so he needed to tell John. He wouldn't be happy, but so what? John was another slimy individual who was hiding his own secrets.

Dave just didn't realise the extent of those secrets.

His phone rang. It was Nico in Corfu again.

'Nico?' Dave still spoke Greek. He was a bit rusty, but it made a change from English.

'Dave, Demetrious is coming on heavy – can you speak to him, please?' Nico sounded desperate.

'Fucking hell, Nico, put him on if he's there,' Dave replied.

'David?' It was Demetrious's gruff, threatening voice.

Dave hated being called David, but knew he had to suck it up.

'We're taking over the hotel,' Demetrious proclaimed.

'How long for?' Dave replied.

'Permanently.'

'What! You can't do that. Look, I could sell it to you at a reasonable price.'

'No, you won't. This is payback time. Don't forget what I know.' Demetrious hesitated, then added, 'That business in Crete? You could go to jail for that if I spoke to the right people.' Demetrious sounded menacing, and Dave knew he couldn't fight it. He blustered but finally agreed that he had no choice. Maybe that was for the best – another piece in the jigsaw that he was trying to finish?

'OK, it's yours, you have it. I'm wiping my hands of it. I'll just make sure the lawyers transfer the ownership legitimately,' Dave said.

'I knew you'd do the right thing.' Demetrious rang off.

Dave thought about Crete – one of his black moments. He had lost money today, but maybe that was fate helping him to wipe his hands of Corfu?

CHAPTER 19 – ISABELLA: 17 JULY

Isabella was upset, she'd been tempted back into an online poker tournament the night before with money she didn't have. Her husband Luca had given her a sizable divorce settlement, but she had a serious gambling problem. She'd blown 500,000 euros on online poker over a two-year period and had managed to stay away from it for five months. She had no income of her own, apart from some stocks and shares, but many of these had now been sold to reduce her debt. Therapy had helped her and the danger that she put herself in had become a reality check, but the temptation was always there. This time she'd made a small profit of 100 euros, but she knew that could easily be a loss of 100,000 if she hadn't backed out when she did. When would she have the strength to never go near it again? She considered destroying her laptop, but she still needed it for regular day to day use. In this day and age, it's impossible not to be online. She felt dirty thinking about what it had done to her, the desperation it caused and what it was leading her to do. She would stop now once and for all.

She had a hair appointment, then after that needed to see her accountant. She wasn't looking forward to it. Accountants were just as corruptible as anyone else in Italy, but he was making a fuss about the debts that Isabella had accrued.

The house in Naples was still mortgaged, but she refused to let go of the lavish lifestyle she'd got used to. Some of the expensive paintings she owned could be sold, but she knew that might look as if she was in trouble if people suddenly noticed they had gone. She knew her accountant was going to say she had no option than to sell, but he must be able to do *something*; the paintings were not hers. Luca had bought most of them when they were married. He just hadn't taken them since he had downsized and moved north.

Quite early in their marriage, they'd bought a house in West Hamble on the south coast of England. This was so Luca could indulge his passion for yachting, as he tried to get involved in Italy's bid for the Admiral's Cup yacht race. Isabella had been naive and had believed the house was in joint names; she'd still used it after the divorce but the solicitor in Winchester had dropped the bombshell that it had been sold, after confirming that it was in Lucas's name only. She'd visited him on the day she met Jake, hoping she could sort something out, but to no avail.

Nine months ago, she'd pleaded with Luca to sell the house and for them to divide the proceeds. It would fetch about one million euros – just enough to pay off her debts – but she was too embarrassed to admit why she wanted to sell, and this had led to a heated debate over the phone when he'd made it clear that the house was his to sell, when *he* wanted to.

There only seemed to be one option left – the one she had dreamed up a year ago when she had met John and they had discussed her past. John was far more dangerous than he appeared, and that excited her. They began a sexual relationship, but that was all it would ever be. This was mainly business; a sort of business she'd never dreamed she would get into. It was he who had suggested that Dave's inheritance could come to her, solving all her money problems. However, what she didn't know was what might be in his will, what the Spanish Law is on inheritance. She was blind to the possible complications.

All she needed was a professional to take Dave out. John was one of the best, and happy to oblige. In return, he would get twenty per cent of his money. Initially, she had dismissed the idea, thinking that he would have a will, that would not include her, but John had skilfully asked him that question several months ago. Dave had been drunk and had said that he knew he had two children somewhere, and he'd left most of his estate to them. Isabella knew she would have to prove she was his daughter, and it would take time, but John assured her there were ways and means. He would use his connections to help her, and he was confident it would work. She was desperate. So, their plan had started there.

Isabella soon found that she was quickly drawn in. She thought she was in control, but John knew he was.

Isabella had one close friend, Chloe. They had grown up together in Rome, and every year went on a skiing holiday in Zermatt, in Switzerland, together. Chloe's husband was very respectable and owned several vineyards in Tuscany. She knew she should confide in Chloe about her situation, but her pride was too strong. She would have to admit to the gambling, and Chloe had quite strong morals.

Isabella had very high standards, and her rather cool exterior had left her with few genuine friends. She was a bit of a snob, strong-minded and sometimes rude. She had no problem with this reputation, but also knew that several of her so-called friends would enjoy her downfall. Lucy Cornish would be one of them. She was a frenemy; their dislike was quite mutual.

No, she wasn't going to let that happen. She felt nothing but contempt for Dave, her one-time father, and now she had the means to make him pay for his neglect, although she was aware that she was playing a high-stakes game.

She looked at herself in the mirror again and winced. Her hair was losing its shine – she hadn't washed it in days and wondered why she'd made a hair appointment. It was an attempt to hang on to respectability, despite the mess she was in. She was gaunt, and lines were appearing where she'd never seen them before, caused by worry – when she might get another knock on the door or be approached by someone reminding her of her obligations? Their patience was running out.

It was another hot day as she stepped out to make her way to the Corso Umberto for her appointment with Gianni. He always gave her a good deal after she'd helped him out when he made the mistake of talking about a relationship he'd had with a member of the Mazzarella clan – a violent mafia-style group who were active in Naples. They were part of the Camorra organisation, which dominated the Campania region of Italy, with their tentacles spreading across southern Europe. No clan member would ever admit to being gay, so when Gianni was caught talking to clients about his new boyfriend he was threatened with the removal of his genitals. He got away with the removal of one testicle, thanks to Isabella. She had known the mother of one of the clan leaders, so was able to plead for mercy. Gianni learned a harsh lesson, and always made sure to give Isabella a good deal at the studio.

She was mentally exhausted after seeing her accountant, Armando. She nodded obediently as he tried to lecture her about the expenses and the size of her debt. She assured him that she had a plan, but it was too early to tell him about it. He had shrugged in despair, talked to her like a child, and shouted at her while she sat there trying to smile at him. She managed to keep cool, which just seemed to antagonise him, but she knew he was right. For now, she just needed to disarm him. It was not his debt, after all, but he was a family friend and was worried about her.

She had one question gnawing away at her. What had happened to Paulo? She didn't like not knowing, as he knew more about her history than most people. She was sure that he had met Dave, but since then there had been silence. Jake was now in Menorca, and she was nervous about what he might find out. It had amused her that he was a rookie investigator; naively, she had thought he would concentrate on events in London, find out what happened all those years ago, and then the second stage of her plan could be implemented. She was troubled after she'd spoken to John again last night. Jake appeared to be brighter than she had thought. Maybe it had been a mistake to involve him in the first place. She might have to think about getting him off the trail somehow and moving things along quicker than envisaged, but she really wanted to find out what happened to Amara. She felt a loyalty to the woman, who had probably been an innocent victim in Dave's dirty dealings.

Did Richard Warr know more? She knew his identity had to be kept out of it, but John was tight-lipped about his father.

She wanted Jake to carry on, but she knew she was walking on a tightrope, and events could slip out of her control.

CHAPTER 20 – ELIAS: 17 JULY

Milly checked her watch, it was 1.30 p.m. She was feeling a bit rushed with only half an hour to get to the studio for an interview with Leopardess. Milly thought about this new grime artist who was, allegedly, from the gritty streets of East London – actually, she was from the leafy backwater of Petersfield, but that wouldn't go down so well with the buying public, or so her record management company thought. She wasn't really a fan of grime. Coast FM only really played this type of music later in the evening and she mused that she was starting to feel a little cynical about the current music scene. She was getting to the age where she became nostalgic about the music of the past, thinking that it had all been better back then.

She grabbed her car keys, a bottle of water and a banana, which was today's lunch. She reversed the car out of her private parking space and headed to the main road which would take her through the New Forest. Once on the straight road she dialled Elias's number, her new Swedish friend.

'Hello, my little dark-haired beauty,' Elias answered.

'Cut the crap, Eli, as much as I like it. Two things: one, is Leopardess there yet?'

'Just arriving now with her entourage, dark

glasses, pout and attitude,' he replied. 'Are you nearly here?'

'Getting there – give me twenty minutes.'

'Tut tut, the boss is not going to be happy.' Elias sounded mischievous.

'Oh, hurdy-gurdy to you. Go and stick a herring sandwich up your arse.' Milly replied. 'Can you ask Mike to keep her amused?' Mike was her producer.

'And the other thing?' Elias asked, sounding even more amused.

'Yes, I want to borrow you for some undercover work, looking into someone for me. You'll need your contacts, and it might need to be done outside station work. I'll tell you all about it later, once I've waved goodbye to the ego that's called Leopardess.'

'Oh, yes? Well, you'd better be a bit nicer to me then,' Elias joked.

'I'm sorry, I just can't do that, my little Scandinavian stud. Go and find a flat-pack wardrobe to build in the meantime.' Now Milly was smiling.

'*Kuksugare*,' Elias said.

'I'm no good at Swedish, but I've a good idea what that means,' Milly replied. 'I hear that's another one of your talents.'

'Whatever,' Elias muttered, ending the call.

Milly smiled to herself as she drove over the level crossing, she felt quite maternal since he arrived at the station two months ago. He was fully embracing life having had a sheltered upbringing in Sweden. He said yes to everything!

Milly checked herself in the rear-view mirror: lipstick applied correctly, hair in place, and mascara not too overdone. It was 1.45 p.m. 'Keep calm,' Milly told herself. She made another quick call to Jake.

'Hey, are you happy if Elias helps with some investigating? He's keen to dig into Richard Warr.'

'Sure. As long as he doesn't want paying?'

'You ok?'

'Yep I'm fine, always happy with any assistance.'

Jake didn't sound like he was in a happy place. She told him she'd ring later.

*

It was busy on the motorway on her way home. Most of the office staff were heading back home and since it was a Thursday, a lot would be working from home tomorrow. Thursday was always the busiest commute home these days. Milly hadn't taken to Leopardess, although the interview went well enough. She would broadcast it tomorrow afternoon. The record company hoped that her music would attract a wider audience in the daytime, so she was doing a tour of radio stations. Naturally, she had a new single out called 'Split the Dick', which was about breaking a man's penis to punish him for sleeping around. Maybe she'd recommend it to

Elias.

Milly felt more relaxed. Elias had his instructions, it was another gorgeous summer's evening, and she had a message from Giles at Original asking if she would be interested in defecting to his radio station. She wasn't going to ring him back straightaway; she was definitely interested, but Original was a much bigger organisation than she was used to, and – crucially – she'd have to work from London at least four days a week. This didn't appeal, so she wanted to talk to Jake about it.

It took nearly an hour for her to get home. There, she headed straight for the fridge. A fresh bottle of Pinot was waiting for her, nice and cold. She grabbed the pizza menu, which was stuck to the fridge door, although she knew she would order a pepperoni. She slid open the patio door and sat down in a deckchair with a big sigh. She would finish this glass, order a pizza, then ring Jake.

CHAPTER 21 – ALAIOR: 26 MAY

Paulo pressed the doorbell a second time, but there was still no reply. He was about to go back down the steps and climb into his car when he heard the shuffling of feet in flip-flops come round the side of the villa.

'Who are you?' Dave asked.

'Forgive me – my name is Paulo Ravenelli.' Paulo knew that he would need to make up a story, and he knew he probably wouldn't be given much time before Dave would try to send him packing.

'And what do you want?' Dave asked.

'Just a few minutes of your time if you'd be so kind.'

Paulo could see Dave was slightly taken off guard, He may not have been used to random callers.

'Are you here to complain about something?' he asked, frowning. 'You're clearly Italian.' He said this in a condescending tone, as if it was an insult.

Paulo mustered a friendly tone. 'Forgive me, but I'm working on behalf of a British bank. Their investigative team is trying to track owners of old accounts which have lapsed and have not been used for some time.'

'I don't have anything to do with the country,' Dave replied. 'Look, I'm not going to have this discussion here – come round the back.'

Paulo was relieved that he hadn't been kicked down the steps yet, but he worried that there would be cracks in his story. He just needed to keep calm and hope that he could find out something that he could go back to Isabella with.

He was feeling nauseous. He followed Dave onto the terrace, making the usual pleasantries about how beautiful the villa was. Dave pulled out a couple of chairs for them. There was a beer fridge under a long table that was still stacked with used plates, dishes, and glasses. Dave explained that he'd held a small party last night and his housekeeper would be along soon to clear up. He offered Paulo a beer. Paulo declined and asked for a soft drink instead. Dave threw him a can of Coke without giving him a choice or offering him a glass.

They sat down.

'So, what exactly are you trying to say to me?' Dave asked.

Paulo took a long swig from the can, suppressing the inevitable belch that resulted. He felt sweat trickle down the back of his neck.

'Well, the Regency Bank in London has a deposit of £64,000 in the name of Amara Welby.'

Dave gripped the arms of his chair more tightly. Paulo noticed this, and it gave him some encouragement. Dave nodded for Paulo to carry on.

'They're trying to trace a number of these

dormant accounts. In most cases, people have died, so the bank wants to trace their next of kin. They could be entitled to the money in these accounts.' Paulo felt that he had the upper hand: so far, he'd been wallowing around, not getting very far, but he could see that Dave was shocked by his words.

'They have reason to believe that you're a relative of Amara's. She disappeared thirty-two years ago. And if she's not alive, you may be entitled to the £64,000.' Paulo felt quite pleased with his excuse for being there.

'So, why are you involved?'

Paulo was growing in confidence but knew this could be his Achilles heel. He blustered on. 'Amara's husband was called Daniel Welby. He disappeared at the same time, but the police believe he went to Italy. The bank contacted my firm, who are corporate investigators, and asked if we could help trace this Daniel or any of his relatives.'

Paulo's hands were sweaty, and he felt a little panicky. He had no more to add, not having thought beyond this explanation. But he knew what Dave's next question would be.

'So how is this connected to me? I still don't know why you're here,' Dave asked. He was appearing cool and more composed again, which unnerved Paulo. He'd supposed that Dave might have shown some sort of reaction, but instead he calmly opened another bottle of Estrella, without offering one to Paulo.

Paulo looked around him, took off his sunglasses and peered directly at Dave, summoning up as much confidence as he could. 'We think you're Daniel Welby,' he said, bracing himself for a reaction.

Dave started to smile which turned into laughter. He turned to Paulo and was almost choking with laughter. It seemed forced.

'This is total bullshit, isn't it?' He smiled at Paulo. 'I'm going to level with you.' Dave paused again and regained his composure. Paulo detected a change in his accent, he was no expert in the English Language, but it sounded a little more London, reminding him of his teacher at college who he remembered came from Ealing. He felt his stomach heave. Dave looked at his bottle of beer.

'I sense you have skeletons in the closet, Mr Ravanelli? You're Italian, after all, so if you tell me the truth, I'll tell you the truth.' His gaze pierced Paulo squarely in the eye and then he slowly nodded. 'I'll go first. I left England thirty-two years ago and became the man you see in front of you now. Dave Constantinou from Nicosia in Cyprus. Before I was twenty-four years old, I was this man you mention, Daniel Welby, part-Greek Cypriot, part-English, brought up in north London. I was married to Amara, and we had two children. Then she went missing and I left England with a new identity. Clearly there's more to that than I'm telling you today, but that's the truth. And I have never admitted that to anyone.'

Paulo had a sense of relief that felt like a victory, it almost seemed like Dave wanted to unburden himself, maybe for the first time. He sensed that his own life might not be in danger, but he was going to need to press Dave a bit more. Until he had done that, Isabella was not going to be satisfied.

The sun was now rapidly sinking behind the small hills to the west of the Alaior, and a pleasant breeze wafted in from the sea to the south.

'Now you?'

'Is there any chance I could have a beer, please?' Paulo could feel his mouth drying up. If there was any occasion that he needed alcohol, it was now.

Dave walked across to the fridge and picked out another two bottles, flipped the tops off and handed one beer to Paulo. He sat down, looking both smug and anxious. Paulo could tell he was trying to convey a certain bravado but was also portraying a look of concern. Paulo had got Dave rattled.

'OK…' Paulo began. 'I'm not sure how much of this is my place to tell you, but I feel it's necessary, and correct under the circumstances.' He gulped down some beer and instantly felt better. 'So, I received a call from a woman in

Naples asking me to investigate Daniel Welby.'

'Hang on,' Dave interrupted. 'So, you're a private investigator?'

Paulo nodded, then carried on. 'She wanted me to find her real parents and gave me details of when and where she was adopted. Her adoptive parents had told her this years ago. I thought this strange, as she could easily have found this out herself, and why not use an English investigator?'

Paulo continued, 'I went to London. The adoption agency that this woman's parents used was council-run and, to cut a long story short, the records showed that she was adopted by Luigi and Sophia Bennetoni, an Italian couple living in Kensington but due to return to Rome shortly afterwards. I believe they were well connected politically, so they were able to get the adoption processed quickly.'

Dave interjected. 'And you were able to trace the real parents as Daniel and Amara Welby.' He paused for effect. 'And here I am, Daniel, aka Dave.'

Paulo nodded. 'I explained the disappearances to my client, but she insisted on me finding out exactly what happened to Amara. This is where I've been hitting a brick wall, as they say in England. To be honest, my client hasn't yet seemed surprised or grateful for anything that I've told her.'

Dave looked puzzled. 'Naples, you say?

Would you care to tell me the name of your client? Or shall I tell you?'

Slowly Dave said, 'Isabella Bellini.'

A pause, then Paulo nodded.

Paulo could see Dave was now off guard and turning this around in his head. Dave took two more gulps of beer, then looked across at his pool, which shimmered gently in the evening sunlight as a breeze rippled across it.

'So that's why she's been so friendly towards me for the past few months,' Dave said aloud, but more to himself.

Paulo shifted in his chair. 'I only told her two weeks ago that you were Daniel, her real father.'

'She's taken you for a fool, Ravenelli – she's known longer than that, I'm sure of it, but I had no idea who she was.'

'It would explain why she wasn't surprised. What's her game then?' Paulo questioned.

'I don't get it – why get you to go to the trouble of finding out what she already knew?' Dave asked. 'I always felt she was devious.'

'Confirmation, maybe? Perhaps she wasn't sure. But now she seems very keen to understand what happened to your wife, her mother,' Paulo replied.

Dave nodded. 'I need another beer.' Dave got another two bottles out of the fridge, handing one to Paulo. 'What a fucking bitch. I know she's technically my daughter, but I don't know her.

What does she want from me? Do you know, Ravanelli?'

'I have no idea,' Paulo said slowly. 'I assumed she wanted to get to know you, to reconcile, and to find out more about her original blood family. To be honest, I find her quite scary. I'm not sure she's someone you want to upset.'

Dave chortled. 'Maybe she got that from me,' he said with a hint of pride in his voice.

A silence fell between them as the sun finally set. Paulo would need to go soon, but he wasn't really any further forward. He went straight for it. 'So, is Amara dead?'

Dave looked across at Paulo, gravely. His eyes were glazed but they also had a look of determination, which suggested that whatever he was going to say next would be the truth. He shook his head at Paulo. 'I just don't know.' He paused again. 'And I don't want to know.' Another pause. 'So, Zoe is Isabella – what happened to Christopher?'

Paulo contemplated his answer. 'That I don't know. I was not asked to look into him.' This had been true up to twenty-four hours ago – Isabella had always said not to worry about Christopher – but yesterday she had said that he was dead.

Dave seemed to suddenly burst into life. 'So how much do I pay you to go away, Mr Ravanelli?' Before Paulo could answer, Dave said, 'I'll transfer 250,000 euros into your account tomorrow if you leave Menorca as soon as possible, go far away from Italy for some time, and have no contact with Isabella. I don't need all this being raked up now. I need to keep in touch with her, even if it's just to put her off the scent. I need your silence after what I've told you, and I'm sure you've broken client confidentiality.'

Without hesitation Paulo nodded. He sensed that the truth about Amara's disappearance was more than a little uncomfortable for Dave, and he was happy to quit. 'I'll take a little trip to New Zealand.'

Dave smiled. 'She's a dangerous woman, but that should be far enough away.'

It was almost dark by the time Paulo left Dave's villa to return to Mahon and his hotel near the airport.

CHAPTER 22 – JOHN: 20 JULY

John put the phone down and smacked his lips. He felt the usual frisson of excitement when the burner phone rang. He would now destroy it in the usual way, with his instructions fully understood. He checked his watch to see how long he had. Three hours before the flight. His special bags were permanently packed, and he was always ready to drop everything. He would tidy a couple of things up then head to Luqa Airport, as it was known locally, or more grandly, Malta International.

John had been 'quiet' for several months now, so he was buzzing to have another job and anxious to get going. His phone rang, and 'Isabella' flashed up on the screen. She would have to wait a couple of days, although he knew how impatient she was. He guessed she finally wanted to move their arrangement on to another stage, but this would require bigger money, so he would have to make his decision on that outcome.

He picked up his tickets from the Air Malta desk. He was travelling as Ricardo Molinari, born in Bari, southern Italy, one of four identifications he used.

The flight to Frankfurt would take just under three hours. It wasn't his ideal location as Germany, along with many of the northern

European countries, were much hotter on security than others, but there shouldn't be a problem. He would collect the gun from a locker usually used for Amazon deliveries situated in a relatively quiet area a couple of kilometres from the airport in Frankfurt.

John checked in and made his way to the La Vallette Club in the Departures area, where he ordered a glass of Merlot and some roasted peanuts. He picked up *The Times*, which had the headline: 'Prime Minister surely can't survive'. More allegations of sleaze – he was allegedly filmed taking a bung for awarding a government contract to a dubious Qatari entrepreneur. It always amused John that the British appeared to take such a moral high ground publicly, but privately were as bent as anyone else.

It was 2.25 p.m. when he took off, and by the time he left Frankfurt Airport it was 5.45 p.m. His target would be in their hotel room at 8 p.m. Intelligence stated they should be alone, but, if not, then John should deal with all occupants of the room. John picked up the gun from the bright orange locker, concealed in an Amazon Prime cardboard box. He put it straight into his bag without opening it, as if it was a pair of new trainers. Always alert when on duty, John scanned the area, but everything looked normal and nobody suspicious caught his eye. He casually walked back to the intercity train station, from where he would catch a train to the

Hilton Garden Inn at the airport, where he would stay the night. Later he would make the short journey to the Hyatt Place Hotel.

A very efficient and pleasant young lady checked him in, and he made his way to the second floor and to Room 213. He had very little unpacking to do. He was on the 9.20 a.m. flight back to Malta in the morning so he wouldn't eat until then. John was never hungry immediately before or after an 'event', as he called it. Immediately after he would return the gun to the locker, go back to his hotel, have a shower to wash away any gun residue, and take out a bottle of rum, which he would probably half finish. His clothes would be wrapped in a bag and sealed, ready to be burned as soon as he got home.

John opened the Amazon box and the case inside. As requested, he had a Glock 17, a 9mm, short recoil, locked-breech semi-automatic pistol with a silencer. John put the gun together, checked his watch, and was ready to head to the hotel.

It was a warm, pleasant evening, and John was enjoying the tension and danger building up inside him. He would also enjoy looking at his bank account in a couple of days' time. It was not a pretty walk to the hotel; he had to walk along the main and access roads to the airport, so he had no chance to savour Frankfurt itself. However, that was of no interest to him today. John walked confidently into the hotel and walked up the stairs to Room 103. He knocked on the door and heard a female voice ask who it was. He was aware of the CCTV cameras around, and careful not to gaze directly at any cameras. He had several disguises, knowing that tomorrow the local police would be looking for a fair-haired man wearing glasses, a cap and blue jacket with the collar turned up. His facial features would be hard to discern.

'Security!' he shouted back, knowing that this answer was something the occupant would be expecting.

'Just a second,' came the reply.

The door opened, and John slipped into the room. He made his way over to the window, checking the room to make sure they were alone. He closed the curtains. 'Miss Buckley?'

'Yes.' She looked puzzled.

John noted that she was younger than he expected – around thirty, with short blonde hair tied tightly back. She was trying to look tough, with no make-up and eyes that seared into his soul.

John said, 'I'm not security.'

He raised the gun and shot her twice in the forehead before her facial expression could change. She fell to the floor, and John made his way to the door. He opened it and looked up and down the corridor. At the far end there was an old lady with her back to him, rounding the corner. She didn't stop; clearly, she had heard nothing.

The gun was back in his rucksack as he headed quietly the opposite way and down the stairs. He saw no one until he reached reception, where a few people were milling about and minding their own business.

John went out through the main door with a smile on his face and headed for the locker, where he was able to put the gun back in its place, ready for collection by persons unknown later that evening. He got back to his room, had a shower, stuffed his clothes in a bag, and opened the rum. He was feeling high. The downside was that he wanted to celebrate in some way but going out into the bright lights of Frankfurt was not an option.

Mission successfully accomplished.

CHAPTER 23 – LYMFORD: 21 JULY

Milly arrived at her desk and sat down. Straightaway she received a text from Elias who was upstairs in the building. He needed to see her, so she said to give her ten minutes. Before anything else she needed to check the playlist for her show this afternoon. Since the buyout, there had already been a change to more bland, predictable music, which you could already hear on a hundred other radio stations across the country. Milly felt her time was now up with this station.

Milly looked up at Elias as he quietly approached her desk. She couldn't help but smile.

'You look thirty-five, not twenty-five, this morning, young man,' she chided him.

'Leave me alone.'

'I heard a few stories about you already this morning.'

'Well, it was Catrina last night,' he said as brightly as he could muster. 'A flight attendant – we really took off together.' He said it without a hint of a smile.

Milly wanted to have a chat with him, but now wasn't the right time. She shook her head at him instead.

'I have news about this character you asked me to look into, Richard Warr.' Elias sounded more upbeat.

'Oh yes, tell me,' Milly said, pleased to think about non-station business.

'Well, I have a friend, Lily, who works in HR for the Met Police. She checked their records and there was a Richard Warr who joined the police in 1986, not long after moving to London from Malta. He mostly served in north London, then went back to Malta in 1996 after his wife died.'

'OK.' Milly sounded interested. 'Did she say any more about what he did? What type of record did he have?'

'She's coming back to me on that. She works with someone who was around at the time and knew of him. They were going to have a catch-up outside the office, which all sounds very clandestine – is that the right word in English?'

Milly nodded. 'Great work, my little smorgasbord.'

Elias raised his eyebrows. 'I do have a name, you know.'

'Oh yeah, you have lots of names, believe me.' Milly laughed at him.

Just then, Mike walked through the door. Milly really needed to have a moan to him about the playlist. 'Seriously, thanks, Eli. Let me know when you hear more.'

*

Once she was on the road home, Milly called Jake. She was about to ring off when he answered, sounding breathless.

'What are you up to?' she asked.

'Running … give me a moment … I've nearly done 10K,' Jake replied.

Milly suddenly felt horny, thinking of Jake out of breath, sweating and about to jump naked in the shower. 'How much longer are you going to stay out there?' she asked.

'I'm not sure. I was thinking about that on the run,' Jake replied, recovering his composure. 'I think I'll go and see Dave. We met in Naples, so I don't need a real excuse. I'll get his number off Isabella and give him a call. After that I'll probably come home. You know Miguel's son I told you about, in the local police?' He carried on without waiting for a response. 'I'm having a drink with them this evening, so I might find out whether Dave's known to the police.'

'I have some news as well. Elias has been investigating Richard Warr. There's not much to report at the moment, but he's digging deeper,' Milly said.

'So, you haven't any news as such?' Jake said sarcastically.

'So funny, I'm losing reception.' Milly ended the call, sure that Jake would ring straight back. She was in the mood to have some fun with him.

He debated whether to ring but decided to have a shower first. By the time he called her, he knew she would be almost back home.

'I have a full-time job to do. I can't just swan around the Mediterranean looking for clues,

Sherlock,' she said with her own dose of sarcasm.

'Yeah, yeah,' Jake replied. 'Bet you miss me, though.'

Silence. Milly wasn't going to give him the pleasure of admitting she did.

'I need to talk to you about something else.' Milly told Jake all about the offer to work in London for Original. She didn't think she could commute every day from Lymford, and she had no desire – or the funds – to rent an apartment in London for four days each week. She liked Coast FM and everyone who worked there, but she knew it wouldn't be the same once it officially became the Crunch.

'What shall I do?' she almost whined to Jake.

'And there's me to consider,' Jake said seriously. There was a pause.

'Umm…I know there is. I'm starting to enjoy your company Mr Stone…..and I don't think I want to see us become ships that pass in the night,' Milly replied. Jake felt his heart skip a beat.

'Well, if you really want my opinion, I would miss having you around during the week. Maybe you need to at least see how this new management goes about things – they may not be so bad. You don't have to like the music if everything else is OK. What is Geoff thinking?'

Geoff Moriarty was the presenter of the breakfast show: the cornerstone of any radio station, whose success often depends on the breakfast show.

'He's nervous – he expects to be replaced. His ratings have dipped a bit and the rumour is they want to get a known name from the past in there. Problem is, other stations have done that before, and it's not worked.' Milly sounded downcast.

Jake was listening to her at the same time as opening the fridge and grabbing some lunch. A slab of cheese, a yogurt, salami, and Cadbury's chocolate brought over from England. He ran his hands through his hair, thinking about his next response.

'Well, it's your decision and I guess it's a tough one. I think you'll just have to go with your gut feel. Sometimes in life you just have to trust it. When your decision is made, you don't look back and regret it because you made the right choice at the time.' Jake hesitated, then added, 'Look at me deciding to accidentally trip up in front of you. Got to make the best of it now.'

'Pah, unlucky me, I say!' Milly responded, smiling.

'I know you don't mean that.'

'No, I don't, you're getting to me Jake Stone!'

She drove under the little railway bridge on the outskirts of Lymford. She planned to pop into the local Co-op for a baguette and a tin of tomato soup – her comfort food. She pulled up outside and asked Jake to text her later. She would go for a walk herself once she'd eaten and checked that Jake's houseboat was OK.

Jake was on the verge of saying 'love you', then reined himself back. 'I am missing you; you know.'

'Me too.'

CHAPTER 24 – MENORCA: 21 JULY

Jake texted Milly at 8.30 p.m. to say he was meeting up with Miguel and his son, Cesar, who was now back from his holiday. They'd booked a table at the Trebol restaurant down on the harbour in Cala Fonts and arranged to meet for an aperitif at Jake's favourite bar on the seafront around the corner from the restaurants.

Miguel and Cesar were already seated when Jake arrived. A cruise liner was passing on its way to dock at Mahon. Jake ordered a mojito, to the amusement of the two Menorcans.

'Have you had one here?' asked Jake enthusiastically.

'Can't say I have,' Cesar said in very good English. Cesar was very tall – well over six feet. He had dark hair, cut very short, and a deep tan. His features were a little bull-like: he had a wide stub nose but narrow eyes. He had a friendly smile that put Jake immediately at ease.

After half an hour of general conversation they moved on to the Trebol restaurant and sat down by the front wall of the restaurant. Jake was keen to have his back to the wall so he could observe the passers-by – he had a natural curiosity about people. Perhaps that was why he was attracted to investigative work. They ordered beers and mused over the menu, which featured mostly fish. Jake chose tuna while

Miguel and Cesar had the calamari. They both knew the waitress so there was a fair bit of chat in Spanish – Jake assumed about Cesar's holiday – before she took their order.

A platter of Mahon cheese and local tomatoes came out as a starter for them to share. Jake decided it was time to talk about why he wanted to meet Cesar.

'I've recently started my own private investigation business, and I was contacted by a woman in Italy. She asked me to investigate a chap who appears to live here in Menorca.' Jake looked around and lowered his voice slightly. 'His name is Dave Constantinou, and I believe he lives out Alaior way. I wondered if you'd come across him. Do you know anything about him?'

Cesar looked serious. He also checked around before leaning into Jake. 'Yes, I know him. I've been to his house a few times, for various reasons. What does this Italian woman want to know?'

'She told me he was a hotelier, and she was thinking of investing in his business, but then she told me the interesting bit: she's just discovered that he's her father. This Dave and his wife used to live in England. Then his wife disappeared. Dave was called Daniel Welby at the time. He then changed his identity and came out to the Mediterranean, cutting all ties with England – including his two children, who were subsequently adopted.'

Cesar scratched his chin. 'He's not a nice person, but is he really bad? We've not been able to prove it. A couple of women have accused him of assault – not sexual, but general bad handling and roughness. He also got angry when he wasn't happy with his meal at a restaurant in Alaior about a year ago – he smashed up a couple of tables, broke a window and swore at the manager, but he always gets away with it.'

'How come?'

'People back off. I think he offers them a ton of euros and they drop any accusations. We all know of him at the department, but he's basically got a clean record. Not uncommon for the rich in this island – or any other place, come to that.'

Jake ran his hands through his hair. 'Have you had any murders, disappearances, anything like that since he's been here?'

'Just one thing, and it was quite recent.' Cesar leaned in closer, as though they were conspiring. 'There was an Italian who came to the island about two months ago. Paulo Ravanelli.'

Jake smiled inwardly, feeling the tingle in his stomach he always felt when he knew he was about to hear something really interesting.

Cesar continued. 'One of the airport hotels contacted us to say that this Paulo had checked in but left without checking out. His hire car was still in the hotel car park, but he seemed to have vanished. No one of that name was booked on a flight away from the island, and all we know is he was planning to meet up with a friend near Alaior. Or so the receptionist told us. It's an open case for us, but we're not sure where to go with it. We have no leads.'

'I wonder if this "friend" was Dave Constantinou,' Jake whispered.

'Well, we recently had an anonymous call from a woman saying she believed that Paulo had gone to see Dave. We went to his house and questioned him, but he denied knowing Paulo. No one has officially reported him missing, so we don't have a lot to go on. His ex-wife in Italy wasn't interested, said she hadn't seen him for months.'

Miguel was clearly confused. Jake wondered if he was struggling to keep up with their conversation; his English was rather poor.

Just then, their meals arrived. The three men ordered more beer. After a few minutes, Jake continued. 'That's interesting. I was told by this Italian woman that Paulo Ravanelli was a PI and she'd employed him to investigate Dave Constantinou, but he'd disappeared. She knew he was on his way to Alaior to confront Dave, but she hasn't heard anything from him since. She contacted me about a month after he vanished. I bet it's the same woman who gave you your anonymous tip-off.'

Jake explained that he had met Dave in

Naples a couple of weeks ago, but he hadn't known the full story then. He had just wanted to get a feel for the kind of person he was. He also explained that Isabella Bellini was a little reluctant to share information and he wasn't sure he trusted her.

'I was thinking of giving Dave a ring tomorrow and asking to go and see him, on the pretext that we met in Naples and we're both in Menorca at the same time, so why not have a drink together.'

Cesar chewed a piece of calamari, then swallowed it. 'Be very careful, Jake. Would you like me to come with you? And watch from a distance?'

Jake considered this. 'That's a kind offer, but I should be fine. He has no reason to suspect anything. He thinks I work for the local council and I'm a writer.'

'Yes, but I still think someone like him is likely to trust and believe no one, so he's unlikely to welcome you. No offence, but you're a young investigator just starting out. He could easily trip you up, and we don't know how dangerous he could be.' Cesar sounded very concerned, which Jake appreciated.

'Thanks so much, Cesar,' Jake said. 'Let me ring him first and I'll come back to you.'

The conversation moved on, and they spent the rest of the evening discussing anything but Dave. Jake sensed he'd found a new friend in

Cesar, although the conversation got lively when they discussed this year's European Cup Final, in which Chelsea had beaten Cesar's beloved Barcelona.

As the three of them were strolling back to the apartment block, a wave of contentment swept over Jake. He was in a happy place, it seemed, for the first time in a few years. He had nothing to worry about, and life seemed simple and interesting. Back in the apartment, he went into the spare bedroom and looked at his guitar, which had been sitting there for a few years. He was tempted to pick it up but closed the door to the bedroom instead and walked away.

CHAPTER 25 – ARRANGEMENTS: 22 JULY

Isabella had come to a decision. She looked at herself in the mirror and thought she'd aged five years in the past twelve months. Her eyes no longer sparkled but had dark brown bags under them. When she started down this road of deceit, she hadn't expected this to happen. She'd realised that she wasn't the hard-nosed bitch she thought she was, and she knew she had to come clean before things went too far. She picked up her phone.

'Jake, I need to see you.'

He was just finishing his breakfast. She sounded worried.

'OK – here in Menorca?' Jake replied.

'I'd rather not. Could you come to Naples in a couple of days? I'll reimburse your expenses immediately,' Isabella said.

'I was going to go and see Dave, then go back to England for a bit,' Jake said cautiously.

Isabella's voice hardened. 'No, don't do that. I've got something really important to tell you. You can decide on your next move after that.'

'You're sounding strange, Isabella. OK, I'll get a flight as soon as I can and let you know when I'll be there.'

*

Jake was puzzled as he threw his phone down on the sofa. At least it would give him the opportunity to get some honesty from Isabella. He decided he would confront her; he was sure she wasn't giving him the full picture. Maybe that's what she planned to do in Naples.

He flicked over the cover of his iPad and pressed the home button. Safari told him there was a flight tomorrow morning with easyJet, which would take just over an hour and a half. He booked himself onto it, then checked availability at the hotel he stayed at previously. They had a vacancy so he booked himself in for one night and texted Isabella to tell her he would be there at 11.30 a.m. and to ask whether he should come straight to her apartment. She said yes and promised to sort out lunch for them.

Well, that has thrown a spanner in my plans, he thought, wandering onto the balcony. He was still keen to contact Dave and decided he would give him a call now to arrange a meeting after he came back from Naples. That couldn't do any harm.

Jake had managed to get Dave's number from Isabella, so he scrolled through and found it, remembering that Dave thought he was Harry Taylor.

'*Hola.*' Dave sounded breathless, but also wary. Jake knew that Dave would not have a clue who was calling him.

'Dave? It's Harry Taylor. We met in Naples at

Isabella Bellini's a couple of weeks ago,' Jake said.

Still sounding wary, Dave replied. 'I remember.' He paused, then manners got the better of him. 'How are you, Mr Taylor?'

'Harry, please. I'm in Menorca at the moment, staying at the family apartment in Es Castell. I wondered if you were interested in meeting up for a drink?'

'For what reason?' Dave asked.

'None at all,' Jake replied. 'Maybe we didn't get off on the right foot in Naples. I was tired that evening, and a bit grumpy.'

'Yes, I didn't find you particularly amiable company,' Dave replied. 'I thought you were a right little shit.'

Jake thought this a bit harsh but gave a fake laugh and ran his hand through his hair. 'Guilty,' he said.

'Look, it's Wednesday today. Why don't you come to Ciutadella on Sunday? I'll book a table at the Smoix restaurant for lunch,' Dave offered.

'Sounds great. How about one o'clock?' Jake said.

'OK, see you then,' Dave replied unenthusiastically.

Jake was feeling pleased with himself. At least he'd be able to tell Isabella he'd arranged a meeting with Dave.

*

When Dave put the phone down after

speaking to Jake, he flipped the lid of his laptop and clicked on a search engine to find out what he could on Harry Taylor. It would not be an uncommon name, so he tried to narrow it down to 'local council' and 'England'. There were a few, but their locations seemed off; he was sure that this Harry said he worked in London. He looked at images and no one came up who appeared remotely like him. This just added to Dave's doubts.

Dave had become successful in his own field through a mixture of greed, suspicion, dishonesty, and an acute ability to sniff out an opportunity. He had a few days to think about what he could use Harry for, sure in the knowledge that Harry wasn't who he said he was. Dave wanted to be ready when they met.

He considered calling Isabella. He kept thinking about her. When Paulo told him that she was his daughter he wanted to blank it out, forget about it, but curiosity got the better of him, so when he received her invitation to go to Naples for dinner he had to accept. But he still didn't understand what her game was. She hadn't tried to approach him directly and ask about the family connection. He had suppressed any feelings for her over the years, he didn't trust her, and he was no longer bothered if she was going to invest in his business, especially now he'd decided to pull out of the Malta deal.

The thought of breaking free again was

getting more tempting. It wouldn't be so easy this time, but he didn't want to face the truth about Amara, and this woman seemed hell-bent on sniffing out the truth.

Dave tapped his fingers on the glass table, frowning as a thought came to him. He got up and walked into the kitchen, looking around but not taking anything in. He opened the family-sized fridge, gazed mesmerically at a bottle of beer then closed the fridge again without taking it. He wandered into the living area and sat down in his favourite chair; his gaze fixed to the floor as if mesmerised by something there.

CHAPTER 26 – NAPLES: 23 JULY

The next day dawned gloomy and continued that way as Jake made his way to the airport. It was a bit of a relief to have the odd cloudy day. The weather would probably be different in Naples. He parked the car then checked in at the easyJet desk. He would be returning to Menorca at 3 p.m. the next day via Ryanair, not his favourite airline, but others were fully booked. He grabbed a coffee and pastry at a café and sat down to wait for his flight. Jake wasn't one to idly scroll through his phone or iPad when he didn't have a reason to.

'I'd rather watch people,' he told Milly once. 'They're much more interesting than seeing a picture on Facebook or Instagram or whatever of someone you don't know having their hair cut at an exclusive salon somewhere.' He'd once stated that 'Twitter is for twats who think life revolves around it when in fact 80% of us don't give a fuck about Twitter' on a crowded train, where most people were scrolling through their phones.

A British family with strong northern accents and skin that was bordering the colour of a post box walked past. Clearly, they had been desperate to get some last-minute sun yesterday. Mother and Father were disagreeing whether little Ariana could open her big tube of Smarties now or wait till they got home. Father said yes, Mother said no. It looked like Mother was winning the argument, and little Ariana was pouting to the point of tears. They headed to the Paulener Bar for a final beer before flying home.

Jake's flight was called, and suddenly the tangerine orange of easyJet was everywhere. There was no mistaking what airline he was getting on. The flight was quick and uneventful, and he touched down and once out of arrivals caught a cab to the hotel, checked in and dumped his bag in his room. It was indeed sunny and very warm in Naples. He texted Isabella to say he would be there between 12.45 and 1 p.m. He was slightly apprehensive as he walked through the Piazza Dante again.

The door to Villa All'Alba was again open and Isabella hurried down the hall towards him. This time she was smiling with her mouth but not her eyes. She was looking paler and older than when he last saw her.

'Thank you for coming, Jake.' She held out her hands as if she was going to grab his face and push his cheeks together. Jake momentarily thought of his mother, who used to do this when he'd been a good boy.

'That's OK,' he said.

'Let's go out on the terrace – it's shady at this time of day. I've got lunch to bring out.' She paused. 'We may need it.'

Jake had no idea what was going on and decided to stop speculating. He'd find out soon enough. The terrace was quite narrow, with only room for two chairs, a table, and various plants in pots. One he recognised as basil, his favourite herb.

The view from the terrace was spectacular. Vesuvius was just off to the right, with smaller hills straight ahead. The suburbs of Naples crept up the sides of the volcano, looking calm and peaceful. The buildings straight ahead were pretty low, which was unusual in this part of the city, but allowed for the view, which made up for the small terrace.

Jake sat down in a black metal chair padded with bright orange cushions; he noticed that the chairs matched the railings around the terrace.

'It's like being back on easyJet,' Jake joked as Isabella came back with a bottle of expensive-looking wine. She held it up, as if seeking Jake's approval. He hadn't heard of it, so just nodded agreeably anyway.

'It's local, from the Amalfi coast,' Isabella said as she poured it into crystal glasses. She went back inside and after a couple of trips the small table was loaded with San Marzano tomatoes, mozzarella, prosciutto, and olive bread. Isabella sat down with a heavy sigh. She glanced at Jake, and he thought he saw a warmth in her face that he hadn't seen before, but also a resignation. He waited patiently while she talked about the terrible state Italy was currently in, the state of the roads and its leaders.

CHAPTER 27 – REVELATION: 23 JULY

Jake shifted in his chair. He was bored of hearing about Italian politicians and their dodgy dealings. He hadn't heard of these people, and he had a natural distrust of politicians. British ones were bad enough, but everyone knew that the Italians were worse. A well-known MP in the British Cabinet had stitched up Jake's father about ten years ago. He'd been caught out awarding a contract to one of his good friends, but had managed to shift the blame to Mr Stone, saying that he was unaware of the contract being agreed. Isaac Stone then found himself on the front page of the *Daily Mail* when all he'd done was arrange the meeting to discuss the contract. Jake wondered why he had gone into the civil service himself. Clearly, he had been influenced by his father, but he had never loved it.

Isabella looked up and smacked her lips. She took off her sunglasses and glanced at Jake. He felt a little unnerved. She looked away again. 'I've not been entirely truthful with you, Jake.'

Jake tensed and nodded. 'Go on.' He could see Isabella trembling.

'I've got myself into a dangerous situation. I'm scared, and I want to get out of it.' She hesitated, then looked directly at Jake. 'I also need to be honest, and I hope you'll forgive me.'

Jake frowned.

Isabella continued. 'Dave Constantinou is my real father; I've known this for quite some time.'

Jake knew this, but did she mean she had known before Paulo had told her? He decided not to say anything and just stared at her, waiting for her to carry on.

Her hand was shaking as she picked up her glass and took a large sip of wine. Jake also picked his glass up, but his hand was still.

Isabella took a deep breath. 'I wanted him killed, but I needed to know what happened to Amara, my real mother. That's why I employed Paulo. He didn't get very far with that, and then he disappeared. He was a fool.'

Jake's eyes widened at the mention of killing Dave. 'And you assumed that he may have come to some harm, so decided to get a new investigator. Me? Who might also come to some harm? We kind of already knew this when we spoke a couple of weeks ago, but are you saying you want me to kill him?'

Isabella was flustered. Jake's calmness was rapidly disappearing into the Neapolitan air. Who is this woman? he thought.

'No,' she said, almost pleadingly.

Jake leaned forward, tightly gripping the arms of his chair. His knuckles went white. He was seething and tried to contain his sudden rage. He leaned back in his chair again and gazed across the rooftops. In a more measured tone, he said, 'I knew you weren't telling the truth. I could sense something wasn't adding up.' He took his gaze off the rooftops and looked at Isabella, who was still shaking.

'Are you asking me to kill Dave?'

'No,' she said quickly. 'I wanted you to investigate Amara's disappearance, as I said. But there's a more important reason why I wanted you to do it.'

Jake interrupted. 'So, who's supposed to kill Dave then? And, more importantly, why?'

'I'll come back to that.' Isabella took a deep breath. 'You, Jake ... are my brother ... and Dave is your real father.'

Jake just looked at her, his mouth open. All colour had drained away from his face, leaving a translucent pallor, as if he'd just opened a door to find a man with a gun in front of him. Incomprehension was written all over him.

CHAPTER 28 – MILLY: 23 JULY

Elias came bounding down the stairs to Milly's desk. She was doing her final prep before her show started at 1 p.m. She was quite excited, as she was going to be talking to an organiser of rave parties from the early 90s. Venues were often in the middle of the countryside and arranged through secret codes and phone calls – all before mobile phones. Covert and illegal, raves were drug-fuelled, went on for twelve hours or more, and invariably upset the local farmers. Milly knew she would have been there – had she not just started primary school at the time.

'I have news,' Elias said excitedly.

'Don't tell me – you've copped off with the boss,' Milly joked.

'She's forty-eight,' he exclaimed. 'I have standards.'

Milly scoffed. 'Come on then, I've a studio waiting for me.'

'Richard Warr,' Elias started. 'Seems he was a bit shady. He was dismissed from the Met Police for dishonourable conduct. He was rumoured to be as corrupt as they come. He was in the pocket of at least one gang, and he obstructed the investigations into several cases that may have implicated them.'

'Interesting,' Milly said. 'Police corruption scandals never seem to be far away; it really makes you think.'

Elias carried on. 'He was on the team that was investigating the disappearance of Amara Welby. Interestingly, though, he received praise from her parents for keeping in touch with them after the investigation had been wound down. His colleagues suspected that he knew more about it, but they could never prove that.'

'So, he may have been keeping close to her parents so he could deflect any thoughts they may have had about who was guilty, but looking like the good guy to them,' Milly said, spinning in her chair and tapping her pen against her teeth.

'Could be.'

'You'd think the police would be on to that and be able to prove it.'

'Unless they didn't want to…'

'Well done, Wallander – you could put Jake out of a job.'

'Thank you, Miss Moneypenny.' Elias clearly pleased with himself.

'There appears to still be some nervousness about disclosing possible corruption, but my contact is on the verge of retirement and doesn't care who he upsets now.'

'Here, have a Twix as a reward.' Milly handed him her remaining chocolate finger from the pack she'd opened for lunch.

Milly's show finished at 4 p.m., so after a quick meeting with producer Mike and Tim, who was on news duty for the day, she got in her car, eager to talk to Jake. She pulled out of the industrial estate where the studios were and joined the motorway. She liked to time it this way so that she just missed the school traffic, but also left before the offices emptied. Milly had been born and brought up in deepest Somerset. Unlike many of her friends, she didn't have a love for city centres. She loved music, she loved her job, and she liked socialising, which didn't always sit well with her dislike of the hustle and bustle of big city life. Small doses were fine, but on her terms.

Milly rang Jake once she'd reached the edge of the New Forest. Her call went to voicemail, so she left a message.

Hi Jakey, got some news for you about Richard Warr. Hope you're OK and all is well in Naples. Give me a call when you can.

She switched the radio on. The talk was about the school holidays – the kids broke up tomorrow, so the roads would be quieter. She smiled to herself, knowing that the presenter, Wesley, hated kids, but he sounded really interested in what they would be doing over the next six weeks, making suggestions to the listeners.

'You'd like to shoot them, Wesley,' she said to the radio.

When she got to the railway line, the

barriers were down. There were six cars in front of her, so she patiently waited for the train to speed pass on its way east. She checked her watch: it was 4.50 p.m. Her phone rang, flashing up 'Jake'.

CHAPTER 29 – NAPLES: 23 JULY

Jake just carried on staring at Isabella. His mouth moved, but no words came out. Eventually he stuttered, 'No, that can't be true. I wasn't adopted. What makes you say that?'

Isabella leaned her chin in her hand, a soft look in her eyes. Jake noticed again they had the same colour of eyes.

'My parents told me only a year ago that I had a brother, Christopher. I already knew about Daniel and Amara Welby, but not Christopher. So, then I decided to find out more. What happened to them? I didn't get very far, but then I had a break. I met John and he told me that his father was in the police force in London in the 1990s, so he'd ask him whether he knew about the case. It was in the news for a couple of weeks until the media got bored when no breakthrough was made.'

Jake stood up and started walking around, his hands taking his hair until it stuck out at an angle like a frozen wave. 'But what makes you think I'm Christopher?'

'Let me explain,' Isabella said, making calming gestures with her hands. 'John came back to me after a couple of weeks and his father —'

'Richard Warr,' Jake interjected.

Isabella nodded. 'His father remembered

the case well and knew that Daniel had a new identity. Dave Constantinou.'

Jake frowned. 'But the police didn't know that for sure. According to them, he just disappeared. They thought he'd gone abroad, but they didn't know his identity.'

'That's because they wanted him to disappear; it was in the best interests of some of the investigating officers. It wasn't hard to trace Dave and what happened to us.'

'But how do you know I'm Christopher?' Jake was shocked and didn't want to believe what he was being told. He watched her closely as he could see her relax somewhat and a part of him could tell she was being truthful.

'The British are pretty good at keeping records if you're looking for them.' Isabella got up. Jake sat back down as she walked into the living room and opened a bureau, pulling out a photocopied piece of paper that was inside a plastic wallet. She came back out onto the terrace and handed it to him.

Jake nervously took it off her. It was headed 'BLC Adoption Centre, Barnet', which Jake knew was in north London, not far from where Daniel and Amara used to live. Epping Forest wasn't too far away along the M25. He scanned the document. Zoe Welby and Christopher Welby, aged five and three. Christopher Welby, adopted by Isaac and Donna Stone of Mortlake Drive, Isleworth. This address, Jake remembered; they had moved from there when he was ten years old to Weybridge. He looked up at Isabella, studied her face and he could see she looked genuinely worried, perhaps a little scared, waiting for his next words.

'I just can't believe it,' Jake stuttered. 'I don't want to believe it.' He glanced across the rooftops again and could see a faint plume of smoke rising from Vesuvius. 'My parents never gave me any indication that I was adopted. It's true that there weren't any baby photos of me, but I saw a birth certificate that had Jake Stone – my name – on it.'

Isabella shrugged and reached out to touch Jake's hand; he pulled back rejecting the gesture. 'I suppose it's not hard to get forged certificates. In Naples, it would be easy.'

Jake stood up again and leaned over the balcony, looking down at the street below. People were going about their business as normal, which seemed wrong. He'd just been told that who he thought he was for thirty-five years was wrong, that Jake Stone didn't exist.

As if she could read his mind, Isabella said, 'You're still Jake Stone, you're still the same person, the same character. I know you're a good person, Jake, and a lot of that will be thanks to your adopted parents. They fashioned you, they moulded you, they loved you. They loved you so much, they always wanted to think of you as their own flesh and blood. In their eyes, that's exactly what you were.'

Jake turned around, his eyes moist, his voice broken. 'I don't know what to say.' Ten minutes ago, Isabella had just been a client; now she was apparently his sister. 'Do you remember? You were five years old – you must have some memories, albeit vague?'

'Not really – there are a few flashbacks that came back to me over the years, but not enough for me to think I was in England, had a brother, or had different parents. I suppose I largely blanked life out until Italy.'

Jake seemed to compose himself but stayed standing. He couldn't sit down while his mind was racing over the past. He remembered all the days out they had as a family. He had often asked why he couldn't have a brother or sister – a question that his parents never really answered. They must have been expecting him to mention something about his past life. Jake remembered them often asking him if he remembered when he was very young. His earliest memory was a vague one: he was five years old, and they went on holiday to Cala Galdana in Menorca. That was when his parents must have first thought about buying the apartment. He had no memories before that, although he still had James, his little panda bear which his parents said he had as a new-born baby.

'Look, I can't stay,' Jake said, 'but can I come back tomorrow and have a copy of the certificate? I need to go back to England. I'm not saying I don't believe you, but my aunt still lives there, and I need to talk to her about this.'

'I have a copy for you here already.' She walked to the bureau and pulled it out from a drawer, also kept neatly in a plastic wallet. They both stood there but Jake found he couldn't make eye contact.

'We still have a bit to talk about, so will you come back soon?' Isabella said, looking at his downcast face.

Jake hesitated, then said, 'Yes, yes, I will. I may bring Milly for moral support.'

Isabella smiled. 'That would be nice.'

Jake walked down the steps of the villa. The sun was scorching again, but he was unaware of it. He put his sunglasses on and ran his hand through his untidy hair. He was sweating. His black Imagine Dragons T-shirt, which proudly displayed tour dates from three years ago, was damp. His cargo shorts stuck to his thighs. He walked back to the hotel in a daze, not noticing the sights and smells of Naples that had fascinated him two weeks ago – or the moped he stepped out in front of, to be greeted by the deafening shouts of its driver. There was a lot he didn't understand, but he had a gut feeling that Isabella was telling the truth – now – and he was going to have to come to terms with it, but at the moment he felt lost.

He wandered around the Piazza for a while then decided to sit down and have a coffee. He gazed across the square, losing track of time, then his phone buzzed. Milly. He really wanted to talk to her but didn't feel he was in the right place to do it now, so he ignored the call, paid for his coffee, and headed back to his hotel.

His room was nice and cool with the air conditioning on. He looked at himself in the bathroom mirror.

'Who are you?' he asked. He was bedraggled – hair all over the place, dried sweat across his brow, five days of beard growth. He decided to ring Milly from the balcony, so opened the sliding door and closed it behind him. He sat down and pressed her number.

CHAPTER 30 – LYMFORD: 23 JULY

'Hi Jakey,' Milly said cheerfully as the railway crossing lights stopped flashing and the barriers started to rise. She put her hand on the gearstick, ready to move off.

There was a pause. Jake swallowed. 'You're never going to believe what I've just been told.'

'I'm all ears,' Milly said.

'I'm not Jake Stone, I'm Christopher Welby,' he replied. 'Welby' was quite hard to hear as his voice was breaking up. Milly's car rumbled over the tracks and passed the sign that said 'Lymford 4'.

'What, Dave's son? Sister of Isabella?' she asked, her own voice rising.

'Uh-huh.'

'Jesus Christ.'

Jake gave Milly a rundown of the afternoon's events. By the time he'd finished she was sitting in her car outside her apartment. 'Crikey,' she said eventually – not a word she'd said for years.

'A bit of an understatement,' Jake said, a hint of sarcastic amusement in his voice. 'Look, I'm coming back to England tomorrow. Any chance you can pick me up from Gatwick? I took the train there and don't fancy the trip back to Lymford on it.'

'Yep, sure. I have no show tomorrow, so

I've got nothing to do that can't wait till the weekend.'

'Cool.' Jake sounded relieved. 'I'd better get on and book a flight. I'll text you later with the details.'

'No worries,' Milly said. 'I'll look forward to seeing you.'

Unknown to her, Jake smiled for the first time for hours, thinking how lucky he was to have her. He wasn't sure what he would have done otherwise, or who he would have talked to. His affection for her was getting stronger by the day.

'Me too.' Jake put his phone down on the small table and let out a long sigh. He doubted he would sleep much tonight.

Milly walked up to her front door and put the key in the lock. Just as she did, she thought she heard movement from inside. She gently opened the door, so she could see the small hallway and the fridge in her kitchen beyond it. Someone was standing in front of the fridge. Milly stopped dead with fright.

*

Jake stood up and saw the bottle of rum on the dressing room table at the end of his bed. He always carried his own glass when he travelled; he couldn't bear to use hotel ones, for some reason. He didn't trust they'd been cleaned properly, although he didn't think twice about the bed linen, the toilet, or the shower.

He grabbed his bag and closed the sliding door. He needed to be in the cool room for a while. He would have a large shot of rum then go for a shower. He lay down on the bed, propped up on two pillows, and turned the TV to Sky News. He wanted to think about something else for a while. He downed the rum in two gulps.

Two hours later, he checked his phone. He'd slept, and it was now 8.30 p.m. He lay there with no enthusiasm to get up and do anything, but he knew he had to book his flight. He swung his legs over and sat on the edge of his bed, rubbing his head. He flicked on the iPad and checked flights from Naples to London. There was availability on a BA flight, but it was going to Heathrow. He'd better make sure Milly knows it's not Gatwick, he thought. It would arrive at 12.45 p.m. He texted the details to her, stripped off his clothes and went for a shower.

Ten minutes later he came out of the bathroom and checked his phone. No response from Milly. He rang her number but after a minute or so it went to voicemail. He left a message. He felt a flutter of annoyance – or was it concern? – that she hadn't responded. What was she doing?

Jake suddenly remembered that he was due to meet Dave on Sunday, and it was now Thursday. He wondered whether to return to Menorca on Saturday but decided it would all be too much. He needed to spend some time at home. He wanted to meet up with Dave, but he needed to get his head round the situation first. What should he say to him? He brought up Dave's number and sent a text.

Sorry – won't be able to make Sunday now, as I need to get back to England. I'll ring again to rearrange.

That's a shame. I'm in Menorca for a while now so give me a call when you're back over.

Jake was surprised at the convivial response. This was his real father – how would he get his head round that?

Unusually for him, he wasn't hungry this evening. He was tempted by more rum, though, so he took out a packet of Texas BBQ Pringles from his bag to soak it up with. He lay on the bed again and waited for Milly to respond.

CHAPTER 31 – LYMFORD: 24 JULY

Milly looked at her phone. It said 6.30 a.m. She was still in shock over what had happened the night before. She felt as though she hadn't slept for a minute, listening out for any movement inside the apartment, ready to pounce, or hide in a corner, she wasn't sure which.

The man standing in front of the fridge as she came through her front door was a man called Colin, or that's what he told her – a harmless name, but it didn't suit his persona. He had been looking for Jake down at the houseboat and had met Jake's neighbour, Sandra. She lived on one of the other two boats that were alongside his. She was about seventy-five, very short, with wiry, unkempt hair and a weather-beaten face. Sandra was watering her plants on top of the boat. Not one to miss a trick, she asked him if she could help.

She'd suggested that Jake might be at Milly's place, and helpfully gave him her address. Jake said to Milly once that Sandra meant well but was a 'nosy old cow.'

Colin was in his seventies and had retired from the police force long ago.

'Who the fuck are you?' Milly had cried out when she saw him standing there. 'How the fuck did you get in?'

Colin gave her a lopsided, patronising smile.

'Locks are not a problem for me, darlin.' He had a London accent. He continued to stand there. Milly was still frozen to the spot. She thought about going back out the door, but she couldn't move. She was scared like she'd never been scared before. What was she going to do? She dug into her reserves of courage and found a little indignation that this man had intruded and invaded her space.

She studied him while he was trying to psych her out with silence. He was tall, over six feet for sure, imposing, with a full head of grey hair brushed straight back from his forehead. He had a craggy face and a look about him that said he would be hard to warm to. Milly was determined not to show that she was scared.

'Well, I'm waiting for an answer,' she said as coolly as she could.

'So, I gather you're the girlfriend of some chap called Jake Stone?' His tone was menacing and made 'girlfriend' sound like a crime.

'Maybe,' Milly replied defiantly, a steely look in her eyes.

Colin lifted his jumper, took out a long, sharp knife from his belt and walked towards her. She remembered thinking, 'No, this doesn't happen in Lymford.'

Her courage was waning as he lifted the knife to head height and stopped about three feet from her.

'I'm not a very nice person, you know. Forty

years in the Met Police and most of the time I was corrupt – half of us were. It allowed me to buy the Mrs and me a nice mansion in Ascot, where we could enjoy our retirement. Now this boyfriend of yours has come along, poking into a case I was personally involved in. So, I need to try and tie up a few loose ends.' He stopped as if he was checking what he was about to say, choosing his words carefully. 'Believe me, I'm not just protecting myself, there's others your boyfriend really doesn't want to upset.'

Part of Milly wanted to laugh. Colin sounded so stereotypical, as if she was watching an old episode of *The Sweeney*.

She looked down at her hands. She was still holding her keys, and her left hand was shaking. Her gaze lifted again, and he was grinning. Not a pleasant sight: he had yellow, misshapen teeth. Nevertheless, she was not going to be intimidated. She boldly moved to one side, so she was closer to a heavy glass ornament in the shape of the Chrysler Building in New York – a holiday souvenir.

'So, what's he going to find that scares you so much?' she asked.

Colin frowned. 'Smart bitch,' he spat.

Milly was used to thinking quickly at work, so started to rationalise things in her head. Summoning up more courage, she said, 'The police have moved on since your day. Corruption is rare, and if you kill me it won't take much to trace it back to you. You may be able to keep events quiet from thirty years ago, but you don't want a modern death to get in the way and complicate things.' Milly could see this unnerved Colin.

Her phone beeped. A text, probably from Jake. Her phone had been in her hand. 'I may have switched this on to record when I saw you...'

Colin grunted. 'You may think you're all that, missy, but I can cause you damage in other ways if you don't get that bloke to back off. Tell him to keep his nose out and you two will be OK. If he keeps on, then...' He paused. 'Then things will get a bit dirty.'

Milly's stomach lurched again, and she had a sudden need to go to the toilet. She ignored it. 'You haven't told me exactly what my boyfriend is investigating,' Milly said, staring him directly in the eyes.

'Don't be smart. We both know what I'm talking about.'

'How do you know?' Milly asked. She could tell he was musing this over, trying to decide whether to tell her.

'The woman who vanished has a sister that's alive and kicking. She knew if she wanted to stay that way, she had to give us the name of the person she met for coffee recently.' The menace was back in his voice. 'She duly obliged and needed little persuasion when I popped round to see her. Actually, we're old friends. I'm just a small cog in this story; there's bigger fish than me who have an interest.'

'Bullshit,' Milly blurted out. She was desperate to see the back of him but couldn't help herself. Colin sneered at her. 'You'll have to see then, won't you love.'

Milly gave a defeated nod, hoping he would leave, but also intrigued. Instead, Colin changed his tone and asked cheerfully if he could have a cold drink.

'What?' Milly exclaimed. 'You've made your point and I'll pass it on. Message received loud and clear.'

Colin just raised his eyebrows. 'Coke, lemonade, orange juice is fine.'

Milly said nothing but went to the fridge and pulled out a can of Coke Zero. 'Here.' She lobbed it at him, making him drop the knife.

'You're a feisty one, you are,' he said as he caught the can. He picked up the knife and she watched him casually wander to the balcony, as if he had been invited. He sat down and opened the can. The drink fizzed, spilling some of its contents over Colin's trousers. He sat there for a few minutes in silence. Milly stayed indoors. She was thinking that she should do something, then realised that this was just one of the intimidatory tactics that people like him used. The thought came to her that she could easily wrap the Chrysler Building around his head while he sat there. Instead, she shouted to him.

'Then you can fuck off out of here!' Her phone rang. This time she could see it was Jake.

'Leave it!' Colin shouted. Milly contemplated defying him, but decided that the more compliant she was, the quicker he'd leave.

After another five minutes he got up and wandered back into the apartment. He stood in front of Milly, menace clear on his face. With steely determination she walked to the door and opened it. She beckoned him to leave.

'You're warned, darlin,' I still have power and your boyfriend is a cheap loser.' He walked out of the door and Milly slammed it behind him.

She was shaking. She ran to the toilet and burst into tears, full of relief that he'd gone. She sat there, rocking, for a few minutes. She assured herself he was gone and wouldn't be back, so she composed herself and walked back into the living room, determined to reclaim her space and be strong. She grabbed a bottle of wine from the fridge, pulled a glass out of the cupboard, nearly dropping it, and filled it to the brim. She drank half the glass, then gasped for air. She swung round to face the front door and started laughing hysterically. 'Have I just been on a movie set?' she said out loud, fearing she may be going mad.

She paced around the apartment trying to collect her thoughts before phoning Jake. She knew Colin had been serious, but how seriously should they take him? Was he a relic from the past? Surely, he'd immediately be in trouble if she went to the police. Should she tell them at the station? Trouble was that the news people would want a story. Maybe she'd just tell Elias. She knew she was an independent woman, but right now all she wanted was to speak to Jake. She picked up the phone and called him, desperate to hear his voice.

CHAPTER 32 – JOHN: 24 JULY

John was fed up and getting impatient. He had a job to do, but he couldn't get on with it. Isabella was dithering: he felt that she was going to back out altogether. It was time to get all this business finished with; it had gone on for far too long.

He was driving across Malta for a meeting with one of his business associates. One of his legitimate business associates – it had to be when you're dealing with the church. Catholicism was important here. Whatever the church did within itself was up to it and almost without reproach, but its dealings with the outside world were as straight as any could be.

John didn't really like religion of any kind. He led a double life: property developer with a contract killing side-line. Both were lucrative – one was legal and, mostly, above board; the other not so. He enjoyed them both and he was waiting for Isabella to give him the nod to take Dave out.

He had a short drive from Sliema to St Paul's Bay. It would only take about twenty minutes, but he was lost in memories of how he had got into this life of crime. From an early age he had known that his dad wasn't a straightforward copper in London; there were always quiet, secretive meetings going on in their three-bed semi in Watford. Tough-looking men would come in and out, always nice to him, but he often found them scary. He didn't see much of his father until they suddenly decided to move back to Malta as a family. He didn't understand why at the time, but a few years later his dad explained it all to him. He had to.

John became interested in a life of crime himself. He taught himself how to use a gun and at the age of twenty-two started mixing with the small Maltese underworld. There he came under the wing of Pablo Vincenzi, a Maltese Italian who had strong connections with the mafia in Naples. John decided he didn't want to be part of a gang and get involved in all the politics that go with it, so he decided to work alone as a contract killer. He justified it by telling himself he was ridding the world of people it didn't need. Later, he didn't need to justify it. He liked the job, and he liked the rewards even more.

Once his name was known, he would be contacted with details of the hit, and he would have to decide whether to accept or reject it, depending on the degree of risk. He always avoided high-profile targets and it was an unwritten rule that you don't hit someone you know – that's why he was uncomfortable about the Naples meeting. He maintained a connection with the Neapolitan gangs and was introduced to Isabella through a mutual friend. She was pretty much clean herself, but had a job he might be interested in. Dave Constantinou.

This had turned out not to be

straightforward, and he only kept going because of his physical interest in her. She was able to pull his strings, which he now resented. He had pretended to be interested in Dave's ideas for a hotel in Malta as part of his legitimate business, but the truth was that it would never come to anything – only he and Isabella knew that. Now Dave was looking to pull out, which was fine with John but didn't stop him pretending to be pissed off. It served a purpose.

Now Isabella wasn't giving him the nod to kill Dave off. After that, the plan had been to go for Jake, the brother and son. It was all too messy. John liked a clean job, to know as little as necessary. Go in, kill quick, get out, see the money in his account and forget all about it. This time, he'd made the fatal error of complicating it. What Isabella didn't know was that he had engineered their first meeting nearly a year ago when a price had been put on her head. This had been arranged by the Boatman, as Giancarlo Morte was known. He was an arranger who kept his own hands clean, a middleman who was valued and protected by gangs, hitmen, and politicians.

Isabella had racked up gambling debts, and this had led to her upsetting the wrong people. It seemed that she couldn't repay the money she owed, and they were getting restless. She thought she was smart, but she was foolish not to understand how ruthless they could be.

Isabella thought she could make a deal with the gangs, but she wasn't important enough and had nothing to bring to the table. The Boatman contacted John for a different type of job – to get to know Isabella, ready for the nod to go in for the kill, when the time was right. He accepted this, unaware how complicated the situation would become, and against his better judgement. He was also aware that his father was manipulating him, and he was the one person he couldn't stand up to.

Richard Warr controlled everything and everyone he dealt with. John loved and was terrified of him in equal measure. He had often tried to break away from his influence, but every time he was pulled back. He knew that, as long as his dad was alive, he'd never truly be his own man.

CHAPTER 33 – HOME AGAIN: 24 JULY

Jake's plane landed at 12.55 p.m. and taxied to Terminal 5. It occurred to him that he'd taken more flights in the last six weeks than he had for several years prior to that. At least he wasn't paying for them.

He was in a hurry to see Milly. She'd sounded very upset and shocked by the events of last night, and he felt guilty. It was his fault this had happened. He'd barely slept, racked with guilt, and would have flown home in the middle of the night, had there been a flight. He knew she was trying to put on a brave face over the phone – she'd tried to make light of it, even calling it 'exciting', but he knew her well enough to know that it was a front. He wanted to get home to protect her.

The English weather was still behaving itself, although it wasn't as hot as it had been. Milly was standing in the arrivals hall with a big smile, in a yellow vest top and short beige shorts. Jake strode over to her and gave her a hug as if he'd been away for a year.

'Let me look at you. I'm so sorry you went through that.' They were drawing the attention of the other travellers and greeters. Milly smiled and assured him she was fine, but he could see that she wasn't her normal confident self; the stuffing had been knocked out of her.

Once out of Heathrow they headed for the M3. Milly started to tell him how scared she had been the night before. She was close to tears. Jake kept apologising, and she kept reassuring him he wasn't to blame.

'Wait till I see that mouthy old cow.' He was upset that Sandra had given out Milly's address and hit the dash with the palm of his hand.

'I'm so angry with her, with this Colin idiot and what I've put you through. It's really made me stop and think.'

'Let's forget that for now. How do you feel about your new family?' Milly asked a little tentatively. She sounded keen to change the subject.

'Fucking hell,' Jake blurted out, as if he'd just been told. 'She's full of fucking bullshit. I still can't process it. I'm pretty sure she's told me a whole fucking pack of lies and I don't know what's true now. So many things don't fucking add up.'

'But you believe her? That she's your sister?' Milly asked, looking across at him and frowning. A Jaguar swung in front of her, causing her to brake.

'Fucking idiot!' Jake shouted, his tension still simmering away, his thoughts swinging from Colin to Isabella and back again.

Milly squeezed his thigh. 'Less of the fucks, thank you.' She smiled again and added, 'Until we get home, that is!' For the first time for a while, Jake smiled, and he felt calmer. He tried to focus on Milly and started to feel pride that she was his girlfriend. 'How many miles to go?' he asked, sounding excited.

Milly smiled back and gently squeezed his groin area with her left hand.

'Shit,' Jake said softly.

'I can't go back to that apartment on my own,' she said, more serious, 'at least not for a couple of nights.'

'There's no way I'm going to let you,' Jake replied. 'Welcome to the cosiness of the houseboat.'

A silence descended in the car except for the hum of tyres on tarmac. They passed Fleet Services, and Jake's stomach started to rumble.

'Do you want me to give up the case?' he asked, bearing in mind the scare Milly had had the night before.

She hesitated before she replied. 'No. I've been thinking about that. At first, I thought yes, then I thought about it further. This Colin was washed up, elderly and living in the past. He won't want to risk prison again at his age. The truth about Amara needs to be found out – after all, she's your real mother.' She looked at Jake, who was gazing out of the window, watching a Chinook helicopter hover over the fields.

'She'll never be that,' Jake said emphatically. 'Isabella will never be my sister, and Dave Constantinou will definitely never be my father.'

He looked down at his feet. His trainers were scuffed and worse for wear. 'Look at these trainers, might pop into town tomorrow and look for new ones. Think I need a bit of normality for a day.' As he said this he thought that he needed to speak to Fiona and Geoff.

As they passed Basingstoke and approached the A303 turn-off, Jake turned to Milly. 'I know I was in a hurry to get home, but do you mind if we go and see my uncle and aunt first?'

'Where do they live?' Milly replied, looking puzzled.

'Micheldever – it's only a few minutes away. I'll check if they're in.' Jake rang their number, and Fiona sounded delighted to hear from him. They'd just got in from a village hall committee meeting, so it was a good time to drop by.

The village was archetypal English: thatched cottages, farms, an attractive church, a river. As they descended a slight hill to the edge of the village, there were combine harvesters on both sides of the road. The good weather had meant an early harvest this year, and the smell of the newly cut wheat was comforting.

Jake had always got on well with Geoff and Fiona – they had been a real comfort when his parents died – but this would be a tricky conversation. Until yesterday, he had thought they were his only living relatives.

They turned into the drive of the attractive brick-and-slate-tiled house. The scrunching of the gravel in the drive announced Jake and Milly's arrival. Fiona came out with a wide smile and a tea towel over her shoulder. As Jake opened the car door, she took hold of it, clearly eager to give him a hug. Jake thought that whatever they knew, he was not going to be annoyed with them.

'Nice to see you, Auntie,' he said, returning her smile and stepping back. She didn't seem to want to let him go. She was in her mid-sixties, but still as active as a thirty-year-old.

'May I introduce you to Milly.'

She was already out of the car and admiring the purple hydrangeas that lined the fence which faced the main road through the village.

'Ooh yes, we've often heard you on the radio – lovely to meet you.' Fiona kissed Milly on both cheeks.

'What a lovely house … and village,' Milly said. 'I'm pretty sure I've never been here before.'

Fiona smiled approvingly. 'Come around to the patio – the wine's chilled but obviously you can have something else if you prefer.' She led the way round the side of the house, which opened up into a small, but neat, garden, with a meadow and the river beyond.

They all sat down and had no hesitation in deciding on wine. Milly decided to have just one glass. Geoff came out of the greenhouse – a tall, round-faced man wearing a baseball cap and jeans, even though he was nearly seventy. Jake laughed. 'I see you're still down with the kids, Geoff,' he said to his uncle as he bounded up the garden, his hand outstretched.

'Well, you know us – we don't believe in acting our age,' he said, taking the cap off and throwing it onto a chair. He sat down. They chinked glasses and took a sip of wine. With a sigh, Jake sank back into his chair.

CHAPTER 34 – ISABELLA: 24 JULY

Isabella was scared. It was dawning on her that she wasn't as hard as she thought she was. She thought her emotions would have been totally in check, and that emotionless skin she'd been wearing most of her life would see her through, and that her plans to solve her debts would be coming to fruition.

It was 11 a.m. All she'd had to drink was an espresso, which sat uncomfortably in her stomach, which was churning. It was decision time. It was a choice between debts or death. She wished she had someone she could talk to about it all, but the way she'd led her life meant the few close friends she had would fall heavily on one side or the other. There was no one to give a balanced view. Morally, there was only one thing to do, but that would probably end up with her own death. She thought she would feel better after confessing to Jake, but it just seemed to complicate everything further. She felt a huge weight pressing down on her, and she wasn't sure she could fight it off. She had more to say to Jake but knew yesterday wasn't the right moment. For the first time, she felt an emotional pull towards Jake. He would have lots of questions, but they could wait for another day, although time was not on their side. She had still told a few lies, which she may or may not decide to be honest about. She wished the clock could be turned back, and that the reason she had contacted Jake in the first place was different. The first time she met him, there was a recognition she hadn't expected, which would make her whole plan more difficult.

She needed to get out of the villa – in fact, she needed to get out of Naples, to think. She no longer owned a car, so she decided to catch the train to Sorrento. Her favourite restaurant was a short walk from the station, and she was on good terms with the manager. He would be sure to fit her in for lunch. The train would take an hour, giving her time to think rationally. She couldn't be bothered to put any make-up on; she brushed her hair with her hands and slipped on an old pair of trainers.

She packed an overnight bag, just in case. She glanced around her apartment as if she was leaving it for the last time. Some instinct made her think that, when she saw it again, things might be different. At the moment she didn't know which direction her life was going in. She shut the door behind her and put her sunglasses on. The sky was blue, but the air was oppressive, seeming to match her own mood.

She caught a taxi to the station. It was the normal eventful journey: the driver was angry, scooters weaved around between the traffic, and horns blared. She entered the vast concourse of

Naples station and bought her ticket. When she reached the platform and saw the train waiting, she was surprised. It had been years since she'd taken this train, and she hadn't realised how outdated it was, with graffiti scrawled across the carriages. She got in and sat down. There was no air conditioning, but at this time of day it was quite quiet. She took out a bottle of water and gulped down two mouthfuls, then waited for the train to leave.

She had to think.

Her debts had mounted until they had reached a level that was almost meaningless. When 10,000 euros became 50,000 and then 500,000, they were just another number. She couldn't see her way out. Hope always lay in the one bet, the one chip, the one poker hand that would wipe the debts away. But that hadn't happened, and her despair deepened. She had to find another way out. She had thought of one, a highly risky way out, but she no longer felt that she had an option. Naples was an unforgiving place if you owe money, and the threats were almost daily now.

The train pulled out of Napoli Garibaldi station and headed through the suburbs towards Pompeii. It was noisy and she knew it would stop frequently; she now wished she'd taken the cleaner, more modern Campania Express.

Her desperation had peaked almost a year ago when she'd got in touch with Giancarlo, a former gang member who had decided to go straight and start up his own boat hire company, ferrying tourists around the Bay of Naples and out to Capri. He maintained his contacts and made sure he kept his nose clean, never implicating the gangs, but he was lucky; others who had left the gangs found themselves encased in concrete or anchored to the bottom of the bay.

Giancarlo introduced her to John. Isabella explained to him that she had a wealthy father who had disowned her as a child, but that DNA would prove they were blood relatives. She believed that he had no other living relatives apart from a brother. She eventually concluded that if she could kill them both, then maybe she would inherit a vast fortune. John seemed keen to help, but she was totally unaware that their meeting had been carefully set up by Giancarlo. Her debts were the common denominator, but John had an ulterior motive.

Isabella hired Paulo to investigate her family and find out if Amara was dead. He failed to do this, so she turned to her unknown brother. She didn't expect to feel curious about him. Instead of distancing herself from Dave and Jake, she felt the need to meet them, so she arranged an elaborate plot that would see all three of them meet in her house, with John. She knew now that this had been a big mistake.

Her dislike of Dave was strong and

unshaking, but her feelings for Jake were different. She liked him. To contemplate his death was a step too far, but without his death the whole plan was in jeopardy. It would mean him inheriting half of Dave's fortune but, more importantly, it would risk the whole plan being unveiled. She was sure that Jake wouldn't buy into it and keep quiet.

She glanced out of the train window, watching Vesuvius get closer and closer. Its classic volcanic shape was almost perfectly symmetrical from this angle. Soon they would reach Pompeii. She thought about what had happened to that city in AD 79: when apparent corruption and debauchery swept through it, nature had intervened and it was wiped out, with everyone being buried in molten rock and ash. How could she escape her own true awakening?

Answers were not coming easy to Isabella. She bent forward and cupped her hands around her face. She wept quietly as she felt the massive weight of loneliness hit her like the train itself. For the first time, she wondered if she could go on. What did she have to live for? When had she become a bad person? What was the point of Isabella Bellini? She gazed out across the bay: a big, blue expanse of water that you could lose yourself in and never return. Maybe this would be her way out…

CHAPTER 35 – HAMPSHIRE: 24 JULY

Jake was both relaxing and feeling tense at the same time. The sun was shining, and they'd had a walk through the village, soaking up the tranquillity of an English summer village scene. As they turned back into the drive Jake decided it was time to talk about why they were here, why they suddenly turned up at his uncles and aunt's house without a real warning. He turned to Fiona with a serious look on his face.

'I've got something I really need to talk to you about.'

'I can tell,' Fiona replied. She almost looked relieved.

'Can we go back and sit down?' The conversation had skirted around why they had suddenly dropped in. They settled back into chairs on the patio and Geoff hastily brought out another bottle of wine.

'Well,' Jake started, realising he hadn't rehearsed this. 'My heritage, where I come from. I'm adopted, aren't I?' He looked directly, and intently at Fiona, who gasped slightly.

'Jake, I love you as if you were my own. But you're right,' she hesitated, 'and I begged Donna to tell you years ago, but she was scared, scared she'd lose you. You'd never be just her little Jake anymore,' Fiona hesitated again, 'you had a sister.'

Jake nodded. 'I know. She contacted me over a month ago, out of the blue, but has only just told me about our relationship. I tell you she's quite a remarkable woman, and I'm not sure I like her very much.

Fiona fiddled with her glass. 'I'm so sorry Jake, I really am.'

'It's ok, I get it. To be honest I'm not blaming anyone, but it's obviously been a shock.'

'Are you sure? I'd be livid!'

'Strangely, no. I've had time to think about it on my own and know that I couldn't have wished for a better childhood.' Jake's voice started to break so Milly reached out and grabbed his hand. 'They were great parents and I truly loved them.' Jake struggled to hold back a few tears so decided to let them fall. Fiona grabbed his other hand and dabbed her own eyes with a tissue. In turn Milly managed to grab a napkin off the table and blew her nose. Geoff topped up the glasses.

'So, tell us what happened when your sister contacted you.' Geoff asked.

'Isabella, she's Italian.' Jake regained his composure, 'and it's a pretty interesting story so far.' He told them both what had happened in the last few weeks, and they seemed genuinely shocked. Fiona sat back in her chair after twenty minutes of Jake talking, which he found quite cathartic.

'I swear, me and Geoff didn't really know anything much about your background. We knew you were from North London, you'd been abandoned, with your parents possibly dead. But that was about it. I just can't believe you're investigating your own mother's death, or possible death.'

'I know, you wouldn't believe it would you?' Jake felt a strange relief that he could share a story about his family, with his family. Geoff stepped in.

'Well, one thing is for sure, you two are not going home tonight. I'll get another bottle.' Jake smiled and wiped another tear from his eye.

CHAPTER 36 – JOHN: 25 JULY

John woke up with a dead arm. It was under Leanne's head, and he gently tried to extricate it, but the lack of feeling made it more difficult. She stirred but remained asleep, much to John's relief. He wanted some quiet time. He got out of bed and put on a pair of shorts. He decided to use the toilet at the other end of his apartment, so as not to disturb Leanne, and made himself a coffee as quietly as possible. It was a warm morning but still early. Malta was just coming to life. The best part of the day.

He put water on to boil, put coffee in the jug, and waited. Once he'd poured the water into the jug, he had a few minutes to collect his thoughts. Today, he would decide what to do. Give Isabella an ultimatum for him to kill Dave and Jake, resurrect the job to take her out, or walk away from both. He'd led a charmed life and he had a nagging feeling that carrying on with this job was risky.

He poured the coffee and walked silently out to the balcony. This was John's flat, and his wife never came here. It had a spectacular view over Valletta Harbour, but all was quiet this morning. The blue sky and the low sun reflected off the water, creating a calming effect. This was one of the reasons John loved living here.

Not one for sentiment, especially when a hit

was involved, John knew that he'd got to know Isabella too well. She was interesting, elusive, and had a dark, steely determination about her. It wasn't such a coincidence that she wanted him for a job at the same time he'd been asked to kill her. John had a strong reputation in Naples, built up over ten years. He'd only once had to abandon a hit, because there were too many witnesses around, and he'd never got close to being caught. John afforded himself a smug smile as he sipped his Colombian coffee.

He put the china cup down on the small table next to him. He'd made a decision. He was not going to go ahead with Isabella's plan to kill Dave and Jake. It was never going to work – what had he been thinking? It could be months or years before Isabella was able to pay him. She was deluding herself into thinking this was the answer: kill her relatives and their estates would be settled in her favour before the wolves knocked at her door. He'd known this in the back of his mind for some time, but finally he had a moment of clarity. He cursed himself for not thinking it through properly at the start. It was so unlike him, and he was annoyed by his weakness. He'd been seduced by her and let his dick rule his head. He must never do that again. He had also been encouraged by his dad, who he knew had his own agenda. It was his idea that he should take both jobs – Dave and Jake first, then Isabella. John had never told his dad the whole story, but he knew it linked back to his time in London and the Welby family.

The question he had to think about now was, should he carry out the hit on Isabella?

CHAPTER 37 – HAMPSHIRE: 25 JULY

Jake reckoned he'd got about four hours' sleep. It was light outside, but he could hear rain falling steadily onto the patio at the back of the house. He and Milly had stayed in Micheldever overnight, after an afternoon and evening of relentless talking and drinking. He lay on his back in the king-size bed in the guest room and let out a long, loud sigh. Milly stirred. He looked across, but she still seemed to be asleep. She had been intrigued by the revelations of the day before, while Jake was struggling to come to terms with them.

He looked at the quilt cover. John Lewis, of course, which Fiona loved; she used to work at Peter Jones in Sloane Square. He'd enjoyed the previous evening, and he felt he'd reconnected with his uncle and aunt, who he'd barely seen in the last year. Sadly, he had found that they reminded him of his lost parents, and he'd been desperate to move on, start a new life, but now he knew they'd been hurting too. They could have helped each other more to deal with their sudden loss.

Jake could hear movement downstairs, so he picked up his phone to check the time. It was 7.38 a.m. He wasn't getting up yet. He wanted to talk to Milly, but she was breathing heavily. He coughed and sighed again, hoping it would wake her up. Nothing. He was busting for the toilet, so decided to go to the en-suite. He got up and, leaving the door open, he directed his flow into the centre of the pan to create the maximum sound of water on water. After a few seconds Milly shouted, 'God, I hate that noise – couldn't you close the door?'

Jake smiled at the bathroom cabinet in front of him. 'Sorry!' he called back. 'Didn't think.' Despite the volume of alcohol he'd drunk the previous day, he was feeling remarkably OK. Milly, on the other hand, was not, and went straight for the paracetamol by the side of the bed. She swallowed them without water, gagging on the second one. Jake climbed back into bed, putting on his 'troubled' face.

Milly's eyes were barely open, and her head lolled to one side as she propped herself up on her elbows. 'Is that rain?' she mumbled.

'Uh-huh.'

'Are you OK this morning?'

'Yeah. Just been thinking how lucky I was to be adopted by Mum and Dad, I suppose. God knows what life would have been like if I hadn't been adopted. It's just so weird to imagine.'

Milly shook her head to try and clear it somehow, but it just made her brain rattle in her skull and made her headache worse.

'You know, I worried that you'd get annoyed, but I was proud of you.' Milly strung the sentence together, although it was an effort and rather stuttery.

Jake laid back in the pillow and thought how he'd met these people without knowing they were his family. According to Fiona, all Isaac and Donna Stone had known was that Christopher came from a Greek Cypriot family in north London, and his parents had disappeared. He had a sister, but the authorities had split them up. The Stones then had the son they had always wanted and changed his name to Jake by deed poll. In the end, what Jake had told Geoff and Fiona had been a greater surprise than what they could tell Jake.

'I still can't believe that I'm 75% Greek Cypriot,' Jake said as he turned to face Milly, pulling the duvet over his shoulders.

'You don't really look it,' she said. 'Your 25% English is definitely dominant in your looks, but you can be a bit hot-headed.' Her face was straight. 'Maybe a bit irrational at times.'

'Alright, alright,' Jake said. 'I'm not sure that's a sign of Greek Cypriot heritage anyway, that could apply to loads of cultures.'

'Just saying.'

Jake sniggered, 'however, I've always liked halloumi – and remember that succulent lamb kleftiko I had in that restaurant a few weeks ago? I loved it, and that's a Cypriot dish.' Jake rolled over onto his back and added, 'It's so weird.'

'So, what's next?' Milly asked.

'Um, that's what kept me awake most of the

night,' he said. 'Isabella has some lies to explain. I need to ask Dave about Amara's disappearance and find out what John's role really is in all of this.' Jake sighed heavily, got out of bed and pulled the curtains apart so he could see the rain falling outside. He ran his hand through his hair and returned to bed.

'Well, I've been thinking as well. I'm not sure I want you to go on with this, but I know you will. It's got nothing to do with my visitor the other night, but more the risk it's putting you in. I'll say no more.' Milly turned to Jake. He held her gaze for a few moments and grabbed her hand, then looked away again. He suddenly felt quite emotional and wondered to himself what he'd done to have been lucky enough to meet Milly.

He picked up his phone just as a text came through from Isabella. He read it out loud.

Hope you're OK, Jake. We have more to talk about. Hope to see you soon.

'That's my sister. It feels so weird to say. Thing is, I'm not sure I like her. I certainly don't like Dave. They may be my blood relatives, but I can't see myself ever calling them family.'

Milly shifted across the bed and snuggled up to him. 'So, now you've had time to think about it, you don't resent Isaac and Donna?'

'It's a good question, it would be easy to resent them for not telling me, but I can't ask them to tell me about it now. As it was, I had a happy upbringing, none the wiser. If they'd told me, I probably would have had years of trouble finding them and been really disappointed now that I know what my real parents were like.'

'What about Isabella?'

'Yep, a sister would have been nice. I do remember as a teenager having recurrent dreams where I had a sister. Maybe that was a latent memory locked away.'

'Do you know what, Jake Stone?' Milly said, her voice a little clearer now as the paracetamol started to kick in, 'you can be a bit of an idiot sometimes, but I think I love you.'

Jake smiled back. 'You're hard work sometimes, but I think I love you too.'

The smell of frying bacon had started to waft up the stairs. Jake decided the pull of the bacon was stronger than the pull of the bed, so he popped his T-shirt on and padded down the stairs. He poured himself a cup of coffee from the cafetière.

'I always said you did the best fry-ups,' he said, as Fiona got the eggs ready.

'I thought I'd make a start, although I have the worst hangover I've had for years.'

'Tell Milly about it,' Jake said, getting the milk out of the fridge.

Fiona looked up, tongs in hand. 'Oh, poor lamb. She's a lovely girl, Jake.' She waved the tongs at him. 'You'd better not let her go, young man.' She began to lift the bacon out of the pan. 'I can't believe what she went through the other night – she's got guts.'

Jake nodded approvingly. 'Where's Geoff?'

'He's also a bit delicate. I was thinking, you still don't know why Isabella wanted Dave killed, do you?'

'Nope,' Jake replied, sitting up at the breakfast bar. 'I was still in a state of shock about me being her brother when she said that. I didn't think to ask her why.'

'That's what worries me. This whole thing seems dark and dangerous. I think I would like you to step back from it.' Fiona frowned in concern.

'That's what Milly just said,' Jake replied, 'but I can't. The least I can do is to find out what happened to Amara. Her death has never been confirmed. She could be living a new life in deepest Wales for all we know, under a new name.'

'I'm not sure about that.'

'Why do you say that?'

'I just think at some point she would have tried to find you both.'

'Maybe she was too scared. We don't know the whole story yet, do we?'

Fiona turned away and, with a humph, she reached for the plate of bacon to put in the oven to keep warm.

They were silent for a few moments, but

Fiona's brain was clearly ticking away. 'You know, it doesn't add up. Obviously, Isabella is lying about why she wanted you to get involved if she wants Dave killed. Why contact you at all if she wasn't going to tell you you're her brother right from the start?'

Jake nodded as she talked, knowing where she was going.

'So why get close to you? She could employ anyone to investigate Amara's disappearance. Is your life in danger as well?' Fiona looked worried. 'You're my boy now, and I couldn't bear it if something happened to you.'

Jake was touched. 'Maybe I get my investigative skills from you...'

'Well, that's all I'm going to say ... for now,' Fiona said. Jake knew that she was always happy to voice her opinion, and he loved her for it. He'd never felt so close to her before.

Jake and Milly left Micheldever soon after breakfast, and it took them just under an hour to get home to Lymford. It was Saturday, so Jake went with Milly back into her apartment. After a short while she insisted she would be alright, so he grabbed some fresh clothes from the houseboat. The rain was back after relenting for a couple of hours, and it felt particularly cool by the water. Dog walkers were scurrying along the towpath as quickly as possible, collars up and hats on.

Despite the warnings Milly and Fiona had

given him, Jake had decided to go and meet up with Dave as planned and find out as much as he could about the night Amara disappeared.

CHAPTER 38 – DAVE: 26 JULY

Dave was making plans before he took off for Argentina. He had a lot of loose ends to clear up –and one of them was Harry Taylor. He had been due to meet him today, but Harry had cried off. Dave needed to make sure that their meeting was rearranged as soon as possible.

He was meeting his solicitor the next day, and he was going to tell him his plans. This included selling his businesses and severing all his ties with Europe. This time he wouldn't be changing his name. The thought of leaving made him feel liberated. Once all his assets had been liquidated, he could buy a nice house in the country and lead a simple life. No business deals, no living on the edge. A clean, law-abiding life. He'd be reborn. His secrets would come with him, but he would have some distance from them all.

He sent Jake a text.

Harry, just wondered if you were coming back to the island this week? Would be good to catch up.

Dave put his phone down on the table and went into his study to gather all the papers he would need for his solicitor. He was going to gift the house in Menorca to his housekeeper – she'd protected him and looked after him for years, and had been totally reliable, always knowing but never talking when his business was a bit shady. She lived with her husband in a small, terraced house in Alaior on the main road. She'd always loved the peace and quiet of his villa, and the garden would give her a lot of pleasure.

He gave himself a month to leave Menorca and head to Argentina. A lot of the paperwork could be done after he'd gone, but his solicitor and accountant could deal with most of that; he would just sign what he needed to sign.

He would be leaving no friends behind, but there was one person he needed to see before he left, he would contact her soon. He knew what sort of person he was, and as soon as people got to know him they turned away. Daniel Welby hadn't been the same. He had been naive and easily manipulated, he had a temper – and that's why he had fitted into the gang. He would do what he was asked and was hot-headed enough to react in the ways they wanted. Dave Constantinou was a harder, meaner, nastier version of Daniel. He saw the world without kindness, and he lacked empathy. People were there to be used, abused, and thrown away. He hoped that in Argentina a new person could again emerge: Daniel reborn with a third identity.

He knew he was running away, but Europe was like an old car now: it had got dirty, with bumps and scratches, and his love for it was gone. It didn't love him anymore; it had broken down, leaving him isolated.

Isabella was Zoe. He remembered her as a cute little girl with dark hair that Amara was always putting into pigtails. She hadn't been a happy child, though, unlike Christopher, who constantly giggled and had an endearing habit of running his hands through his hair when he was a little frustrated. Dave had never really taken to Zoe, but when events took over and his life changed, he missed Christopher. In the back of his mind, he'd always hoped that he was alright.

He saw Harry run his hand through his hair in Naples. This was a thought that only came to him a few days ago but he dismissed it then, but also, he remembered that Harry and Isabella had the same eyes, which were the same colour as Amara's. He was starting to believe that Harry was Christopher and now he was in a hurry to know for sure. Would Harry hate him? Dave didn't know what his own emotions were telling him, how much did it mean to him? How much did he care? He knew he had to meet Harry again to find out. Would it derail his plans to go to Argentina? He thought not, but if they both turned out to be his children what was he going to feel when he saw them again. He didn't want to take any responsibility, but it was a strange feeling that both his children, by Amara, had come back into his life after so many years. He reached for a bottle of whisky.

CHAPTER 39 – JAKE: 26 JULY

Jake was on a 'thought walk'. It was Sunday morning and Milly had gone to see her mother, who lived about thirty miles away. He walked down Lymford High Street and popped into Costa for a coffee. While it was being made, he texted Dave.

Back in Menorca in a few days, shall we meet up at that restaurant in Ciutadella?

He was surprised to get a quick reply.

Sure, I'll book the same place at 2 p.m. Thursday?

Perfect.

Jake realised the thought of the meeting made him nervous. He thanked the barista for his coffee and stepped out into the bright sunlight. Summer was back. He walked down the street, heading for the entrance to St James's Park. As he entered the park, he found himself taking it all in, as if for the first time. There was a pavilion to his right and a path down the middle separating two fields. Cricket was being played on one field, with the clunk of bat hitting ball and the shout of 'Run!' followed by the heavy pitter-patter of running between the stumps. Jake smiled. It was one of the most iconic sounds and visions of an English Sunday in summer. And then there was a cheer as a batsman was run out.

On the other field, off to Jake's right, there was an exercise class, in which several women and a man were being put through their paces by the trainer, who was not going easy on them, despite the sun blazing down. Jake could see their sweat from fifty metres away. A breeze gently wafted through the evenly spaced beech trees that lined the path. Jake walked to the end of the field, where a small bridge crossed a stream. The path led to a larger field, then went off to the right down to the bowls club and tennis courts.

The park buzzed with life. Teens were playing volleyball – they were shouting at each other for missing the ball and hitting the net in frustration. All around the edge were runners and dog walkers. This was the site of Lymford's weekly Parkrun.

Jake sat on a bench, carefully clearing off a bottle of Budweiser that had been left behind by some nocturnal revellers. Birds were hopping from tree to tree and shrub to shrub. He thought they were a mixture of blackbirds and starlings, but his knowledge of the species was not the best. He looked up and saw a red kite, which he did recognise. There was a sudden manic twitter in the tree next to him and a magpie landed in front of him. He raised his hand to his forehead and saluted it.

Despite everything going on, Jake felt an enormous feeling of calm and contentment, although he was still troubled by Colin's visit to Milly. He wondered how long this feeling would last.

In the afternoon he went back to his houseboat. Sandra from the next-door boat popped her head up when she saw him coming. She started to fiddle with her plants, glancing Jake's way. He ignored her at first, still unhappy that she'd given Milly's address to Colin. He went on to his own boat and unloaded his shopping onto the bed and put water into the kettle. He had a gnawing feeling inside him and checked if Sandra was still watering her plants. She was.

'Hey Sandra, you nearly got my girlfriend killed the other day.'

'How?'

'You gave her address to a complete stranger.' Jake was trying to keep calm.

'That nice old man? I thought he was a relation.'

'Well, he wasn't, he was a nasty gangster from London.' Jake realised this sounded like he and Milly were mixed up in some organised crime and probably wasn't helping his explanation. He added, 'it was to do with an investigation. He was trying to put me off the scent.'

Sandra looked a little shocked and uttered her apologies.

'Well, if anyone else comes around can you just say you don't know where I am and not give out Milly's address?'

'Of course, of course,' she paused and added, 'it's just a bit exciting though, isn't it?'

Jake allowed a slight smile to emerge and said, 'maybe,' then went back down below deck.

As he flicked open his iPad to book another flight to Menorca, he realised that he was getting fed up with all this travelling. He hoped this would be the last trip for a while. He needed to see Dave, then Isabella. Hopefully then he could come home and concentrate on uncovering the truth about Amara's disappearance. This now had an added importance for him, although he was struggling to feel any sort of emotional connection to her. He ran his hand through his hair and vowed to have a haircut tomorrow.

Just after he'd booked his flight, Milly called to say that she was back. She'd been to Marks & Spencer and had bought them a Thai banquet.

'Yours or mine?' she asked.

'Yours, of course,' Jake replied. 'I'm not leaving you in that apartment on your own just yet.'

'I've had a thought,' Milly said, 'but we'll discuss that later. Come over when you're ready.'

'Oh, it always terrifies me when people say that,' Jake said, a touch of trepidation in his voice. 'See you later.'

He was starving, so he opened a bag of cheese and onion crisps. He wanted to sit on top of the houseboat, get some fresh air, but he couldn't be bothered to speak to nosy Sandra, so he put the fan on and sat on his bed, scrolling through Facebook on his phone. He soon got bored of that and checked the BBC news feed. Nothing much caught his interest until he saw an article on police corruption. He opened it. It was a scathing report on the Metropolitan Police. It alleged institutionalised corruption towards the end of the twentieth century – no surprise there – and it focused on north London, the rave scene, and the gangs that had been in control at the time. Jake wrote down the name of the reporter, Sean Bellow, and decided to get in touch with him.

*

They felt stuffed by the time they had finished the Thai banquet. One bottle of Merlot was gone, with another on the go. They went out to sit on the balcony. In the background Spotify was playing Milly's Daily Mix, which included Radiohead's 'Creep'.

'Your song,' she teased.

It was very humid again, and both wore shorts and T-shirts.

'This weather makes me so horny,' Jake said,

putting his hand on top of hers.

'Charmer,' Milly replied. 'Later – I'm too full at the moment. Anyway, I've got a proposal for you.'

'Go on,' Jake said guardedly.

'What if I do a bit more investigating? I quite enjoyed finding that stuff out with Elias, and I reckon there's more we could discover from his contact, Lily. I could do that while you swan off to Menorca again.'

Slowly Jake nodded and told her about the article he'd read earlier. 'I think it's worth having a chat with him – he may know a lot more than he wrote. Go for it, Miss Moneypenny ... I'm not paying you, though.'

'I can make you pay in other ways, Stone. I'll make you my sex slave.' Milly laughed as she poured some more Merlot into her glass.

'Yes, please.'

With a swift change of tack, Milly looked at him more seriously. 'How are you feeling about things? I thought you might still be upset.'

Jake rolled the edge of his glass against his chin, pondering his answer. 'I was shocked at first, but I don't feel anything much now. I'm not sure why. I've met Dave, I didn't like him, and I'm not sure I like Isabella. Maybe I've just compartmentalised it for now. The life I know is what's important to me.'

Milly leaned across and kissed him on the cheek. Human League's 'Don't You Want Me?'

started to play in the background.

'Yes, I do,' Milly said as she walked inside, laughing.

'Thank god someone does,' Jake shouted back.

CHAPTER 40 – MENORCA: 29/30 JULY

Jake flew into Menorca again, then headed for the apartment. He went upstairs and opened all the windows and the door to the balcony. It was like a sauna, but the heat of the day had now let up as the sun was low on the western horizon.

He was meeting Dave tomorrow, and Milly had already enlisted Elias to track down Sean Bellow. Jake had picked up wine, ham, cheese, and bread at the supermarket and laid it out on the balcony table. He took down a glass from the kitchen cupboard. He stood on the balcony, looking out at the view, and ran his hand through his hair, still getting used to his new cut – he'd gone for a grade four all over. He picked up the glass and took two large gulps of water. He was nervous about tomorrow.

The next day, it took him forty minutes to drive the fifty kilometres to Ciutadella. It was a bit cooler when he reached the west coast, with a layer of thin, high cloud obscuring the sun into a fuzzy milky ball. Jake had always liked Menorca's second town and its original capital. It was a lively place with some lovely Italian-style buildings, a pleasant square, and a different vibe to the rest of Menorca. It was not about beaches here, but about fishing boats, yachts, and rocky outposts. The restaurant was centrally located, so Jake parked in a side street and checked his watch. He was slightly late. His nerves jangling, he walked swiftly down the road and past the square. Then he saw the restaurant cum hotel and the figure of Dave Constantinou, his real father, sitting at a table near the back of the shaded terrace.

Emotion washed over Jake, making him want to turn around and go home. He tried to analyse the feeling: was it rejection, annoyance, anger? He felt nothing positive, and he knew he was going to have to put on an A-grade performance in tolerance and charm. Dave saw him and waved.

Jake walked over and held out his hand.

'Nice to see you again, Harry,' Dave said ebulliently, a big grin on his face.

Jake smiled back, although it took some effort. They both sat down, and Jake noticed Dave's hips struggle to fit between the arm rests of the chair.

'Well, let's get to the first confession of the day. I'm not Harry Taylor.'

'No, I don't think you are.'

Jake had decided that he couldn't be bothered with too much small talk; he wanted to get to the point of the meeting as quickly as possible. 'I'm Jake Stone, and I'm a private investigator.'

At that point a waiter came up to the table with two glasses and a bottle of Primitivo. Dave indicated that he should put them on the table, and they would help themselves. He also told them they weren't ready to order yet.

Dave looked back at Jake and nodded slowly. 'I knew there was something fishy about you.' He poured the wine into both glasses.

Jake fiddled with his watch strap, which was sitting on a layer of sweat around his wrist.

'Go on, explain yourself,' Dave said, sitting back in his chair.

Jake paused. 'Isabella hired me to investigate the disappearance of her mother, Amara Welby. Your wife, when you were Daniel Welby.' Jake noticed that Dave didn't look surprised.

'Bloody bitch,' Dave spat out. 'Why doesn't she just leave it and get on with her life? Why drag that up now?'

'Maybe she wants to find out what happened to her mother. Maybe you killed her thirty-two years ago...'

'And if I did, it would be a waste of time her trying to prove it,' Dave said, leaning forward again and talking in an urgent whisper.

'Why?' Jake replied, a determined look on his face. He was starting to feel an intense dislike for this so-called father of his. The prospect of a meal with him was not appealing. Dave shook his head, his red face seeming to bulge, and his yellow short-sleeved shirt streaked with damp patches.

'If I were you, I'd get out. You're out of your

depth trying to manipulate people who have far more power and influence than you will ever have. I'm dangerous, Isabella is dangerous, and we both have friends and enemies who would happily leave you at the bottom of the Med, never to be found.'

Jake felt winded, and surprisingly hurt, by this comment. As much as he didn't like Dave, he wouldn't have thought he'd want to see his own son dead. 'Would you do that to your own son?' He looked up and stared into Dave's eyes. He noticed they were caramel coloured – more Greek than his and Isabella's were. Dave's face seemed to soften a little as he stared back at Jake. Their eyes locked for a few moments before Dave opened his mouth. 'It dawned on me last week that you could be Christopher, and I've known for a few weeks that Isabella was Zoe.'

'Before the dinner in Naples?'

'Uh-huh. I was interested to find out if I felt anything for her now that I knew. In all honesty, I felt nothing. Too much time has passed. You were both Amara's kids back then; I wasn't around that much, so never really bonded with you. That's not to say I wasn't curious. I did occasionally think about what you might be doing now that you were grown up.'

Jake couldn't look at him anymore. He played with his wine glass as if there was hidden treasure in it. 'How nice of you,' he mumbled. He could feel Dave studying him.

'Look, do you want me to say sorry? Because if you do, you'll need to get into the queue.'

'I just want the truth, that's all.'

Dave bit his lip. 'Have you had a good life, Jake?'

Jake hesitated. 'It's been a bit rocky, but I had a great family life.'

'So, look at me. Would you have had that with me?'

Jake frowned at Dave, knowing what the answer was.

Dave sat back in his chair as if he was bored of the conversation. He looked at the relaxed visitors and locals walking past the restaurant, smiling, and enjoying the ambience of the town. 'I'm leaving for South America soon – permanently, so we probably won't see each other again. I know you think I'm a heartless bastard, but that's just the way it is. I'm not suddenly going to become a father to you.'

Jake reacted abruptly; his eyes wide. He couldn't get the words out quick enough. 'Believe me, that's the last thing I want.' He checked himself before telling Dave what a nasty, odious, selfish twat he was. He still needed some answers. He looked at Dave again and steadied his voice. In a slow, deliberate tone, he asked, 'What happened to Amara? That's what I need to know, nothing else.'

CHAPTER 41 – ISABELLA: 30 JULY

It was nearly a week since her trip to Sorrento, and Isabella was lucky to still be alive. She had been in a trance that day and had been on the verge of throwing herself off the cliffs. Her appetite had gone; she didn't bother with lunch, opting to wander, and keep wandering. The Amalfi coast had always been her place to recharge. It was truly beautiful, and for years she'd wanted Luca to buy a house there so she could spend her time enjoying its – often noisy – beauty, escaping from the dirt and grimness of Naples. He was never keen. She should have done it when they divorced but she had got distracted by her demons, the main one being gambling. She had struggled with depression most of her life. She recognised the signs, but this time refused to resort to the pills that her doctor was more than happy to dish out. She needed a clear mind and to think rationally.

As she gazed out to sea, as blue as an aquamarine gemstone, perched, like the town itself, on the rocky cliff above the shore, she desperately tried to cling on to hope. She wasn't a coward. The answer might be quite simple, but it wasn't a decision she could make on her own. The thought of disappearing to another country came to mind – just like Dave. It must run in the family. But she knew that people can almost always be tracked down unless they're in a government witness protection programme. She would be on her own hiding from the Neapolitan criminals who chased down debts. It was time to pay up – or die.

She decided to swallow her pride and go and see Luca. She could do it over the phone, but she felt the need to get away from Naples, and the clean air of the mountains was quite appealing. This was probably her real last hope. Maybe it was one she should have thought of a long time ago.

Luca was wealthy; she wasn't sure how he had become so rich, and she had never asked. When they were married, she didn't care. They had a lavish lifestyle and they both had lovers, which they thought kept the marriage fresh. In the end it was their downfall, as trust between them broke down. However, they divorced amicably; Luca had always been kind, and was still good for words of advice.

Luca lived in a small village in the Italian Alps called Chiesa. He'd set up a ski school and left behind the world of commerce. He'd met a ski instructor and they apparently lived happily, and simply. Isabella had rung him two days earlier, saying that she needed to see him and would be flying into Milan on 30th July. He booked her into a small hotel in the village. She hired a car from Milan Malpensa airport and drove the Fiat north past Lake Como and up into the Alps. It was the first time she'd been among the mountains in the summer, and it was a strangely enjoyable experience. The twisting mountain roads in summer seemed so much easier than in the winter; then they were busier and icier, often sleety, or snowy.

It took two hours to get to Chiesa. As soon as she got out of the car, she noticed the fresher air. The sun was strong, but there was a welcome relief from the humidity. She grabbed her bag and checked into the hotel, which was a few minutes from Luca's villa. She had arranged to meet him at 8 p.m. so she had an hour to settle in.
*

Luca's villa was surprisingly modest: a two-storey Alpine design similar to the others around it, but with spectacular views. Luca came out to meet her as she walked into the drive. Her first thought was that he looked much older than when she'd last seen him, about a year ago. He was older than her, in his mid-forties, and his thinning hair was rapidly going grey. His skin had a pale brown pallor which appeared almost fake.

He kissed her twice on both cheeks. He was always one to get straight to the point, so he guided her into the villa and asked her pointedly what she wanted. A bottle of wine was already open, and a glass of red had been poured for her. They sat down in a couple of comfy chairs. Isabella exhaled. 'Money and family.'

She paused and took a sip of wine. She took a deep breath and explained that she had got herself into terrible gambling debts and couldn't see a way out. She then went on to explain her plan to kill Dave and Jake and hope to receive their inheritance. This took about thirty minutes, and during this time, Luca's changing facial expressions were his only response. Finally, he said,

'You do know how ridiculous that all is?'

'Yes, yes, I do … and saying it all out loud shocks me to the core.'

'Isabella,' Luca said, as if he was talking to a child, 'I knew there was something wrong when we talked about the house in England being sold. The paintings you've got – I bet they could clear your debts. Sell them, then get yourself into counselling or a self-help group to stop gambling.'

Isabella felt a surge of hope. 'But they're yours – you never actually gave them to me. I assumed at some point you'd come and claim them.'

Luca scoffed. 'Come on, we both know that's why you're here – to ask if you can sell them.' He shrugged. 'I have no need for them. Go ahead.'

Isabella gasped and smiled, for the first time in weeks. 'Not going to lie to you, I hoped that was what you would say, but I never thought you would. Thank you, Luca. Truly. It's like a massive weight has been lifted off my shoulders.'

'The mountain air has been good for me – you can see this house is modest. I've changed, and I'm so glad to be out of the rat race. Promise me you'll sort yourself out.'

Isabella felt a surge of comfort. She wondered why she hadn't come to see him several weeks ago. Her mind had been scrambled and she had been unable to think clearly. She'd distracted herself by trying to find out the truth about Amara's disappearance. It had become complicated and a little dangerous, but it had stopped her thinking about her debts and what to do.

Luca seemed happy to be her sounding board for the evening, and it was soothing her soul like nothing had for months. Isabella went on to tell him about Jake and Amara in more detail. Luca had known that Isabella was adopted, but he seemed fascinated by how the story had developed, which surprised Isabella. By the end of their marriage, they had little to talk about and little interest in each other. He'd mellowed.

Isabella left Luca's villa at about 10.30 p.m., just as the first rumblings of a mountain storm could be heard away to the west. Luca promised to keep in touch, and she in turn assured him she would pay her debts and seek help. Buoyed by the successful evening and several glasses of wine, her journey felt so much easier than the walk up to the villa had been. She felt lighter, brighter, and more optimistic. Could this be a turning point? She was still attracted to Luca, especially the 'new Luca', but she knew their relationship was history. As the thunder rolled across the mountains and the lightning got brighter, Isabella thought about Jake. She hadn't seriously considered it before, but she decided she would like to get to know him better. Maybe they could have some sort of relationship in the future. She felt crushingly guilty that she had considered having him killed.

At that moment there was a blinding flash of light, followed instantaneously by a deafening crash of thunder, as if the village was falling off the edge of the mountain. She was thrown to the ground, and felt a strong shake rise up her body. She then heard another crashing sound – quieter but closer and equally ominous. Something heavy fell across the backs of her legs as the sound died away, and she looked around, just as rain started to fall as if it was being poured from a bucket. Two men came running out of a nearby house, dodging the tree that had fallen on Isabella, and asked if she was OK. Isabella was shocked but felt no pain and started to pull herself up. Two pairs of hands grabbed hold of her and the two men, in their twenties, put her arms around their necks and guided her to a chair underneath an awning owned by a small restaurant. The people inside had seen the tree coming down and thought for a moment it was going to smash straight into them. Isabella sat down, her legs shaking. She then started to smile, which gradually morphed into a laugh. She looked at the two men and managed to say '*Gracias*' several times.

She threw back her head and said to whoever would listen: 'God has been on my side tonight.' She was on a high, for the first time for years and mentally thought it was a sign that things might be changing for the better.

CHAPTER 42 – MENORCA: 30 JULY

Jake was thinking about his meeting with Dave. He didn't know what to believe. Dave seemed adamant that he didn't know what had happened to Amara. Clearly, he was in deep with the gang in London, which was wrapped up with some Met Police officers earning nice little payoffs to keep quiet. Dave had sworn that he'd never seen Amara again after their argument the night she disappeared. According to Dave, the next day he was summoned to see gang leader Jimmy Stefanov and told to skip the country. The gang got his paperwork together, which included a new passport in the name of Dave Constantinou, a ferry crossing from Portsmouth to Caen and an address in Deauville, where he was to lie low for a few weeks.

It occurred to Jake that Isabella had always been convinced that Dave had killed Amara, but so far, no proof had been uncovered. Maybe there was another explanation, but where could that lead him? Was the truth deeper and darker than a domestic killing?

*

Dave decided to go for a walk around the harbour at Ciutadella. He thought he was starting to go soft. He'd just told Jake – not Harry – things he'd never told anyone else. He felt exposed, but also relieved that there was someone he could say 'I didn't do it' to. It was only a few weeks since he'd unburdened his soul to Paulo. His life as Daniel Welby was back to haunt him. Deep down he always knew it would, but maybe he could take some positives from it.

Even though he had carefully nurtured a tough, uncaring attitude for most of his life there was still a trace of humanity about him. Seeing Christopher, as Jake, in front of him, made him remember the little boy crying for his mummy thirty-two years ago. It had had a strange effect on him, which he hadn't expected. He knew he was a bit hard on Jake, but it had been many years since he'd felt an emotional connection with anyone, but there was a part of him that meant no harm to Jake. He might even have learned to like him. Jake was a bit feisty, which Dave approved of. So was Isabella, come to that.

Walking back to his own car, he thought again about the last days of Daniel Welby. When he'd seen Jimmy Stefanov on that fateful morning after the argument the night before, he had looked haggard. Normally he was immaculately dressed: a smart, well-groomed man, supremely confident and in charge of everything and everyone around him. That morning he was worried, dressed in jeans and a tatty T-shirt. His dark hair was messy and his cheeks stubbled.

Daniel was ushered to a house in Rickmansworth by one of the 'heavies', a square-jawed brute with a shaved head who looked like he worked out for twelve hours a day. He stayed there for two days, seeing no one until the brute turned up with his new papers. Daniel knew that something big must have happened, but he had no idea what. He'd learned not to ask questions as he knew he wouldn't get any answers. He took the Underground to Waterloo on 30th April 1991 – the day he was reborn as Dave Constantinou, with Daniel Welby consigned to history. A history that included a general assumption that he'd killed his wife, although he wouldn't find this out for a few weeks.

Once across the Channel and in Caen, he took a cab to Deauville, a smart resort popular with Parisians escaping the city. He was to go to a townhouse on the boulevard overlooking the beach and the English Channel. A key was hidden in a small box, buried in sand by the gate. The key had an elaborate ironwork design shaped like a dolphin. Dave remembered this well as he spent most days staring out the window at the front of the house, watching life go by and waiting for his next instruction.

Finally, one wet, windy morning in late May an unfamiliar woman slipped a letter through his door. He saw her from the window as he watched early holidaymakers shelter along the boulevard. He opened the letter with some trepidation, knowing it would take him down a path he didn't really want, or expect. But he had no choice. That was when Dave hardened up even further.

He was to go to St Malo. The letter gave details of where he could pick up a large parcel of francs, and the keys to an empty shop with a flat above. The shop was his to do what he wanted with. He had so many questions, but his biggest surprise was the PS scrawled at the bottom of the letter. It said that Amara was no longer around, and the children would be taken into care and looked after. Dave never knew whether that meant she'd died, had disappeared like him, or been killed. He suspected the latter. After some time, he realised that he'd been left alone and was free to live his life. It was the cue for him to contact an old friend, and so began the happiest period of his life.

*

Jake passed the airport just as another holiday flight came into land. It was now the school holidays – and time to get out of Menorca and return to Lymford. He'd try to get a flight home tomorrow, and then he wanted to stay at home for a while. He called Milly as he came off the roundabout a couple of kilometres from the apartment. She and Elias had been sleuthing, as he put it, and she had news. She told him would fill him in when he got back, but she was clearly enjoying herself.

CHAPTER 43 – MALTA: 1 AUGUST

John had made his decision. He was on his way to see his father, who lived on the island of Gozo, just to the north of Malta. John sensed that Richard was agitated and, ironically, considering his career choice, he'd always been a little scared of his father. John had been summoned and had dutifully agreed to come and see him that morning.

When they came to live in Malta, twenty-six years ago, his father had been constantly on edge and was always unapproachable. He then met Mary and married her. She adored John, and loyally stood by both of them, devoting her time to making sure that Richard was looked after and doing charity work in Valletta on behalf of the Red Cross. John had always considered Mary as his mother even though he was twelve when his real mother died. As time went on, John came to understand more of the work that Richard was involved in. When he was about twenty, John realised that his father was not necessarily honest. When John was twenty-one, his father made a deliberate attempt to let him into Richard's life, and John started to accompany his father to meetings, where the guns and the import and export of drugs and guns was often discussed.

Richard was clearly grooming John to join

him in his illicit lifestyle. John relished this and was eager to get involved. By the age of twenty-five he had been introduced to Luther Blackhall, a Scot with a love of guns and earning money from contract killing. John did his first kill two years later in a remote village in Spain. He loved it, and truly felt as if he was performing a service for the good of mankind, although he was never told much about the 'sins' of his victims.

*

Gozo was like taking a step back in time. Richard moved there four years ago and seemed to settle into a relaxed way of life, doing very little. Mary, his wife, looked after a couple of Airbnb properties while Richard mostly drank in the bars, slept on the porch and, when he was feeling energetic, went fishing.

John got into the queue at Cirkewwa just as the Gozo Channel Line ferry was starting to load. John was soon on board and the ferry promptly started its 25-minute journey to Mgarr on Gozo, passing the small island of Comino on the way. By 11.30 a.m. John was on his way to the village of Qala, a short drive from the ferry terminal. His father's house was a beautifully restored authentic farmhouse on the edge of the village, appearing like a small castle, and with lovely views across the sea to Malta and Comino. It was built of large limestone blocks, and these were exposed in most of the rooms, giving the house a rustic look. In the summer heat it was lovely and cool, and John always enjoyed going there.

Richard was sitting on the veranda, which was in the shade, scrolling through the BBC news on his phone. Richard looked up, and John could see that he was troubled.

'That bloody woman – what the fuck does she think she's doing?' Richard scowled at John, who silently sat down in the chair opposite him. He knew Richard was talking about Isabella.

John rubbed his top lip between his thumb and forefinger and sighed. 'What exactly is the problem? Isn't it time you told me the whole truth? This started as a job to kill one person, and now it seems we're after three. Obviously, this goes back to your time in England – so what's your involvement?'

Richard snapped back. 'I thought you wanted to know as little as possible. I'm not going into my involvement, but there are things that need to be dealt with. This son of Constantinou – what does he know, and is he a danger?'

'He's quite smart, if in a slightly bumbling way,' John replied. 'He wants to find out what happened to his real mother, and I don't think he'll stop until he knows.'

'I've been putting the frighteners on him – one of the old team from London has been to visit his girlfriend and put the shits up her. He doesn't have a clue what he's getting into.' Richard glanced across at John. 'What have you been told to do?'

'Take out all three.'

'And do you know exactly who's asking?'

'No, but my contact has a London accent, and is about your age.'

Richard knew exactly who had contacted John. He stood up and went into the kitchen and opened the fridge. He pulled out two beers and flipped the lids off. He came back out, handing one to John without asking if he wanted it or not.

'I should never have told you that I knew about the Welby's back in London, so you could pass on the info to that cow in Naples.' Richard looked disgusted with himself.

'At some point she would have found out – she's a very determined woman. You thought you could control the situation.' John was trying to rationalise things, as he knew this was when Richard could get angry. He wasn't good to be around when things were not going his way.

Richard's agitation seemed to lessen. 'Mary's out in the village if you were wondering,' he said. John nodded. His mother, as far as he knew, was oblivious to his secret life, and he never wanted her to find out. He knew she would be devastated to know that he killed people for a living, rather than running hotels around Malta.

John looked at his father. The lines on his face had become more pronounced. He normally appeared so arrogant and confident, but he was troubled this morning, in a way John had rarely

244

seen.

Richard sensed his gaze. 'We need to put this to bed.' He looked intently at John. 'You've got a job to do. I suggest you get on and do it.'

'Three of them?' John asked. Before Richard could reply he said, 'Three in one job makes me nervous – it's three times riskier.'

'Then you need to work for it this time. Get them in one place. I don't know how you'll do it, but you need to do it soon.'

John looked away, seeming transfixed by a blue and white vase that sat in the corner of the veranda, no doubt waiting for a new plant. He sighed heavily. 'That's not how I operate. I'm told where to go and when. I don't organise things.'

'If you don't, then all of this is in danger: my life, your life, your mother's life. You decided on your career, and this is just another day's work. You're entitled to say no, but if you love your family then you won't consider that.'

Silence followed. John felt trapped. He wasn't worried about the hit, just about how he was going to go about it, and the higher risk of being caught. He had always worshipped his father, who had always had an air of mystery and danger about him. Letting him down was not an option. At least if he did it, it would put an end to the charade around Isabella and her new family.

As the ferry trundled back across to Malta, John's mind raced. He needed to plan his strategy, and knew it was going to be a major challenge.

Where, when, and how?

CHAPTER 44 – ENGLAND: 1 AUGUST

Milly was working, so Jake took the train home to Lymford after landing at Luton. This meant a slow trip into London, followed by a stifling Tube ride to Waterloo, then a two-hour journey to Lymford. The train journey took three times longer than flying from Menorca to England, and he was hot, tired, and grumpy when he got off the train at Lymford station. He was relieved that he was going to be spending time at home ... and with Milly. He'd had a stream of texts since he left the apartment in Es Castell over eight hours ago. He only read the ones from her and decided to take a rest from the investigation for the day.

He was pleased to see her waiting for him in the station car park, with a big smile and arms out wide. She hugged him and then – romantically – told him how bad he smelt.

'It's all natural.' He smiled back at her.

Jake checked that Milly was still OK following her little adventure with Colin in her apartment. She assured him again she was fine. They got in her Fiat. Jake stowed his sports bag into the back and put his backpack between his legs as he settled into the passenger seat. Milly made her way out to the main road for the short journey to the marina. Jake unzipped his bag and looked at Milly mischievously. 'I've got something for you.'

'I hope you have.' She giggled. 'But I'm driving at the moment.'

'That's later when I no longer smell.'

Milly loved white Toblerone, but he pulled out an almond version.

'Oh,' Milly said, looking at it with disappointment.

Jake's smile dropped. 'That's not the reaction I like to hear when I give you a present.' He deliberately put on a dejected and sulky face.

'I've just never had one of those. I like a white Toblerone.'

'I couldn't get one, so I thought I'd give it a try.'

'I'm sure it's great,' she replied. 'It's the thought that counts.'

'Yes, it is,' Jake said sarcastically. 'I've got a bottle of Menorcan gin as well.'

'That's more like it,' Milly said more enthusiastically. 'We can open that later.'

'Toblerone-gate averted then?' Jake laughed, running his hand through his hair. He was still not sure whether he liked it this short.

Milly dropped him off and they arranged to meet at hers an hour later. She said she had news about Dave and Amara, but Jake insisted it could wait until tomorrow. The only thing on his mind now was pleasure. The sun was rapidly going down on another warm day.

They both had the next day to themselves, so there was no need to get up early. After a late-morning cup of tea in bed, Milly pulled Jake towards her and felt him harden in her hand. He returned the favour, gently massaging her, moving his hands up her body, caressing her breasts and gently kissing her erect nipple, his tongue exciting her.

Afterwards, they lay back and discussed how hungry they were. It was nearly one, so they decided to get dressed and see if they could get a table at the Black Boar, a gastropub on the outskirts of Lymford. Jake rang up and managed to get a table.

Milly ordered the Goan vegetable curry with basmati rice and flatbread; Jake had a predictable burger with bacon, cheese, and skin-on fries. They planned to have dessert too. Jake always asked for dessert not to be deconstructed – a fashion he didn't approve of. He'd recently visited a pub in the New Forest and was unhappy to discover that the apple crumble had been separated into piles of apple, crumble, and cream with a drizzle of jus over it. Worst of all, it was cold. He complained all the way home and emailed the pub afterwards to say that deconstructed desserts were a nonsense.

'So,' Milly said as she poured some water into a glass, 'tell me about Dave.'

Jake wondered where to start. 'Well, I don't think I would ever get to like him. He now knows who I am, although I think he'd guessed already, but he's adamant he doesn't know what happened to Amara.'

'Your mother,' Milly interjected.

Jake looked at her and frowned. 'Only biologically.' He carried on. 'He was mixed up in all sorts of shit when he was in London. I don't think he knows the extent of it. He was basically told to skip the country with a new identity, and he didn't really know why. I think he didn't want to know. He decided to forget all about me and Isabella as if we'd never existed. He gives the impression that this was easy, but was it really?'

'He must be an incredibly uncaring bastard,' Milly blurted. 'How did you leave it?'

'He's escaping to South America soon – wants to turn his back on everything in Europe and start a new life … again.'

'Bastard,' Milly repeated. 'I hate the bloke, and I've never met him.'

Jake felt uneasy at this remark and fiddled with his napkin. Dave was genetically his father. He felt that it was OK for him to criticise his own family, but it felt uncomfortable when Milly did, no matter the situation.

'He's not going to help. He's told me what he feels safe with. He's warned me off, and I must admit that the way he was talking scared me.'

Milly leaned across the table and took hold of Jake's hand. 'What do you want to do?'

Jake looked defiant. 'I can't leave a question mark; I need to know the truth. If I wasn't personally involved, I'd probably let it go, but we're talking about the woman who gave birth to me.'

'And I can cope with another visit from Colin.' She also looked defiant. 'It's hard for an old man to look as scary as he thought he was.'

Jake bit his lip and grimaced. 'Sorry.'

The dinners arrived, smelling good. The waiter dutifully asked if they wanted any sauces, which they did, ketchup and mayonnaise, then Milly recognised him as someone who worked in the marina at weekends. She smiled at him 'It's Dan, isn't it?'

'Yes,' he replied. 'Milly, isn't it? You're on the radio, aren't you?'

'At the moment,' she replied.

'Oh, I hope you're not leaving. My mum loves you on there.'

'Thanks, Dan,' said Milly.

Dan clearly didn't notice the disappointment on Milly's face. Her hope that she still appealed to a younger audience had been dashed. Dan then made it worse by saying he liked Funk FM as well as Radio 1. After an awkward silence, during which Jake had his hand over his mouth, smirking, Dan scuttled off to collect another order.

They tucked in and said nothing for almost a full minute.

'Well, my news is...' Milly said, stopping there and picking up another mouthful of curry.

'Go on,' Jake said, wiping some cheese off his

chin.

'Elias has made some progress. He found out that there's an anti-corruption team in the Met investigating old cases.'

'Very *Line of Duty*.'

'Seems they take these things very seriously now. Anyway, you know I said about Sean Bellow, the journalist? He put Elias in touch with a DI Steve Crumpler who was stationed in Edgware. He remembers the case and says there were always rumours about a cover-up. He's now in the anti-corruption unit and this case has always been in the background, but they've never had time to investigate it. Anyway, to cut a long story short.'

'As Spandau Ballet would say,' Jake said, chuckling to himself.

Milly ignored him and carried on. 'He would be happy to meet you to find out more. They can then decide whether it's worth reopening as a case.'

'Really? When?'

'I've arranged that – on 4th August. We took the liberty of arranging a meeting in Winchester, at a pub called the William Walker.'

'Well done, Miss Moneypenny. You'll be wanting to be a paid employee soon.'

'There's one condition, though. We're coming with you, me, and Elias. This is getting really tasty now and we're enjoying ourselves.'

CHAPTER 45 – JOHN: 2 AUGUST

John was back in Sliema, thinking about his plan of action. This was going to be a tough job, and potentially his most dangerous. He understood that the reasons for it were far more important than he'd originally thought. This wasn't revenge or the need to ensure an old secret remains buried; there was something more to this, something bigger. It was probably to protect well respected people – perhaps respected individuals who were well known today. John had learned not to be curious, but this time he couldn't help himself. What exactly had his father been mixed up in thirty-two years ago?

He went into his back bedroom and unlocked the cupboard, which was mostly filled with junk. There was a safe hidden under a pile of sweaters. He turned the dial of the combination, and it clicked open. He took out two keys, which accessed his lock-up in a rundown part of Valletta. He wondered which gun he was likely to need. He needed something discreet, but which could fire rapidly. He decided on a Beretta 9000. He would travel into town once it was dark and bring it back to Sliema, ready for when he needed it.

John's guns were like his babies. He cleaned, caressed, and admired them, and was always happy when he had one close to hand. He loved them more than his wife.

Now he needed to work on his strategy. He thought he would start with a phone call to Dave. He might have to do two hits, but he did not relish the thought of going to England; border controls had tightened now that the UK was no longer part of the EU. He needed to get Jake in Naples or Menorca; hopefully this would not be too difficult. He'd been careful to nurture a good relationship with Jake, as he was never sure when he was going to need him, for good or bad.

His anonymous phone call had promised him a considerable sum of money for taking out all three of the Welbys – a sum he hadn't discussed with his father, and clearly a measure of the high-profile secret that these three were unknowingly caught up in. Isabella was going to be his key now: he had time to properly use her and work towards his end game. He'd just received a phone call from her that made the whole situation a little simpler for him.

CHAPTER 46 – NAPLES: 3 AUGUST

Isabella put her phone down, puzzled. John had sounded very friendly on the phone – there was nothing unusual in that, as he was a very personable chap, but the day before she'd told him to forget any thoughts of killing Dave and Jake. He'd taken this in his stride and had seemed unfazed when she thought he would have been angry, and it would be the end of their friendship. She was fearing a backlash – she knew it would look like she'd chickened out – but surely he would understand that her madness of a few weeks ago had been stupid and she now had another way out of her situation?

She had no idea that his agenda was different, and he was doing the manipulating. He had taken her news with good grace and promised to keep in touch, and so his phone call the next day was a surprise to her.

'Hi Isabella, hope you're OK this morning?'

'Not bad, John. I didn't expect to hear from you again so soon.'

'Well, I was thinking now that we have a different agenda, maybe we could have a bit of fun. Actually enjoy ourselves.'

'What were you thinking?' Isabella was unnerved.

'All this talk of Menorca, and I've never actually been there. Maybe we could go there for a few days, just you and me, to relax and see the sights? We could talk about normal life and find out more about each other.'

Isabella couldn't deny that it was an attractive proposition. He didn't mention Dave, so she told him she would think about it and get back to him in the next couple of days.

She was sitting in her favourite café in the Piazza Dante sipping a double espresso; she needed the caffeine after a few sleepless nights. After her brush with death in Chiesa, she'd made some decisions. Her mind was now clearer. She would get an art dealer to value the paintings and sell them as soon as possible. She would tell Jake the whole truth and hope that maybe they could have some sort of relationship in the future, and she would attempt to be a nicer person all round. She didn't know what she thought of John now that she didn't need him for Dave. He was good-looking and had an exciting, dangerous air about him. She smiled. A Maltese James Bond, she thought. Above all, though, she still wanted to know about Amara. And Jake was essential to that.

Jake had called yesterday. Their conversation had been stilted and awkward, but he explained how he'd met Dave, and how Dave had denied knowing what happened to Amara and had denied killing her himself. Isabella was not convinced, but it sowed a seed of doubt in her mind that hadn't been there since before she hired Paulo.

After paying for her coffee, she got up and strode into the main part of the square, which was heaving with tourists. She thought again about whether she would turn back the clock and concluded that she wished she'd never got into this. She should have left everything alone. If Dave was innocent, she would feel bad that she'd arranged for him to be killed, even if he was an odious little twat.

Naples was sweltering and tourists were everywhere, pushing, dawdling, and constantly taking out their phones and taking photos. The school holidays had started and, after the restrictions of the last few years, most of Europe was anxious to travel.

She suddenly felt a great need to get out of Naples as soon as possible, so she decided to take John up on his offer of a few days in Menorca, but first she needed to contact her so-called debt recovery agent before she became a statistic herself. This was going to be another difficult conversation, and she'd need to convince him that her plan to sell the paintings would work. She had an ace up her sleeve: a rising star of the Neapolitan underworld and someone gaining a fearsome reputation was Luca's illegitimate son, Gino. Gino was born before Luca and Isabella had married. Luca was a teenager when he became a father, Gino's mother a one-night stand, but Luca had kept in touch with Gino and Isabella had seen him regularly when he'd been younger. They lost contact as Gino's life took him on a different path, but they were still on speaking terms, and he was aware of her situation.

CHAPTER 47 – WINCHESTER: 4 AUGUST

Elias had volunteered to drive them all to Winchester. Jake was a little unsure this was wise; Elias was keen to get involved but he preferred it just to be him and Milly. She'd assured Jake that Elias wouldn't interfere and was just trying to help. Jake reluctantly agreed.

'What junction do we come off?' he said to Jake as they sped up the M3,

'The first one – junction 11,' Jake replied. 'We'll park in Tower Street and walk from there into the town.'

Jake was on tenterhooks, as he felt this could be a breakthrough that might lead to the truth. He was as keen as Isabella was to find out the truth. He'd spoken to her the day before and said that they still had things to sort out, and he needed to see her again. They ended the call with nothing settled, and their conversation strained.

They came off the motorway and across two roundabouts. They drove straight on for a couple of miles until they were in the centre of the city.

'Turn left here at the traffic lights, bear round to your right and the car park is there,' Jake said.

Once parked, they walked down the same hill that Jake had walked down two months ago when he first met Isabella. They walked past the Ivy, and Jake spontaneously took Milly's hand. 'I promise to take you there one day soon,' he smiled at her as he said it.

They turned right into the square then left again past a few more restaurants. The William Walker was on the corner close to the cathedral. Steve Crumpler was sitting in the corner, reading a newspaper, and nursing a pint of London Pride. He stood up when the group approached him. Jake held out his hand. Elias went to the bar and ordered drinks, while Jake and Milly sat down after making their introductions.

'Nice city, this,' Steve said. 'Never been 'ere before.' His accent was pure London, not quite cockney, but not far off. Steve was tall, over six foot tall, with thinning strawberry blonde hair, a slender build, narrow features, and a ruddy face.

'Yeah, it is,' Jake replied. 'I'm south-west London myself.' He could hear himself exaggerate his own, slight, London accent in response to Steve.

Elias handed the drinks round then sat down. Milly and Elias stuck to Coke, but Jake needed a pint of beer. They all took a sip and looked at each other. Steve spoke first. 'So, tell me your side of the story and I'll tell you what I know.'

Jake explained how Isabella had contacted him to try and find out what happened to Amara, how he'd discovered he was Daniel Welby's son, and that Daniel was now Dave, living in Menorca. Steve explained how his department had a long list of cold cases linked to alleged cases of police corruption that had been closed, with the investigations not having been as thorough as they should have been.

'Has it really been that bad over the years?' Jake frowned at him.

'No wonder public confidence is so low in the force,' Milly chipped in unhelpfully. Jake looked at her with a 'back off' expression.

Steve shrugged. 'There's a huge push to stamp out anything left that suggests corruption, and to investigate these old cases. I'm proud to be part of this, but it doesn't always make us popular. The Met is huge and there's still some people working in it who are nervous about the past. I'm still not sure it's as clean as we'd like it.' Jake was surprised at Steve's honesty. He opened a bag of peanuts and started to eat them. 'I read through Amara's file about a year ago – what there was of it. It troubles me when there's a missing person and the case seems to have been closed far too quickly. It almost looks like they stopped working on it after a few weeks, then waited a decent amount of time before knocking the investigation on its head. I'd be lying if I said it was unusual, but it's an interesting one.'

'So will you help?' Jake asked.

'Yep, that's why I'm here. I spoke to my boss and agreed to pick this up, since we know that

Daniel is still alive and kicking.' Steve chewed another couple of peanuts.

Jake could smell the sweetness of crushed peanuts in his mouth from his seat opposite. Not pleasant.

'So, what has Daniel – or Dave – told you?' Steve asked Jake, who explained his recent meeting with Dave and how he had denied knowing exactly what happened.

'There are a few officers on the investigating team I'm going to look into first. A couple of them are dead, one lives in Malta, and another is retired.'

'The Malta one will be Richard Warr, I guess,' Jake said.

Steve raised his eyebrows and nodded. 'Have you come across him?'

Jake explained how he'd met his son in Naples, and he seemed to be helping Isabella.

'That's interesting. Bit of a coincidence. I wonder why?' Steve frowned. He seemed to frown a lot. 'Look, let's work together on this,' he said to Jake. Jake nodded.

'Sometimes they're not corrupt; sometimes they're under orders,' Steve said.

'There's a bigger picture, you mean?' Milly asked, clearly struggling to keep quiet.

'Uh-huh,' Steve replied. 'Sometimes a much bigger picture. Some of the programmes you see on TV are exaggerated, if you're a Line of Duty fan, or some of the investigative journalism pieces the BBC like to do. But historically there have been cover-ups and people protecting themselves. That's not gone away yet, but it's becoming harder to do, and there are still some powerful individuals who will go to great lengths to protect themselves.'

CHAPTER 48 – NAPLES/ LYMFORD: 6 AUGUST

Isabella was feeling a bit better. The darkness of two weeks ago had lifted somewhat and she was looking forward to her trip to Menorca with John. A couple of paintings were going to be auctioned in three weeks' time and expected to fetch about 200,000 euros. This would keep the wolf from the door, but she had been given an ultimatum to repay her debt fully by the end of September. Gino had helped.

She still needed to see Jake, as she had more explaining to do. John had suggested she see if she could meet him in Menorca, so she sent him a text.

Hi Jake. I know you will have more questions for me. John and I are going to Menorca next week so I wondered if we could get together?

Isabella was impatient and always expected people to reply almost as soon as she sent them texts. It was several hours before she got a response.

I'll see what I can arrange. Will come back to you asap.

Isabella checked her watch. It was 7.30 p.m., and she was bored. That was the time she'd often contact her bookmaker or go online and play poker. She'd gone to her first Gamblers' Anonymous meeting yesterday and was still determined to stop. It was like a drug, though: the more she thought about it, the more the desire to gamble took hold. She had a knot in her stomach. If she wasn't careful, it would ruin her evening, as nothing else would be able to enter her thoughts. She needed a diversion.

She contacted a young friend of hers, Rodrigo. He was twenty-five and worked in a nearby pizza shop. She texted him to see if he was free for a bit of fun.

*

Although it had only been two days, Jake was enjoying his downtime in Lymford. He felt his own investigations had mostly involved travelling and getting caught up in his own emotions. Milly and Elias had been a great help and he felt a little guilty how much they'd done. Although, as Milly said he hadn't expected to be major player in the story.

He'd been running, had repainted part of the boat, and had arranged to watch a pre-season friendly between Chelsea and Napoli – ironic, he thought. He was listening to Milly on the radio and cooking a chilli when he received a text from Isabella. As 'Creep' by Radiohead started to pump out from the digital radio, he put his mind back to the investigation and pondered what to do.

He hadn't heard from Steve since their meeting in Winchester, and he wasn't sure what else he could do without going to see Isabella – and maybe Dave as well. He should probably have told them that a proper police investigation was under way, but he had decided to leave it for a while and text her this evening. He wasn't seeing Milly tonight as she was playing cricket for Lymford Ladies, a newly formed team that was playing in the Hampshire Evening Cricket League. He rang her to let her know he was probably going out to Menorca again in a couple of days, and to see if she could join him.

It was 6.30 p.m. when he texted Isabella back. He would check plane times and make arrangements. He had something else on his mind now: should he move in with Milly? She'd suggested it yesterday during a particularly enjoyable day trip to the Isle of Wight. He'd managed to deflect the subject. In many ways he felt flattered, he still felt she was too good for him, but their bond was definitely getting stronger. His immediate thought was not to say yes, and she didn't pursue it further. Maybe she just said it in a weak moment but if she mentions it again he needs to be prepared. He decided to go for a walk and weigh up the pros and cons.

The warm, sunny weather was still holding on and the ground was cracked and parched.

As Jake stepped off the houseboat and onto the towpath, there was a strong smell of charcoal. Needless to say, plenty of meat was being under- or overcooked in an attempt to embrace the great outdoors while summer was still here. Jake loved the smell of a barbecue but didn't enjoy the palaver associated with hosting one. The sun was getting lower, and the evenings were noticeably losing their light, slowly but surely. He donned his baseball cap and headed away from the town.

*

Isabella was walking back to her apartment when John called. She was exhausted after a hot and steamy session with Rodrigo.

'Hi,' he said, sounding distant. 'I've got a friend's place in Mahon for a week from tomorrow. Shall I meet you there?'

Isabella was taken aback, but quite liked his spontaneity. She had nothing planned, so she said she would try and get a seat from Naples to Menorca the day after tomorrow, 8th August. She would find out if Dave was there so she could arrange for them to meet.

She turned the key in her lock and thought about something else John had suggested. Maybe it was time for her and Jake to meet Dave together – the first time the three of them would have been together since they all knew they were related. It had been a month since the dinner in her apartment, when Jake had no idea that he was in the same room as his father and sister.

*

Dave was still unravelling his life, preparing for his departure for Argentina. He had gifted his hotel in Corfu to Demetrious – an insurance policy to ensure his name was kept clean over an incident where a woman accidentally died three years ago. As it happened in Crete, he needed to make sure the Greek authorities would never catch up with him. She'd drowned in a pool at an apartment he owned after taking a cocktail of drugs he supplied. He was there and Demetrious had pinned the blame on an innocent man for him.

Dave's other tangible assets were all being sold, apart from the house in Menorca, which he would give to his housekeeper. Most of his bank accounts were being consolidated into one account in the Cayman Islands. He was starting to feel positive and optimistic: it was the right time to go, but he thought he should make peace with Isabella and Jake before he went. He would never see them again once he'd left Europe.

CHAPTER 49 – MENORCA: 8 AUGUST

Jake had failed to decide whether he wanted to move in with Milly. He still liked his independence, so decided to give himself a bit more time. He managed to book a flight from Bournemouth to Mahon for the 8th of August. He texted Milly to see if she could make it, which she couldn't due to work commitments. Included was an emergency meeting about the future direction of the station. They compromised, though: she would come out on the 11th and book her own ticket the next day. Jake texted Isabella to say he would contact her when he got to Es Castell. He closed the iPad, spooned some chilli into a bowl and grabbed a large packet of Doritos. The TV was on, so he sat at his small table and watched a repeat of *Only Fools and Horses*.

Jake and Isabella landed two hours apart in Menorca. John landed half an hour before Isabella, so waited for her in the arrivals hall. John's courier had arrived at the small lock-up in Valletta two nights before and taken the Beretta, and a spare, and moved them to a motorboat in the harbour. The boat then crossed to Sicily, where it anchored until morning. At first light the courier sped across the Med to Mahon and, under the cover of darkness and using the key given to her by John, smuggled the guns into the townhouse he was going to be staying in.

John was waiting for Isabella with a big smile on his face. She was surprised when he announced he'd booked two hire cars in case they wanted to do different things on particular days. Their house was right on the harbour in the northern part of Mahon.

*

As they left the airport, Jake was already in his apartment south of the capital.

Since he'd seen Steve, he couldn't stop thinking about John; something had been nagging at him. He didn't mind coincidences, but Richard Warr's son being friendly with Isabella seemed a bit of a stretch. He needed to understand where they had met to be sure it was just a coincidence.

John and Isabella stocked up on food and drink, then she made a salad with salami and local cheese while John opened a bottle of Prosecco. They sat on the balcony and took in the view across the harbour. John had gone quiet after his earlier exuberance.

'I think I'm going to try and arrange to see Dave tomorrow,' she said after cutting a slice of crusty bread, still warm from the bakery next door. John tried to hide his pleasure at the news. That was what he had been hoping to hear. He calmly asked, 'With Jake?'

'I'll ring them both later to confirm, but that's the plan.'

John smiled, but not for the reason Isabella thought. 'I'll leave you to it – let it be a family reunion.'

She rolled her eyes. 'Not much of a family. What will you do?'

'Have a look around Mahon, do a bit of shopping.'

*

Jake was studying his map of Menorca to check where Dave lived. Now they were here, he wondered if it was worth going to see him with Isabella. It would be a strange family reunion, but he could kill two birds with one stone. When John was around, he decided he'd be careful what he said to Isabella; John didn't need to know that a DCI in London was looking into his father's activities. Jake rang Dave and asked if he was free to see them in the next couple of days. Dave confirmed he was, so Jake said he would get back to him once he'd spoken to Isabella.

*

Dave nervously put his phone back in his pocket. Panic hit him: he had agreed to see both of his estranged kids again. He knew it was the right thing to do, but it wasn't something he had expected a few months ago, when he had been in blissful ignorance of their existence. The Naples meeting was one thing, but events had moved on since then. He paced the room for a few minutes then walked out to the kitchen and leaned on the table, his palms flat down. He could call off their meeting when Jake phoned back, but he thought it would bring some closure before he flew off to another continent to live. He was hopeful he could convince them that he hadn't killed Amara.

*

'I was thinking the same,' Jake said when Isabella suggested they go and see Dave.

'I spoke to him earlier to suggest it,' he added. 'Said I'd confirm later, so shall we say 10.30?'

Isabella's voice trembled when she said that she would pick him up. Jake texted her his address then confirmed with Dave that they'd see him tomorrow morning. Dave also sent his address, which Jake entered into his phone.

All was set for a family get-together tomorrow morning. I have time to prepare myself, Jake thought. It suddenly struck him how much his alcohol consumption had increased in recent days; he seemed to be surrounding himself with drinkers. He shrugged and pulled a bottle of beer from the fridge. The meeting tomorrow was a good reason to have a beer tonight, but he must speak to Miguel first as he might need Cesar.

*

Isabella had similar thoughts as she strolled across to the kitchen table and poured herself a glass of Valpolicella: however, there hadn't been many days in the last few years that she hadn't drunk alcohol. She'd taken the cork out half an hour ago to let it breathe – a habit she'd got from Luigi, her adopted father, many years ago. John had disappeared for a while, so she went looking for him. He bumped into her just as he was coming out of one of the spare rooms, which was stuffed with junk. He appeared momentarily flustered, but quickly regained his composure and smiled warmly at her.

'Ah, just what I needed, vino,' he said, and took her hand and guided her back to the kitchen so he could pour himself a glass and take her away from the room where he'd hidden the guns.

'Why were you in there?' she asked.

'Just nosing.'

CHAPTER 50 – DAVE'S/ LONDON: 9 AUGUST

The next day promised to be cloudless. According to the forecast, it would be one of the hottest days of the year so far. Neither Dave, Jake or Isabella had slept well, partly due to the heat and partly from wondering how the meeting would go.

John had slept soundly.

Isabella had a white Seat Ibiza hire car, while John's was grey. She set off at 10 a.m. and wound around the outskirts of Mahon. Thanks to Google Maps, she found herself in Jake's road by 10.25 a.m. He was looking over the balcony, waiting for her.

*

Back in London, Steve was poring over the case notes from Amara's disappearance. CCTV was not available; some petrol stations and buildings had it, but any footage would be long gone, so any intel on where she had gone after leaving the house was down to eyewitness statements. One neighbour had seen her heading down Rowley Lane, where she could join the Barnet by-pass. She could then go right to Edgware and London or left towards South Mimms and the M25. Someone else had seen her red Astra going towards the town centre, possibly to Watford.

One detective who had worked on the case was Eric Chivers. He was now seventy-four and enjoying retirement in Norfolk. According to his records he had an exemplary record, but there were hints that he led a lavish lifestyle, with holidays in the Caribbean and a second home in Vannes on the Brittany coast. Maybe that wasn't exceptional for someone who had risen to his level in the Met, but Steve felt a tickle of suspicion.

Steve sat back in his chair, chewing on his pen, which had 'Portugal' written down the side. He had a golfing weekend in Vilamoura in June and always picked up a new pen whenever he went abroad. He had fifteen in his top drawer, which he kept locked, so his colleagues didn't nick them. He sat opposite Jenny, an enthusiastic detective who was new to the team.

Jenny started filling him in on her investigations. She'd discovered that Stelia had a Facebook profile, although she posted little on there. Her avatar was a photo of a ginger cat. Flicking through her history, she found a lot of cat pictures but very few humans. 'Not much of a life, by the look of it.' Steve had arranged for them both to see her the next day.

Steve opened a packet of cheese and onion crisps, picked up at Tesco Express on his way to work.

Jenny grunted. 'This is interesting,' she said, still staring at the screen. 'This Stelia appears to have lived in Cyprus before coming back to London in 2012. There's a post showing her next to a removal truck with a comment – "Back to England". I'll investigate when she went there.'

Steve nodded. 'Look into her finances – see if she worked much. I'm not going to go easy on her tomorrow. I can't believe she doesn't know more than she told Jake a few weeks ago.'

'OK, boss,' she replied, smiling. She was clearly relishing this new case, which was assigned to just the two of them for now. 'I don't like the look of this Eric Chivers either,' she added, screwing up her face. 'He's fat, has ridiculously long grey hair tied into a ponytail, and eyes that seem to bulge out of the screen.'

'Is that fattist or looks-ist?' Steve asked her, laughing to himself.

She scoffed and got up to grab a coffee. Steve recalled the interest she had generated when she joined the department. She had the clearest complexion of anyone he'd ever seen. Long dark hair, a happy smile, and light brown eyes that oozed enthusiasm. She tried to dress down for the job, but her natural beauty was hard to conceal. She shouted across to him to ask if he wanted a coffee, although he never drank anything other than Coke Zero at work.

Steve was looking through the paper cuttings for the time Amara had disappeared and noticed an article on drug's bust at a rave in a field outside Tring. The bust was led by Jerry

Ellis, one of the Amara investigators, who had since died. Steve made a note of this.

*

Jake waved to Isabella as she got out of the Seat. 'I'll be down in a second.'

*

To her relief, Jake greeted Isabella by kissing her on both cheeks. She hadn't been sure how he'd be after the revelations of a couple of weeks ago.

*

It would take them about twenty minutes to get to Dave's, so they had time for a bit more honesty. She turned the Seat around. Once they were on the main road, he picked at his nails, not wanting to look directly at her. He'd never really looked at her up to now, to see what similarities there were between them, but it would be interesting to make some comparisons today. He remembered reading somewhere that, as time goes on, children adopted at a very young age tend to look more like their adoptive parents. He cleared his throat and fixed his eyes at her. 'So, were you deliberately putting me in danger asking me to take on this job, even though you knew we were brother and sister?'

This still felt like a very odd thing to say – that he had a sister. Isabella kept quiet until she pulled off the roundabout leading out of the Mahon suburbs.

'It's not as easy as that.' Jake looked at

her, she'd visibly tensed and seemed to be considering her response.

'I was confused and naive when I contacted you.'

'Naive? In what way?' Jake asked. Again, he was starting to feel annoyed, but he decided to give her the benefit of doubt.

'I became curious to know what you were like, but I didn't necessarily think I needed to tell you that Dave was our father. When Paulo vanished and I knew you were an investigator, it seemed a great opportunity. My head wasn't in a good place.'

'And what about John? What's that all about?' Jake asked.

'What do you mean?'

'He's the son of a bloke who was involved in investigating Amara's disappearance. Bit of a long shot, that. What's the story with you two?'

Jake could tell she was uncomfortable and her concentration on the road lapsed as she came very close to a moped rider while overtaking. Fortunately, they were now on a straight bit of road.

Rather weakly she said, 'I don't know. We met about a year ago and both knew Dave – him through business, me manipulating the situation knowing he was Daniel Welby.'

'Do you trust him?' He knew she was rattled. 'Because I'm telling you I don't, and at the moment I don't trust you.'

Isabella mumbled that she was sorry. An uneasy silence fell between them.

She pulled onto the main road going west past IKEA, while a white VW Golf left Es Castell about ten minutes after Jake and Isabella.

CHAPTER 51 – DAVE'S/ KINGSTON: 9 AUGUST

Steve and Jenny met at McDonald's. She just wanted a coffee, but Steve needed a sausage and egg McMuffin. Steve's wife was a nurse and often on long shifts, so he was used to not seeing her at breakfast time. He would rather get fast food than put bread in the toaster or cereal in a bowl at home.

'Tell you what I found out last night,' Jenny said, blowing on the coffee. Luckily, a written warning on the side indicated that its contents might be hot.

'Go on.' Steve grunted.

'Stelia hadn't worked since Amara disappeared, then she got a job in Sainsbury's last year. She used to work at Debenhams in Watford but left a month after Dave skipped the country.'

Steve bit into the McMuffin and swallowed before replying. 'So, what have we got here? What are the factors? Drugs, money, disappearances, lies?'

'And a police investigation that was thin and short, to say the least,' Jenny added.

Steve nodded. They cleared up and walked back out to the car.

'Eric Chivers is going to be the key here. We might also have to make a trip to Malta,' Steve said as they climbed into the car. 'We need to try and talk to this Richard Warr and his son. Could be a very interesting conversation.'

Jenny hesitated. 'How high do you think all this goes?'

Steve just raised his eyebrows and shrugged.

*

Just as Steve and Jenny were pulling up outside Stelia's, Jake and Isabella were pulling up outside Dave's villa. They had exchanged small talk over the last few minutes, but there was still an air of tension between them.

'Nice,' Jake said as they got out of the vehicle.

'Actually, smaller than I thought. He's a rich man,' Isabella said. 'He could probably buy half of Menorca if he wanted to.'

They looked around. The heat was almost intolerable, and the day had a long time to go before it would cool. There was no sign of Dave, so they walked around the side of the villa and found a gate that was open. They walked through to the pool area, which was clean and inviting. There was a peach orchard the other side of a low wall at the back of the pool. Dave came out carrying a big jug of sangria.

'Welcome to my villa,' he said without smiling. He put the jug down on a glass table where three glasses had already been arranged. 'Come and sit down.'

Isabella sat down in the middle, with Jake to her right and Dave to her left. He poured the sangria into glasses, and they all sat back in an awkward silence.

'It's weak,' Dave said. 'Too much alcohol is not good in this heat.'

Jake and Isabella mumbled agreement. They all took a sip. Jake was impatient to get to the point and agitated. 'Look, this is strange for all of us. This isn't a family reunion – quite frankly, as far as I'm concerned you two aren't family. My family died eighteen months ago and I'm not looking for a replacement. Having said that, what happened to our real mother is important, and I want to know everything you can tell us that may help us to discover the truth. I also wanted to let you know that there's an anti-corruption unit investigating the case back in London.'

Dave and Isabella gave Jake a surprised look.

Dave shifted in his seat. 'You may be playing with fire there, my boy.'

'I'm not your boy,' Jake retorted, 'so come on – tell us some truths.'

'I don't know everything you want to know, and I can't add much more to what we discussed in Ciutadella.' Dave hesitated. 'I'm not a good man. Back then I was involved in gangs. It was quite brutal, and I admit I injured quite a few people. Amara hated it, but I'd become immune to it, and I liked the money. I'm not defending myself, but I got sucked in, then pressure was put on me. I enjoyed the glamour of it all.'

'But why did you have to leave?' Isabella asked.

'Leave rather than be killed you mean? I wasn't stupid, I knew who the Stefanov's were dealing with, who their clients were. I know who they are now.'

'What do you mean?' Jake asked. Dave hesitated and looked away.

'I've said enough. That I will need to keep to myself, to my grave.' Jake and Isabella glanced at each other. Isabella spoke.

'But then doesn't that mean they should have silenced you, for good.'

'I had an insurance policy.' Dave was still looking away and a few moments of silence followed. Jake and Isabella were waiting for him to expand on this. When Dave turned back to them Jake could tell there were a lot of thoughts running through his head, his features softened, maybe he would say more. Dave continued.

'There was a lot of tension about at the time. I got the feeling that something big was about to break, although I was never party to the decisions being made, but it had got to the point where you didn't go against them. You obediently followed their orders.'

'But Amara.' Isabella chipped in. 'Could she still be alive?'

'I give that a 10% chance, but I don't know

for sure.'

Jake's turn. 'If she is dead, why? Why would she have needed to be killed?'

Dave smiled. 'Families are complex, aren't they? Look at us.'

'You're being obtuse now. Surely, we have a right to know what you know. What was your insurance policy?'

Jake could tell Dave was thinking hard.

'You know I was safest as Dave Constantinou, new identity, new life, don't look back. Forget Amara and you two, save my own skin.' He carried on talking.

*

John saw the Seat parked in front of the villa ahead of him. The neighbourhood was very quiet. He parked about two hundred metres away and looked around before getting out of the car. Keeping to the sparse shade of a hedge, he walked stealthily up to the villa, which he'd researched on Google Street View. What he didn't notice was a white Golf parked just fifty metres from him. It didn't seem unusual as it was outside another villa, but Cesar was sitting inside watching John. As John made a wide arc around the side of the villa, Cesar got out of his car. He had a holster hidden under his baggy polo shirt and a gun tucked into his regulation police trousers.

*

Cesar's heart was pumping hard, but his twenty years of police training and his instincts told him where John was going to position himself.

He'd taken precautions. Although he wasn't necessarily expecting trouble, he'd called his unit in Mahon; they were on stand-by, ready to come out if needed. Cesar radioed back to them, as he now knew this situation would need armed police back-up.

*

Steve parked the car outside 31 Salisbury Avenue, Kingston, the home of Stelia Markou. It was a standard 1930s semi with bow windows and a stained-glass front door that had seen better days. He pressed the doorbell, then a little woman in a none-too-clean beige blouse and beige shawl, despite the heat, appeared from nowhere. Steve knew immediately she was going to be a little odd.

'You must be the DCI,' she said rather meekly.

'Yes, DCI Steve Crumpler, and this is DS Jenny Uhugu.'

They held up their badges for inspection. Stelia squinted at them and beckoned them to follow her round the side of the house to the back garden. This was surprisingly neat and tidy. The lawn was brown due to the summer sun and lack of rainfall, but the flower beds were well tended and neat. She had a nice patio area which looked as though it had just been jet-washed, and there was a table and chairs for six people.

Steve thought this a little odd, as she didn't seem to be a sociable person. They all sat down, and she poured out glasses of lemonade from a jug, whether they wanted them or not.

'Now, how can I help you?' she asked. 'There seems to be quite a bit of interest in Amara recently, poor soul.'

'I believe that you met Jake Stone recently,' Steve started.

'Yes, we had coffee. A nice young man.'

'And you mentioned Richard Warr to him – an investigating officer who was in regular contact with your parents?'

Stelia looked oddly at Steve, as if she was confused or hadn't heard what he said. 'Did I? Oh, I'm not sure. I don't remember the name.'

Steve stared at her, frowning. 'Are you sure?'

'I'm not a stupid old woman. This Jake must have made a mistake.'

Steve glanced at Jenny.

'Jake says that you said that you thought Daniel had killed her and buried her in Epping Forest?'

'Yes,' Stelia said, raising her voice and sounding defiant. 'He did it, I know he did. I just do.'

'But you've no proof of it? From what we can uncover the police found nothing that pointed to him.' Jenny asked.

'No, I haven't.' Stelia shook her head.

Steve raised his eyebrows, realising that she

was not going to be reliable, but Jenny wasn't finished yet.

'So, what about the police? Do you think they did a good job?'

'I think so – I can't really remember. It was a long time ago.'

'But surely you don't if Daniel wasn't arrested?' Stelia was starting to look agitated.

'Look miss, they tried , I don't doubt that, but he was a nasty piece of work that Daniel.'

'Well, this is at odds with what you said to Jake just a few weeks ago.' Jenny was starting to get frustrated. Steve recognised the signs. All young detectives go through it, she'll get used to it, he thought. Stelia was trembling. She tried to pick up her glass but had to put it down again. Steve decided to go in a bit harder.

'What was your relationship with Amara? How did you get on?'

'Fine!' Stelia's hackles were now up.

'And the gang's, did you have anything to do with them?'

'No, of course not.'

'Really Miss Markou? I suggest you're not telling us the whole truth.'

'You can suggest all you like young man.'

Steve took out a piece of paper from his jacket pocket, opened it up, and looked at Stelia. It was actually a letter confirming a hospital appointment for his wife, but it was enough to make Stelia frown, and he could tell she was nervous at what it might say.

Steve left that hanging and decided to change tack a little.

'So, you worked in Debenhams, then you went to Cyprus and lived a nice life. We've seen a picture of your home. Very nice.' He paused. 'So where did you get the money from?'

She looked indignant. 'I had savings.'

'You told Jake you wondered what had happened to Zoe and Christopher. It wouldn't have been hard to find out, so why didn't you try?'

Stelia turned her head away, seeming lost for words. She turned back to Steve and opened her mouth. Nothing came out.

Steve spoke instead. 'May I suggest that you were told what to say if you were asked that question, eh? Who told you what to say? You have no idea what happened to Amara, do you? Or if you do, you're protecting the person who hurt her. Why would you protect your sister's killer?'

Steve could see Jenny bite her lip, but he could also tell she was enjoying this: seeing liars squirm was always something of a victory and made detective work even more rewarding.

'Stop it, stop it, stop it!' Stelia shouted frantically. 'Please leave – I can't cope with this.' She pulled out a tissue and blew her nose.

'I ask you again, what was your relationship like with Amara?' She ignored him. 'We'll go,'

Steve said, 'but we'll be back. One last thing...'

Stelia struggled to raise her face to look at him.

They got up to go.

'Jake Stone is Christopher. Your real-life nephew.'

The colour visibly drained from Stelia's face, then it sagged, and she started to cry. Neither Steve not Jenny offered her any comfort.

CHAPTER 52 – MENORCA: 9 AUGUST

John crept around the side of the villa, keeping well hidden. His adrenaline was pumping hard – he almost felt euphoric, full of anticipation, knowing that he was moments away from bringing down his prey. His senses were heightened, and the result this time could be a triple reward, very lucrative.

*

Cesar was weighing up his position. He was going to have to be careful, as there was not a lot of protection, just the fruit trees. He decided it would be safest to get right behind John, where there would be less risk of him being seen. He'd keep at about fifty metres. He crept around, staying as low as possible. He could tell that John was used to this; he wasn't an opportunist or someone new to killing. He would most likely have a high degree of awareness, and Cesar felt exposed.

He had been only too pleased to help Jake out, but he had never really expected it would come to a shootout. His nerves were on edge, and his heart pounded. Armed police were on their way from the capital, but they were unlikely to be here before any action started.

*

John was now at a forty-five-degree angle to the three targets. The wall was dotted with small holes as part of the brickwork. This was fortunate. He found a small hole that separated the orchard from the pool area; looking through that would save him having to pop his head up above the top of the wall. They were about thirty metres away, and clustered close together. He regretted not being able to bring his automatic rifle, as the whole thing would have been over in about three seconds. There was more of a risk with the Beretta semi-automatic pistol as there was more of a gap between shots. John had chosen his clothes carefully: a beige T-shirt and shorts to allow him to blend into the surroundings, topped with a beige baseball cap to hide his dark hair. He thought he heard a sound behind him, so he whirled around and scanned the orchard. Everything seemed fine, but he had a nagging sense that he was not alone. He felt a little trapped. Any movement he made now would alert his targets, and he'd have to abort.

He looked again. Nothing.

*

Cesar crouched behind a peach tree and some branches that had been cut down and laid on the ground, which provided good cover. The sweet smell of rapidly ripening fruit hung in the air, but he was oblivious, his senses were elevated, and he was focused on John and John alone; nothing else was happening in the world. He froze as he saw John turn towards him and muttered a prayer. John turned back around; he clearly couldn't see Cesar.

With sweat trickling down his back, Cesar slowly pulled his own gun out, hoping his recent training wouldn't let him down. There were a lot of trees in the orchard, and he didn't have a completely clear line of sight to John.

*

Dave was explaining his future to Jake and Isabella. He'd told them more than he expected. It was quite cathartic. He noticed that Jake was now more relaxed while Isabella was still tense. Bit of a hard one, he thought ... but she is my flesh and blood, so what do I expect? He thought he heard a rustle in the orchard beyond the wall. Probably just a lizard, or a breeze kicking in.

*

The sun was almost directly overhead. Even the Mediterranean native John was finding it hot. His hands were sweating, but any movement to dry them on his T-shirt would be risky. He inched down slightly, the barrel of the gun resting in the gap. His eye line was perfect for the small gathering. He decided to take Jake out first, as he felt he was the one most likely to tell the police about whatever it was his father had been involved in thirty years ago. He would then shoot Dave, then Isabella. It should all be over in less than four seconds.

*

Cesar could feel his heart pounding as if it

was trying to jump out of his chest. He steadied himself on one knee and raised his gun gently, resting his straight right arm on his left hand. He had to decide whether to shoot first. He'd never been in this situation, and momentarily thought about the repercussions. He wasn't officially on duty, but this was life or death. He hesitated.

*

John had Jake's head in his sight. He squeezed the trigger, just as a fly buzzed in front of his right eye. It was just enough. Jake staggered backwards, falling to the ground. John had hit him, but not his head; the fly had disrupted John's concentration at the wrong moment. He was about to fire again when he heard another sound behind him and felt a heavy thud against his leg. John didn't have time to look around, but he knew he'd been hit. He staggered but summoned immense willpower to remain where he was. He ignored the excruciating pain that was starting to fill his body and took aim at Isabella. Dave had leapt to his feet and had jumped in front of her. The bullet left the barrel and hit Dave in the chest. He collapsed like a detonated chimney.

Cesar fired again. This time he got John in the back. He screamed and seemed to freeze before falling forward. His head hit the wall. Cesar held his gun high and walked towards John. Blood was streaming onto the dirt and trickling around the base of the nearby peach tree. John was still breathing, but he was making a gurgling sound. Cesar grabbed the gun from John's bloodied hand, pushed him to one side, then jumped over the wall and ran around the pool to the terrace.

Isabella was frozen, her mouth open and a glass still in her hand. Cesar came rushing towards her and he could see fear in her eyes, then bewilderment, and finally relief when Cesar shouted, 'Police!' and assured her she was safe. Jake was on the ground, having been pushed backwards by the force of the bullet. Blood seeped from his shoulder. He was conscious.

Dave was dead. The bullet appeared as though it had gone straight through his heart.

Cesar leaned over Jake. 'Can you hear me, Jake?'

Jake opened his eyes and tried to turn his head, but it was too painful. 'Yes.'

'Just stay there and don't move. I'll get the paramedics here as quickly as possible.' Cesar found a small towel and wrapped it tightly around Jake's shoulder and underneath his armpit to help stem the blood flow. Jake screamed as pain shot through his body. Cesar dialled 112 for the emergency services and explained the situation. They said they would be here in about fifteen minutes.

*

Isabella looked around, trying to take in what happened. Dave was clearly dead at her feet, so she stepped across him to Jake and bent down at his right side. She took his hand and wiped his brow with a napkin she took from the table.

'You're going to be fine.' Her voice shook as she tried to reassure him.

Jake managed a weak smile. 'This is a fine mess you got me into.' He winced as his shoulder moved. 'What about Dave?'

'He's dead, I'm afraid – a bullet straight to the chest, by the look of it,' she replied, wiping his brow again. Blood was starting to show through the towel, increasing Isabella's concern.

'I think he saved you.' Isabella gasped and nodded, tears in her eyes.

Cesar came across and Isabella looked at him, puzzled. 'Where did you come from?'

'Menorcan police. My father is a friend of Jake's parents, or was, and Jake asked if I would follow him to the villa. He was a bit concerned that your friend might be setting you up. Seems like his instincts were right, but I never thought there would be a shootout.'

'Thank God you came,' Isabella said, looking up at Cesar but still holding Jake's hand. 'Did he want to kill all of us?'

'Seems like it. He's dead now, so the danger is over,' Cesar reassured her.

Isabella put her hand to her chest and looked all around. John's right arm rested on top of the wall, but the rest of him was not visible. His cap had flown across the wall and landed on the slabs just behind the pool. Dave was prostrate on the ground, flat on his back, his large stomach no longer rising and falling. Blood was coming out of the back of his head. She looked back at Jake. 'I'm so sorry,' she repeated.

The distant sound of ambulances came into earshot and gradually got louder. Almost as soon as the sirens stopped, paramedics came running around the side of the villa. Cesar moved forward to explain the situation, and they brought out a stretcher and placed it next to Jake. A loud exchange in Spanish followed. Jake's eyes kept closing and opening again with every shriek of pain. They gave him a sedative, then waited a couple of minutes for it to take effect. They unwrapped the towel. Blood welled on his upper left side, just below the shoulder. Isabella winced.

Slowly but carefully, they manoeuvred Jake onto the stretcher. He was in a lot of pain but trying to hold it together. More stretchers were brought out to carry John and Dave, but there was no hurry; there was nothing to be done for them.

Shortly three policemen arrived. Cesar gave them a full description of events while Isabella climbed into the back of the ambulance with Jake. It sped off in the direction of Mahon, its lights flashing and its siren blasting.

CHAPTER 53 – LONDON: 10 AUGUST

Steve was at his desk when his phone rang. He didn't recognise the number, which was clearly from abroad. 'DCI Steve Crumpler.'

A weak voice came back at him, and he turned up the volume on the phone.

'Steve, it's Jake Stone in Menorca.'

'Jake are you OK?' he asked. He looked at Jenny and she raised her head to look at him.

'Not exactly,' Jake replied, then described the events of the day before. He kept raising his eyes at Jenny which he could tell was making her impatient. He was quite enjoying the suspense. It was a full ten minutes before Steve ended the call and updated Jenny. 'Well, I think Richard Warr needs more investigation. His son has just shot dead Dave and injured Jake. Isabella was there as well, but she was unharmed.'

'You reckon he wanted all three of them dead to cover up what happened years ago?' Jenny asked.

'Without a doubt,' Steve said, swinging round in his chair as he said it. 'Fancy a trip to Norfolk to see Mr Chivers?'

'I'd prefer Malta, but go on then,' Jenny replied.

Steve made a call to check that Eric Chivers was there. He picked up the phone within three rings and sounded quite frail. Steve was careful not to give Eric any detail except to say it was police business. This would cover a multitude of possibilities but would keep him guessing.

They left London at 9 a.m. It took three hours to get to the village of Reedham, between Norwich and Lowestoft. Their chat was minimal and mostly related to the case. Jenny was clearly quite private, but Steve got the impression she was very much career-oriented and was being fast-tracked through the force. She mentioned a boyfriend, but not in glowing terms. He played a lot of sport which, combined with her job, left them little time to see each other. Steve thought the boyfriend's time might be up. A familiar story for detectives.

The village was retirement central, with lots of bungalows with elderly people tending their gardens, getting the daily paper from the local shop, and walking slowly along the streets with sticks and frames. However, the village had a picturesque setting on the broad, with a pub and lots of benches alongside the water. The flat landscape disappeared into the distance beyond. Since it was the height of the holiday season, several boats were passing up and down the water. Steve could see how calm this could be as a holiday: there was a real sense of tranquillity as people quietly sat on decks reading, drinking tea, or just looking.

Steve and Jenny arrived at a large bungalow on a corner plot that appeared pretty modern, probably built a few years ago. They pulled up outside, got out and stretched. Eric was standing at the window to the left of the door, not making any pretence to be watching them discreetly. They walked up to the door, their badges ready. The door opened before they could ring the doorbell and Eric stood there. He looked like an old hippy, long straggly hair and in need of a shower. He had a pensive look on his face. Steve introduced them both and Eric ushered them into his spacious lounge, which was packed with knick-knacks and trinkets, something Steve hated. There were two sofas and a chair. The chair was clearly where Eric spent a lot of time, as it was stained, and the cushion was squashed out of shape. He had a flat-screen TV which was on, with the opening credits of *Loose Women* playing.

Eric hadn't yet spoken, so Steve started. 'Thank you for seeing us today, Mr Chivers.'

Eric nodded but still didn't respond.

'We're here because we're investigating a case from 1991. The disappearance of Amara Welby.' He paused. Eric stiffened. He still said nothing, so Steve continued. 'I believe you were on the investigating team at the time, and we're curious to find out why the investigation seems to have been, shall I say, brief, and the case closed pretty quickly. Bearing in mind there was no real evidence of what happened to her.'

Eric looked impassively at Steve.

'The suspicion was always that her husband killed her, so I'd like to know what you think.' Steve decided to stop there and wait for Eric to say something.

Eric cleared his throat. 'Why exactly do you want to know?'

'We're from the anti-corruption unit at the Met,' Steve replied, waiting for the reaction in the old man's eyes.

'You've got your work cut out for you. You'd need a team five hundred strong to go through the cases falling under that category. How serious are you? About uncovering the truth, I mean.' This time it was Eric's turn to look hard at Steve.

'Very serious, especially since the Daniel Morgan case,' Jenny answered. Daniel Morgan had been killed in a pub car park in south London in 1987, and an enquiry had alleged a history of cover-up by the police, preventing any investigation getting to the truth. It was alleged that Morgan had been about to blow the whistle on institutionalised corruption within the force. No one had ever been charged with his murder.

Eric sighed. 'Thank God.'

Steve and Jenny looked at him, surprised by his reaction. His demeanour changed.

He coughed and then carried on. 'There were four of us involved in that case. Three of them were making a lot more money from drugs than the police payroll. The other one was me.'

'Go on,' Steve said.

'I can tell you the truth, as I know it, but you'll never be able to bring anyone to court.'

'Why?' asked Jenny. A deep frown creased her forehead.

'Daniel Welby's gang, the Stefanovs, was controlled at a much higher level in the police and...' He hesitated. 'Let me just say that if the masterminds behind some of the drug deals were known publicly, the shockwaves would take years to die down.'

Steve and Jenny looked at each other. Jenny spoke next. 'What about Amara?'

Eric glanced down at his watch. He seemed to be getting agitated. He stood up and slowly walked to the window, holding the back of the sofa to keep him steady. He looked out of the window and spoke with his back to them. 'She was a bright woman – much brighter than that idiot Welby. She could see what he couldn't, but she confided in the wrong person. This person went to the top, saying that Amara had worked out who the Stefanovs were in cahoots with, and she was planning to leak something to the press.'

'Did Daniel know this information too?' Steve asked.

'I'm not sure, maybe, but I don't think so – they wouldn't have helped him to skip the country if he did. They thought he might still be useful with a new identity abroad – he could create another market just across the Channel.'

'So, Daniel's ignorance saved him, but Amara had to go?' Jenny said.

Eric came back to his chair and sat down heavily. The chair creaked. There was a long pause. 'It's a big relief to talk about this,' he said. 'I haven't mentioned it to anyone for over twenty-five years. I've got to the point where I don't care if it gets me into trouble. Life has been pretty good to me, but this was an unhappy time.'

'I swear that talking to us won't get you into bother,' Steve tried to reassure him.

'It's not your lot I'm worried about.'

Steve could tell that Eric was on a roll, so he was determined to get as much out of him as possible. 'Tell me...' Steve put on his most convivial voice, 'who was this wrong person Amara talked to?'

'Her sister. Stelia, I think her name was. She was the girlfriend of one of the Stefanov's and she got in well over her head. Thought she even had some power herself, but she was incredibly naive.

Steve and Jenny looked at each other again. Steve was getting that joyous feeling in the pit of his stomach that said they were about to crack the case. He could barely contain a smile. 'So, she was involved as well?'

'Yep – she was clever as well, but not clever enough to realise the consequences of her actions.'

'And those consequences were?'

'Amara had to be done away with, quickly. So, they used a corrupt detective to do it, then made sure he was part of the investigating team, so he could cover up her death by planting red herrings. I was the token good cop, and I was eventually paid off to keep quiet.'

Steve cleared his throat. 'So corrupt officers were deliberately placed in the team to investigate Amara's disappearance? Is that what you're saying?

Eric nodded.

'So, who killed her?'

Eric seemed to be summoning up the courage to make this final confession. He looked back at them and said slowly, as if for dramatic effect, 'Richard Warr.' He smiled as if he was enjoying himself now. 'You'll find her body – or rather, you won't – deep in concrete, where she was dropped during the building of a new roundabout in Slough.'

Steve and Jenny glanced at each other briefly, intrigued.

Eric paused. 'I wasn't supposed to know that, but I was a bloody good detective after all. But I always pretended to be ignorant about what might have happened. And that might have saved my life. I survived by keeping quiet, and in return I was paid handsomely. I was corrupt too, in my own way.' Eric struggled out of his chair, clearly restless, and stood in front of them. 'I know your intentions are good and honourable, but I don't believe you'll ever be able to reveal the real crooks, the real people who were controlling the drug supply in north London. It's just too big.'

'C'mon, you've told us this much. Give us a name,' Jenny said.

Eric looked at her. He seemed to be fighting an internal battle. Would he tell them or not? He shook his head. 'I'll just say this….' He paused. 'You know some of them very well, and that is all I will say. I trust this is all off the record?'

Once again, Steve and Jenny just looked at each other and after all of his years in the Met even Steve was surprised.

CHAPTER 54 – MENORCA: 11 AUGUST

Everything was very white and bright; it was too much for Jake's eyes, so he closed them again. He knew he was in hospital. He knew he'd been shot, and he knew he was lucky to be alive, but for now he just wanted to sleep. He felt himself drifting off again, loving the feeling of letting go into the comforting embrace of unconsciousness.

*

Milly came back into the room with a cafeteria baguette in hand and a hot coffee. She was in dire need of the caffeine. She'd barely slept since she heard about Jake's shooting. She'd arrived that morning, coming straight to Mahon Hospital from the airport. Jake hadn't been conscious enough to know she was there. He was going to be okay, but he was still quite heavily sedated. The bullet hadn't gone in too deep, so it was just a case of making sure it started to heal and no infection set in. The door opened and Cesar joined her. They had met earlier. Milly unwrapped the plastic from her cheese and ham baguette. The TV was on in the corner, showing another news report of the Alaior shooting. Jake's face was now well known across the Balearics, and Cesar was rapidly becoming a national hero.

'You know, I kept saying I wanted to come to

Menorca. Finally, I came, and he has to make it a dramatic one,' she said, nodding at Jake.

Cesar chuckled. 'He gave me one of the most dramatic days of my working life,' he said with a smile.

Milly took a bite of her baguette, suddenly realising how hungry she was. 'Well, thank you for being there. It was a stroke of luck that he asked you at the last minute to follow him.'

Cesar nodded. 'Are you staying at the apartment tonight?'

'Yes, I think so. I could stay here, but there doesn't seem much point. He's going to live and will probably be asleep most of the time.'

'Well, give me a call on this number' – Cesar handed Milly a post-it note – 'and I'll give you a lift. I'm going to be around Mahon until 7 p.m. so I can take you to Es Castell then. I'm going to have to try and keep a low profile for a while, away from the media.'

'That's brilliant, thanks, Cesar. I can't wait to see it, but it will be strange Jake not being there.'

As if from far away, Jake could hear voices, familiar voices, comforting voices. They got louder, then there was silence, and he heard a door close. He forced his eyes open and tried to focus. It hurt to move his head, but then he saw Milly's smile.

'Am I a legend or what?' he muttered.

Milly leaned over and kissed him on the lips.

'More of a bell-end, I'd say. It's Cesar who's the legend.' She sat on the edge of the bed and took his hand.

He managed a half-smile then descended back into dreamland, where he was sailing across the Solent on a warm sunny day.

Milly had updated Steve on Jake's condition. Steve was pleased that Jake would be alright, and he was able to tell Milly what would happen next. So far, he'd put in an extradition request to try to get Richard Warr over to England for questioning, but he suspected that it wouldn't succeed. Why would Richard think he was so much at risk that he needed to get John to kill the remaining members of the Welby family?

This bothered him. He felt they were missing something. Maybe Richard thought time had moved on and the authorities wouldn't hesitate to prosecute him, and others would be happy to hang him out to dry. That would be a gamble, though, because he would be sure to name names. What motivated him? Had he been given orders?

Whatever happened, Amara's body would not be retrieved, but he was sure she would be able to rest in peace in Slough. Jenny would be happy to question every north London policeman who had been in the force in the early 90s. Steve knew they were going to have to tread carefully and be very sure of their facts. They might have to drop Richard Warr as a target for the murder of Amara, but they would need dogged persistence to uncover the corruption. Steve wasn't sure what stance the Menorcan authorities would take over the events at Dave's in Alaior.

CHAPTER 55 – MALTA/ NAPLES: 18 AUGUST

Richard Warr had not often felt scared in his life. He was always in control, and this trait had been passed on to his son. John was now dead, and it felt as though it had almost been at Richard's own hands. It hadn't been supposed to work out like this. He had meant to get rid of the remains of the Welby family, as they were in danger of resurrecting the truth about what had happened in the early 90s. The press may have been stifled and paid off in the UK, but they wouldn't be across the world. It wasn't Amara's murder that was the problem, but the web of lies, deceit and corruption linked to it. Also, in the age of social media, the greatest untruths are believed by an element of society, and stories then take on their own momentum. Would Richard now become the scapegoat? The establishment would spin the story that they made a mistake in protecting him carrying out the numerous killings that were made under their name, in the pursuit of wealth for some and pleasure for others.

Richard Warr had always thought that Eric Chivers should have been killed. He knew too much. Leaving him alive had been a big risk, but he'd been saved – paid off, but Richard knew that he was continually monitored. No, there would now be regrouping going on, and he knew he was the most vulnerable.

He walked around the village of Qala, where everybody knew him – or they thought they knew him. His wife Mary didn't really know him. She was inconsolable, spending hours a day in the local church dressed in black, clutching her rosary and rocking backwards and forwards. She still thought that John was a property developer and nothing else. The double lives of her son and her husband were a blind spot to her.

John's body would arrive in Malta tomorrow from the morgue in Mahon Hospital, and his funeral was in two days' time. Richard couldn't wait to get that over with. He knew there would be a couple of people from the UK there who he wouldn't know. They would be 'representatives,' making sure if there were any stones unturned they would be turning them back over as quickly as possible.

He found his favourite spot and sat down on a large rock that gave him a view over the sea, which sparkled, as it always did during the summer in these islands in the middle of the Mediterranean. He thought about the people who had been protected all these years. He thought about Amara's death and what a complicated web it was – corrupt police officers, gangs that were free to do whatever they wanted, drug dealers capitalising on the booming rave and club culture, those who were involved in the manufacture and distribution of ecstasy. The need for them to remain anonymous had resulted in several deaths as well as treachery – such as Stelia ratting on her own sister in a vain attempt to prove her worth.

Richard was scared; these faces were big news. They were some of the biggest names known to most people around the world. In the 1990's they were small time politicians, later they rose the ranks to hold the top jobs in British Government. Sportsmen were drug clients, they went on to Olympic golds and feted around the world, always criticising the use of drugs in Russia while themselves being protected by members of the International Olympic Committee. Then there were the police, and him, cosy with the gangs. The suppliers had long gone into other legitimate and illegitimate businesses, or died, but many of the clients were still around and still protected by the security services. They all wanted the Welby's silenced to quell any rumours. Now the plan to eliminate them had backfired, it would be too risky to try it again. The message he got on the burner phone yesterday had been simple:

Damage limitation to be enforced.

What this meant for Richard, he wasn't sure.

Isabella had spent the past few days making arrangements. She had decided that her life needed to change and, as much as she loved Naples, it was time for a new start. She had little inclination to mourn the death of Dave Constantinou. Maybe she should, but it just wasn't there. He wasn't a nice man and never had been, but she would get part of his inheritance. She discovered that he'd recently added some codicils to his will, which meant that she and Jake would receive something from his estate – enough to pay off her remaining debts and buy a nice place in Tuscany, ironically among the British expats to whom she now felt some connection. Deep down she knew that life had made Dave hard, but clearly there was still some softness about him. And after all, who was she to judge?

She was happy that she could draw a line under her past, but also hopeful that she would be able to build a relationship with Jake. She felt guilty that just a few weeks ago she had been prepared to feed him to the lions. That made her realise how hard she'd become. She had a feeling that Jake would be a good influence on her, if he would let her in.

She looked around her apartment. Some of the walls were bare where paintings had gone for auction. The dining room table caught her eye – where they had all met for the first time just six weeks ago. Then, Jake didn't have a clue who they really were. It made her shiver to think they, quite literally, had dodged a bullet.

CHAPTER 56 – HAMPSHIRE: AUGUST 29

The persistent summer heat had broken, and a cool, misty, drizzly wave had blown in from the west. Milly helped Jake out of the car. He'd lost quite a bit of weight and Milly had been telling him to eat more. He'd lost his appetite, but it was coming back, and he was looking forward to eating as much as he wanted for a few weeks.

'Can you just help me with my jacket?' he said, wincing each time he had to move his shoulder. He'd reduced his reliance on painkillers. Sex was still sometimes a challenge, but they were inventive.

'I'm sure you can start doing this yourself now,' she said, pulling his bright blue rain jacket together and zipping it up.

He'd enjoyed Milly fussing over him, but he'd missed Chelsea's first two home games of the season and he was desperate to get to the next one in two weeks, so he'd decided he would make a rapid recovery as from next week.

Steve pulled into the car park in his BMW, Jenny in the passenger seat. They'd arranged to meet for lunch in a pub just off the M3 near Basingstoke. Steve got out of the car and waved to them.

'The pub name is appropriate!' he called.

Jake looked at the sign, which said the Sun Inn, and laughed. 'You're not wrong there.' The four of them greeted each other then walked inside the pub.

Elias and Isabella were already there, sitting down. They seemed to be getting on fine, apparently laughing at the numerous quirks of British behaviour.

'Technically, I am British as well,' she reminded him. 'Maybe I will need to improve my sarcasm.'

Everyone sat down, ordered drinks, and started to look at the menu in silence. Elias broke the silence, saying he would order a halloumi burger, then turned his attention to Jenny. 'So, how long have you been working with Steve?' he asked.

'Oh, not long, a few months,' she said, without looking at him. She was more interested in the menu.

Jake glanced up. 'Come on then, Steve, I'm dying for an update.' He could hardly contain himself.

Steve took off his glasses, after deciding he was going to have posh sausage and mash, then rubbed his eyes. 'Well, put it this way, like I said on the phone, we know that Richard Warr killed Amara, and where she's buried. We'll never find her body, and it seems that Richard will never be brought to justice. Extradition was blocked, we've been told that in no uncertain terms.' He looked at Jenny. 'We've been told to forget about trying to get a prosecution for the murder.'

'So, what can you do?' asked Milly.

He shrugged. 'There's a real drive to get rid of corruption in the Met, but this is too big. I think we'd be able to get some low-level prosecutions for corruption, but we won't get to the heart of it. All the trails lead deliberately to Richard Warr, and we've uncovered a lot about the Stefanov's, but go deeper than that and there's a well-constructed wall.

Jake frowned. 'When you say "big", what exactly do you mean?'

Steve explained that he didn't really know the extent of it, but clearly people involved in the gangs in the nineties were still wielding power, be they suppliers, dealers, or clients.

'What about the gang members themselves, are any still around?' Jake asked.

'Doesn't seem like it, they appear to have gone abroad or just disappeared as well. We found one running a very nice hotel in the Lake District, known as Jim Higgins, formerly known as Matej Stefanov. He denied all knowledge and wasn't saying a thing.'

The waitress came and took their orders. All the women opted for salads. Everyone turned their attention to Steve again.

'Three days ago, we found out that Eric Chivers had a fatal heart attack. There will be a post mortem, but I suspect it won't have been natural causes, even though that's what will be on the death certificate. Eric was never going to confess publicly what he said to us, but certain people will have known we went to see him, and that put him at risk. He was very brave speaking to us.' He paused and took a sip of water. 'And I didn't say just now. This morning I heard that Richard Warr's body was found washed up on a beach in Gozo. They're saying he probably took his own life, but I wonder...'

Isabella spoke for the first time. 'What about me and Jake? Are we still in danger?'

Steve frowned, looking unsure. 'I'm sure you'll be fine. They've got to the people who could tell the whole truth. No one else can prove anything, but my advice is to stop investigating and let it drop. I still wonder why Dave wasn't killed when Amara was knocked off though.' Milly grabbed Jake's hand and gave it a squeeze.

Jake looked at Isabella. 'I think we know that, it was almost the last thing that he told us in Menorca.' Jake leaned in, making sure no one else was in earshot.

'We've been holding out on you a little Steve, but one of Dave's clients back in the day was the Home Secretary, he used to exclusively deal with her. He let her know that he had a video of her snorting a line of coke and it was locked in a safe at a friend's house. It was the one person in the world he trusted. He told this friend if he goes missing then to pass the tape to a newspaper.'

'But he did go missing?' Jenny said.

'When he got to France, he passed the message on that he was safe but had a new identity.'

'Come on Jake, tell us who that is?' Steve almost begged. 'The video might still be with them.'

'Well, I haven't been totally idle since I got back from Menorca. Me and Milly took a drive to Weston-Super-Mare after tracking down a Michelle Constantinou, she's Dave's daughter.' Both Jake and Milly were smiling, loving this twist of fate.

'Wow,' Steve was intrigued. 'But Constantinou, she's got Dave's name. He had a daughter after he left England?'

'Yep. Seems Daniel Welby had a mistress in Bath, he gave her the video a while before his disappearance, and he showed a copy to the Home Secretary as proof. Blackmailed her. He then contacted his mistress after he'd been in France six months, and she joined him. By that time the gang was breaking up, people had lost interest or forgotten about Dave, and the clients had moved on. I reckon the clients left it in the hands of certain members of the Met to tidy things up.'

'And,' Jenny stuttered, 'the Home Secretary soon became the Prime Minster, am I right in thinking?' Jake nodded, with a huge grin on his face. 'And it's the same party in government now!'

Steve looked at Jake, 'then you come along and start making the ends loose again, which needed tying back up.'

'I suppose so. With Isabella's help.'

Isabella looked embarrassed. 'But my motives were not good, for which I will never stop apologising for. One day Jake will forgive me.' He smiled at her, 'I'm almost there.'

'Blimey, as you say in the UK.' Elias added to the conversation. 'So, the people ordered to tidy up were Richard Warr, and this Colin who scared the shit out of Milly?'

'Seems like it.' Both Jake and Steve were nodding.

'What happened to Michelle's mother?' Jenny asked.

Milly's turn to add to the story. 'Well, her name was Louise, seems like her and Dave drifted apart, she came back to England with Michelle and set up home in Weston. Michelle has got pictures of Dave. I have to say he was a surprisingly handsome devil back in the late nineties.'

'You say was, is she dead?'

'Sadly, she died of COVID in 2020.'

Steve turned to Jake again. 'So, Dave started to tell you about Louise just before he was shot?'

'Yep, he literally had just told us that we had

another sister, Michelle, told us where she was…
then bang! It's really sad. He seemed to be finally
unburdening himself to us, making peace before
he went off to Argentina.'

'Did Dave and Louise marry, or did Michelle
just take his surname?' Jenny asked.

'No, they married in 1997 and Michelle was
born a year later.'

Everybody sat back, deep in thought, just in
time for the food to be delivered. Once everyone
had dinner in front of them, Steve sipped on a
local pint of beer from a New Forest brewery,
then looked at Jake again.

'It all adds up now. Eric Chivers was on the
brink of telling us more but held back. I think
the remains of former police corruption will take
a while to go away. There're still the people, and
enough power in the background to get things
"dealt with." Dave was probably lucky to have
survived so long. Maybe moving around Europe
helped him, although I'm not sure he exactly
kept himself under the radar.'

'Maybe.' Jake said. 'What about your end,
what about Stelia? I was totally taken in by her,'

Jenny nodded. 'We think she's a smiling
assassin – much more important and dangerous
than she looks. She was also a part of the
Stefanov gang but she's no danger now. She will
want to carry on keeping her head low.'

'She basically dobbed Richard Warr in,
saying his name to let it be known, but then

saying he was the good guy. Devious bitch.'

'Yes, but...' Steve hesitated. 'She played a dangerous game there, and I'm not sure I fully understand it. Why say anything at all? Maybe it was just a thrill for her, and she couldn't help it. Life had become mundane for her.'

Isabella flicked her hair back. Jake ran his hand through his growing hair.

'Well, I won't be meeting up with my aunt. I don't suppose there's anything else we want to know,' Isabella said. 'Having said that we've still got an aunt in a nursing home.'

Jake agreed and added that nothing was to be reported on the radio, looking at Elias as he said it. Elias nodded but added that Sean Bellow had been regularly contacting him for information, but he knew how to keep his mouth shut.

'This really is big, isn't it?' Milly said.

'Don't think we'll ever really know how much.' Steve was clearly enjoying himself. 'I can understand you wanting to know everything Jake, but it's best not to.'

'No, I'm happy to live in the present and look to the future.' Jake glanced across at Milly and smiled.

Isabella had rented a VW Polo from Hertz at Heathrow Airport. Jake had insisted that she stay with him and Milly in Milly's apartment for a couple of days. After lunch they all headed out to the car park. At the roundabout to get on to the M3 Steve and Jenny turned left, heading to London, and the rest turned right, heading for the coast.

'I'm glad we're going our way and not theirs,' Jake said to Milly as they accelerated down the slip road.

'Yep ... and I meant to say, I've decided to turn down the job offer from Original. It would mean spending too much time in London. I'll stay where I am and weigh up my options.'

Jake looked across at her, raised his good arm and tickled the back of her neck. 'I'm pleased,' he said. He then checked his mirror to make sure Isabella was behind them. They would not be going straight home to Lymford; he wanted his uncle and aunt to meet Isabella first.

CHAPTER 57 – LYMFORD: AUGUST 30

The next day dawned brighter and warmer. Milly left for the radio station early as she had prep to do; she was interviewing the band Bastille later and she was very excited. She still got a thrill whenever she interviewed a band, even though she'd done it many times.

Jake grabbed a cup of coffee and met Isabella on the balcony – the first time they'd been alone since she'd told him she was his sister back in Naples.

'I don't think an apology is remotely enough,' she said, 'but I'm so sorry for putting you in danger. I didn't expect to feel anything for you; I was just going to use you for my own aims. I'm a cold, heartless bitch.'

Jake pondered his answer. Part of him was still a little angry. 'It just seems incredible that you thought the way to pay your debts off was to get me and Dave killed. I think I know you a bit now, and you really must have lost your mind.'

Isabella gazed across the rooftops to the ferry trundling across to the Isle of Wight from Lymford. 'I know – I'd gone down so far and hadn't realised it. Thank God for my ex-husband. But as for John Warr, what a devious bastard. He got me really believing in him when all along he was setting me up for his own pleasure and to save his father's back, and whoever else back here.'

Jake shook his head. 'A master of deception, that one. Cesar told me that they reckon he could have killed over thirty people in the last fifteen years.'

Isabella chuckled. 'Don't forget, I live in Naples, so that doesn't seem so shocking.' She paused, took a sip of coffee, and shook her head.

'You know that Steve tracked down Paulo?' Jake remembered that Isabella had missed that conversation. 'He's on his way back from New Zealand. He'd been scouring the internet for news, and when he read that John and Dave had been killed, he wasn't sure whether to return.'

'Is he OK?'

'Apparently. Wants to get back to Italy and restart his life. He's actually quite grateful to you.'

'What a terrible business.' Isabella appeared to drift off, gazing across towards the English Channel. After a few moments she said, 'You know, I never did find out how Dave got that scar across his cheek.'

'I can help you there,' Jake responded. 'Jenny found out that the Stefanovs did it – a warning she thinks, once he left England, to keep quiet.'

Isabella glanced at Jake and raised her eyebrows. She looked away again and repeated, 'What a terrible business. One day I hope you'll forgive me.'

Jake gazed towards the sea as well, thinking

about what he was going to say, wanting to be sure he meant it. 'Yes, but I've gained a sister, though,' he said. 'I have another living relative again, which is nice. Anyway, what sister hasn't wanted to kill her younger brother?' Jake chuckled.

'Yes, and I have a lovely brother, and a new half-sister.' Isabella replied, smiling.

'Yes, you have. You're very lucky.'

Jake turned the radio on. Human League were playing on CoastFM.

ACKNOWLEDGEMENTS

To Lucy for nagging me to write down an idea for the first chapter, which came from a dream, and Brenda for her hours of constructive editing advice.

Thanks also to Richie Cumberlidge at More Visuals for his cover design, and Jane and Margaret for their professional editing skills, as well as numerous others who have helped me along the way.

Printed in Great Britain
by Amazon